Sophia

Book Seven
The Sacred Women's Circle Series

Judith Ashley

Windtree Press
HILLSBORO, OREGON

Windtree Press
Hillsboro, OR
http://windtreepress.com

Publisher's Note: This is a work of fiction. Names, characters, places, and incidents are a product of the author's imagination. Locales and public names are sometimes used for atmospheric purposes. Any resemblance to actual people, living or dead, or to businesses, companies, events, institutions, or locales is completely coincidental.

Book Layout ©2013 BookDesignTemplates.com
Book Cover by Christy Caughie
Editing Services by Kelly Schaub

Ordering Information:
Quantity sales. Special discounts are available on quantity purchases by corporations, associations, and others. For details, contact the "Special Sales Department" at the address above.

Sophia/Judith Ashley – 1st Edition
ISBN 9781940064635

Acknowledgements:

My village for *Sophia* includes, as always, my first reader, Lois. My fellow Blog Queen, Sarah Raplee, who held my hand and helped me make the scene where Cam is shot so much better. My editor, Kelly Schaub, who took extra time to explain her comments. And, last but in no ways least, to the #RCRWFTB group and the Goal Writing Challenge group. Without your encouragement and support to keep my tush in the chair and my fingers on the keyboard, the seven books in the original series would not yet be completed.

1 A Volunteer

November 2005

Sophia Stewart pulled her car to the curb on the residential street. Even though she couldn't see any house numbers, she knew the drab grey house across from her was the one. There was a porch but no stairs. Even in the light of a late November afternoon the over-grown bushes hid the deteriorating, dilapidated building from further scrutiny.

There is a difference in the color if a white house is neglected and turns grey rather than grey being the original color. Shutters were dark but Sophia could not ascertain what the original color might have been. Paint peeled down to bare wood and chips of it lay on the ground.

Remembering her training, Sophia checked that her cell phone was on. Slipping it into her coat pocket, she made sure her ear piece was in place. Her badge clipped to her collar, she picked up her notepad and pen and headed across the street.

Her mission was to check on Mr. Stanton, an elderly man, who lived at this address. Neighbors had called adult protective services concerned about him being exploited by a younger man. Her job was to make an after normal-business-hours visit. A friendly 'how are things going' check to add her observations to what the workers saw during the work week.

Making her way down the overgrown side path, Sophia watched her step because of the mud and moss. At the bottom, dull light shone through a filthy sliding door, the entrance to the daylight basement. A glance up at the dark windows on the upper floor confirmed that Mr. Stanton lived in this part of the house.

Her gaze took in the scene on the other side of the glass as she knocked. Two men sat at a table, a television on across the room. From the door Sophia didn't see a kitchen, only empty take out cartons and pizza boxes piled on chairs or the floor.

The younger of the two men rose and came to the door.

"Yeh." There was something in how he looked at her that set her nerves on edge. She clutched the notepad to her chest.

"Hi, I'm Sophia, a volunteer with Fremont County. I've been asked to check on Mr. Stanton this evening." She held up her identification. Leaning to the side, she said, "Mr. Stanton?"

The older man stood, and holding on to the table and backs of chairs slowly made his way towards her.

"Hi, Mr. Stanton. I'm Sophia. How are you doing today?"

"I'm good. I've got my friend here if I need anything."

"I'm glad you have someone who comes by and helps you out."

"Oh, he don't come by. He stays here with me. We're fixing the place up."

"What kinds of things do you think you need to do to fix it up?"

Mr. Stanton grabbed a jacket and stepped out the door. "Look at all this." His gesture was wide. "I own all this. Me and Randy was thinking if'n we cleared this lower part of the lot, we could build apartment buildings."

Sophia took in the thicket of blackberry vines that were taller than she was. "How steep is the hill?"

"Pretty steep. When spring comes, we'll get rid of those berry vines."

"How tall will your new building be? It'd be a shame to block the view from the house."

"Yep, Randy and me are working on the house this winter."

"Oh really? What are you plans? I watch the Home and Garden network and love the programs where they come in and renovate older homes." Sophia didn't have to fake interest, she did want to know about their plans.

Mr. Stanton invited her in and told Randy to clear off a chair for 'the lady'. While Randy did as Mr. Stanton asked, he did not appear to be happy about it.

Sitting at the table with both men, Sophia listened and asked questions about the renovation on the house. She even made a suggestion when the talk centered on the kitchen. "Be sure you have a surface for baking. And women want a window over the kitchen sink. Even with a dishwasher, some things are always washed by hand."

Randy participated in the conversation by reporting what he would do to help. He knew the best electricians and plumbers, could get Mr. Stanton a great deal on flooring, cabinets. He also made comments that created a sense of unease.

The house needed a "woman's touch".

Why didn't she come with him and he'd give her a tour. He paused and winked before adding "of the upstairs."

If Mr. Stanton had offered, she'd have gone. Since Randy had angled his body so she brushed against him when she'd followed Mr. Stanton into the house, following him anywhere was definitely unwise. Add to that both men had been drinking. Even if Randy had been stone-cold sober, she wouldn't have followed him anywhere alone.

It was apparent the younger man was at the very least taking advantage of Mr. Stanton. After a relatively short period of time, Sophia believed it was more likely Randy was exploiting him. Every service Sophia mentioned, Randy popped in with how he was already doing it or if Mr. Stanton needed it, Randy could do it.

With Mr. Stanton, who Randy referred to as Mr. S, agreeing with everything Randy said, there was nothing more to discuss. A glance behind her showed her she'd spent much more time with Mr. Stanton and Randy than she'd planned.

It was dark!

"Oh my, how the time has flown." Sophia stood and gathered up her still blank note pad and pen. She'd slipped her coat off her shoulders when she'd sat down. Before she could reach for it, Randy had it in his hands.

"Here, let me help the lady into her coat."

He touched her neck and she shivered in revulsion.

Mr. Stanton beamed.

At the door, she said her goodbyes again. Thanked Mr. Stanton for his hospitality and wished him well on his projects.

Stepping out into the night, she felt Randy's presence.

"Let me help you up the path." He brushed her hair to the side. Her stomach lurched and a spike of fear skittered down her spine.

"I'm fine. Really, I don't want you to go to any bother." Sophia purposefully kept her voice friendly instinctively knowing this man would feed on her fear.

"Not a bother to escort a lovely lady." He reached for her hand and grabbed thin air.

Shoving her hand in her coat pocket, she felt her cell phone. By touch she dialed 1, where she'd programed 911. When the 911 operator came on, she made sure her conversation to Randy was clear and informative.

"Thank you for your offer to help but I'm making my way up the path just fine."

She reached the path and started up.

"I think Mr. Stanton needs you. He shouldn't be left alone for very long."

Randy was only a step behind.

"I can make it past this slippery part without taking your hand. In fact, it would be better if you didn't touch me. It throws me off balance."

She hoped the 911 operator could hear Randy. He wasn't as subtle here as he was when talking about taking her on a tour of the house. Here in the dark, he was more specific about taking her on a very different tour. Assuring her she'd like what he showed her, that she'd even be grateful if she gave him a chance.

The 911 operator had asked her if she needed help and she'd managed a 'yes' without saying 'yes' to Randy's veiled invitations.

"Randy, my car is at the top of the path on N. Wine. I really can make it to my car without your assistance."

"I wouldn't be much of a gentleman if I just left you here. No telling what could happen to a pretty lady like you along a deserted path like this."

One more turn in the path and she'd be able to see the top and safety. She urged her legs to move more quickly but the path was muddy. Slipping and falling would be disastrous, so she concentrated on where her feet were and trudged forward.

Just before the turn, Sophia's coat caught on a branch.

Not a branch—Randy.

"Let me go." Sophia shouted and swung her elbow back, connecting with air.

Randy laughed. His arm wrapped around her and he took a step back.

"I said let me go!" Sophia put every ounce of force into her voice and twisted in an effort to free herself.

"Sophia, is that you?"

The 911 operator had been with her, encouraging her, telling her help was on the way. Now the operator said an off-duty officer was on the scene.

"Yes, it's me."

"Guess you don't need my help anymore," Randy said, letting go of her coat.

Caught off balance, Sophia stumbled, her hands landing on a mossy patch. Regaining her footing, she scampered around the curve in the path into the arms of her savior.

He kept his arm around her and leaned down.

"I've got you. I won't let you fall." Peppermint breath that overlaid whiskey wafted across her cheek.

She was safe. Shaky but safe.

They crossed the uneven ground and gained the sidewalk.

"My car is right across the street." Sophia stepped away from the man. "Thank you." Her voice shaky as she shivered in her warm coat. "He grabbed me and was trying to pull me backwards." Her eyes filled with unshed tears.

"How are you doing?" he asked, leaning down to see her more clearly in the dim light of a street lamp a few houses away.

"I'm just glad I don't have anyone else to check on tonight. I think getting myself home will be enough of a challenge."

She started towards her car and stumbled.

He caught her and steadied her.

"I've another idea. There's a great little diner not far from here. Follow me. We'll get a cup of coffee and see how you're feeling after you've been clear of this for a while.

"Your car keys?"

Sophia fumbled in her coat pocket and pulled them out. She leaned against the car and clicked the remote to unlock the door.

"Change of plans," the officer said taking her key from her, relocking the doors and setting the alarm. His arm around her shoulders, he steered her to his car parked in front of hers.

"We're going to get that coffee and then I'll bring you back. You're not in any shape to drive right now."

Sophia couldn't believe she was so shaky, almost teary when nothing had actually happened to her. But the officer was right, driving wasn't a smart thing to do right now and sitting in her car in front of Mr. Stanton's house wasn't either.

"I don't drink coffee," she managed. "But I do drink tea.

"And my hands." She held them up in the weak light. They were dirty. "I stumbled when he let go of my coat."

"Don't worry, we'll get them cleaned up."

2 A Hero

Cameron Mitchell kept his hand on the woman's elbow as he guided her to his car. He knew who Randy Brown was. Not really a small time crook, he'd moved up the ladder some. He'd served time for rape and theft so Cam knew he was more than capable and willing to assault the lady beside him. Brown also knew who he was and Cam was certain he recognized his voice. They'd had enough run-ins over the years.

A bone deep weariness claimed him body and soul. *What I wouldn't do for three fingers of scotch.*

Glad he had an unmarked car, he opened the front passenger door and assisted the lady in.

She was trembling.

Cam got a blanket from the trunk and a couple packages of sanitizing wipes for her hands. She used two wipes for each hand.

"Let's get you away from here." Cam wrapped the blanket around her shoulders.

"I can manage." Sophia said in a wobbly voice when he tried to put her seatbelt on.

"I know you can." He left her to finish the job and rounded the car.

Fastening his own seatbelt, Cam turned to the woman. "I'm Captain Cameron Mitchell, Fremont Police Department, North Precinct. Now let's get that tea and you can tell me who you are and what happened."

Sophia practiced her deep breathing in an effort to calm herself. *I've never felt such fear.* She wrapped her arms around her torso in an effort to stop the tremors. *Would rocking help?* She shook her head when that idea popped into her mind. *Concentrate on the here and now.* Sophia pulled the shoulder strap to hold her even more firmly in place. She paid attention to where they were as the officer drove out of the neighborhood and onto the busy main street.

Less than five minutes passed before they pulled into the parking lot of a restaurant. With ease Cam backed his car into an empty spot under a bright overhead light.

"Before we go in, I've a couple of questions." He pulled out a small pad and pencil from a shirt pocket.

"Your name?"

"Sophia Stewart. Do you want my address?"

When he nodded, she gave him that information.

"And your date of birth?"

He sat there, pencil posed, waiting for her answer.

She sat there, her mind whirling with bits and pieces of what had happened.

"You will probably think it strange that I want to look at my driver's license. My brain—well, it seems to short out—I mean—."

Cam put the notepad and pencil away. "Let's get you that tea. It'll help."

Before Sophia could unbuckle the seatbelt and pull off the blanket, he was there, opening her door, offering his hand to help her out.

And she took it.

He felt her tremble and sway, saw tears welling in her eyes and thought about calling for EMT's to check her out or even for him to take her to the ED for observations.

When they turned toward the restaurant, she held on tight. He guided her left hand behind him and patted it in place at his waist. He settled his right hand on her shoulder and pulled her close. The top of her head came to his shoulder, just under his chin. A hint of her vanilla scent wafted on the air.

They walked into the diner and he nodded or gave short answers to the people he knew who were there. First stop was the women's restroom. He waited a discrete distance from the door until she emerged. She'd washed her hands and face, a few wet spots decorated her coat.

His favorite booth was available. He held his hand out for her coat and then had Sophia, Ms. Stewart he reminded himself, slide in first.

Once settled beside her, he waved the waitress over.

"I'll have coffee with the works and she'll have tea."

The waitress looked over at Sophia. "We have black and a couple of herbal ones."

"Do you have chamomile?" Sophia kept her clenched hands under the table.

"We do. Is that all?"

Cam looked over at Sophia. "Hungry?"

She shook her head.

The waitress left.

"I know my birth date." Sophia gave it to him as well as repeated her address. It was amazing how much calmer she was sitting in a well-lit diner with a large police officer next to her.

"Feeling any better?"

Sophia nodded.

"Tell me what happened, starting with why you were at Stanton's place."

"I'm a volunteer with the Safe Elders Program."

"I know about them. So, you were asked to check on Stanton?"

"Yes."

"And?"

"I got there while it was still light and thought I'd be gone before dark. He really is a delightful man and we got to talking. Before I realized it, it was dark outside. Mr. Brown insisted on walking me out and Mr. Stanton was so pleased that he was doing that—well, I refused as politely as I could but he just kept pushing."

The waitress arrived with coffee and tea along with cream, sugar and some lemon. Sophia took some time fixing her tea, letting the tea bag steep a bit in the hot water. She breathed deeply of the calming aroma of chamomile before setting the cup down.

"The path is very dark, no lighting along the way at all. And it's overgrown so the ambient light isn't much help either. I made sure I was ahead of him, thinking that would be better than being behind him." She looked over at Cam, the question in her eyes.

"You did the right thing."

"He kept, he was so close and he was saying—saying—." Her face burned. She put her hands up to her cheeks but they too were heated from the hot tea.

"All I could think about was to keep talking so the 911 operator might figure out where I was and what was happening."

She'd swiveled on the bench and was facing him. "How did you find me?"

"You did say enough that dispatch knew where you were."

"There are two really bad spots on the path. One covered with moss and the other muddy. I wanted to hurry but thought if I fell, he—he'd—he'd a-a-attack me." A shudder racked her body and she wrapped her arms around herself.

"I just kept going. Kept talking and kept moving. I was so close to the top and thought I'd made it when he grabbed for me. I managed to shrug him off but he caught the back of my coat.

"I told him in as firm a voice as I could muster to let go of me. I jerked away and he lost his hold. But then he latched on to my coat again. It was buttoned against the weather and I didn't think I could get it unbuttoned and slip out of it before he pulled me back down the path.

"The 911 operator had said someone was coming and I was to do what I was told.

"When I heard you call out, I also heard the 911 operation say someone was there. So, I answered.

"I fell onto my hands when Randy let go because I was leaning forward. He took off back down the path."

Sophia's hands shook so hard, she didn't dare pick up her tea. Her stomach wasn't even receptive. And her head throbbed as she talked.

She gripped her hands together to minimize the tremors. Tears welled but she blinked them back. Her gaze locked with his. "He would have raped me, wouldn't he? He would have if you hadn't come."

"Do you want the answer to that question here? Or when we are back in the car? Or do you even want an answer?" Cam watched her carefully as he asked those three questions. She had large dark brown doe-like eyes. In the harsh diner's light, her brown hair had subtle streaks of red and gold. The urge was strong to reach out and stroke his knuckles over her fine toned skin, to feel her softness, to pull her against him and tell her everything was okay. But almost thirty years on the force had engrained in him a rigid self-control.

His eyes never left hers, even when he took a sip of his cooling coffee. He waited for an answer, taking a moment to relish her soft vanilla scent.

"No, not here." Sophia looked away, picked up her tea with both hands and took a sip.

"How are you doing now?" Cam asked attempting to determine whether she was safe to drive.

"I'm still a bit shaky."

He looked at her address. It was a couple miles away. Could she drive that by herself? "Do you have someone you can call? Someone who can come and take you home? I'm not sure it's wise for you to drive."

Sophia looked at her watch. It was after nine and while she knew she could call any one of The Circle who was in town, it was late. *I can do this. It's only a few miles away.*

"Not really. It's only a few miles. I'm sure I can get there on my own."

Cam noted her knuckles were white from holding the cup. The tremors that had been very visible were less so but still there.

"Here's what we'll do. I'll take you home and you can come back tomorrow and get your car. Or you can call someone to come and drive you and your car home.

"What we're not doing is having you drive yourself." His voice was firm but not harsh.

"I can take a taxi." The idea popped into her mind and out her mouth before it registered.

"You could."

She'd turned as white as the snow on the mountains. For a moment he thought she might pass out.

Haunted yet luminous shimmering brown eyes seemed to grow bigger. "Why am I so frightened? Nothing happened?"

"Something did happen, Ms. Stewart. You were followed and threatened.

"Finished with your tea?" Cam set his coffee cup in the middle of the table. At her nod, he took the tea cup from her hand and set it next to his. *They look like they belong together.* He shook his head after a second glance. Sliding out of the booth, he held out his hand.

Sophia, her gaze still on him, reached out. He took her hand and helped her out of the booth. Tossing a fiver on the table, he tucked her hand in his arm and led her out.

"What do you have to do tomorrow?" he asked as they approached his car.

"I was going to bake cookies."

"I'm going to take you home. I'll call you around eleven and if you don't have someone able to bring you back to pick up your car, I'll do it."

"Are you sure you won't get into trouble?"

"Ms. Stewart, I'm not on duty. Haven't been since fifteen minutes before your call came in. I was on my way home when I heard dispatch ask who was close to your location. I was, so given what was happening, I responded.

"You need to talk to the Safe Elders Program folks tonight and file a report with them.

"Do you want to press charges?"

"I-I-I don't know."

"I'll tell you now, that Brown didn't say anything explicit enough that the District Attorney will do anything. Even though he has a record and I'm as positive as you are that his intent was to rape you, he didn't say anything that couldn't be interpreted in a harmless way."

Sophia stopped, her grip on Captain Mitchell's arm tightened. "But you believe he was going to rape me."

"I know he would have if you hadn't gotten away. That's why you need to let the Safe Elders people know what happened. No one should check on Stanton by themselves. No one should go at night. And, better yet, this is one situation when you want to either ask for police escort or ask the police to check on him."

"I'll call the manager when I get home. I know they wanted someone to check on him every day over the weekend."

"Not a good idea. Have the manager ask the police to do the checks. You can use my name."

Sophia was able to buckle her seatbelt on her own. They did go by her car because Cam convinced her to see how she felt about driving home after moving her car four blocks to a well-lit street. He watched her from his rearview mirror. She made it but it looked more like a kid taking his first solo drive than an experienced driver.

He wrote down the street and cross street where they left her car glad she didn't argue when he said he'd take her home. She did buckle her seat belt and even got her cell phone out and called the manager. Her version of what happened was sanitized. She was uncomfortable with Mr. Brown and in talking to Captain Mitchell, was told she had reason and that no one should check on Mr. Stanton alone day or night.

He pulled into the driveway of a ranch-style house. All the homes in this subdivision had double lots. He could see in his headlights that the yard was well cared for.

Sophia, Ms. Stewart he reminded himself, got out of the car. He put the car in park and set the hand brake.

"The house is dark. No one's home or they've gone to bed."

"I live alone."

At the front door, Cam held up the small flashlight he always carried in his jacket pocket so she could unlock the door. As soon as it opened, he heard the beeping of an alarm system.

She hurried in to turn it off.

Cam closed the door and strode to his car. He backed out and drove away before he gave his second thoughts a chance to win.

Those second thoughts had him following her in and checking the place out. With the alarm system she had and the fact that she used it, there were no intruders waiting for her. He'd always had a strong need to protect others. A strong need that had been worn down over his time as a police officer.

In his car, he backed out of the driveway and headed back to the precinct to write up his report. He could still smell her vanilla scent, still hear the thread of fear in her voice. A question ran through his mind as he pulled into the station's parking lot.

What was there about Sophia Stewart, an obviously independent woman that said she needed someone?

He couldn't answer that question now and didn't want to find out.

3 Tried and True Recipes Soothe

Unable to sleep Sophia got out the makings for cinnamon rolls. Once the basic recipe was rising, she mixed cinnamon and sugar in one bowl. In another she added chopped pecans to brown sugar and butter setting it on heat to make the caramelized goodness that turned her basic sweet roll recipe into pecan sticky buns. While the yeast dough rose, she whipped up a batch of peanut butter chocolate chip cookies.

Even though her busy hands did nothing to quiet her mind or stop the 'what if's' that still ran riot through her even in her own kitchen, the smell of yeast dough rising along with the aromas of cinnamon and caramel, peanut butter and chocolate soothed.

While the cookies were baking and the sweet roll dough was rising, Sophia sat at the counter sipping another cup of chamomile tea. Acknowledging she wasn't helping herself by ruminating on 'what if', she focused her mind on the future.

What was she going to do in a few hours when it was daylight?

After mulling things over, she was thankful she had options. In the end she decided to take a taxi to get her car. And then she'd take a batch of her cookies to the precinct. Maybe Captain Mitchell would be there and she could thank him again.

He'd left so quickly last night, when she'd turned back to the front door to thank him again, the front door was closed and he was gone.

In the quiet of the night, the smells of cinnamon and pecan sticky buns baking wafting through the house, Sophia thought about the troubled officer. What was it about him that told her he was troubled? That was a harder question to answer.

It's like knowing I was in danger with Randy. I knew I was safe with Captain Mitchell.

She, along with her circle sisters, practiced their energy work. They were all more connected to each other on an energetic level and could sense when one of The Circle was in trouble. No one was in trouble right now, but she knew everyone was busy.

Gabriella and Elizabeth were in Italy and Ireland respectively. Lily was off with Jackson. Ashley was balancing her family, checking on Lily's clients and recovering from her mastectomy. Diana was also balancing the balls of her life— her daughter, Madison Michelle; her classes; consulting clients and actually at the top of her list—her husband, Matthew. Hunter and Grant were in Eugene visiting with Logan this weekend.

There was no doubt in her mind if she called any one of them, they'd come. But it seemed like an intrusion in already busy lives to ask them for a ride. And she'd not had the time to tell The Circle about her decision to volunteer with the Safe Elders Program. It would be impossible to ask for a ride and not have to tell whomever picked her up how her car had ended up where it was. The decision to call a taxi was the sensible choice. That decision made, cookies and sweet rolls cooling, Sophia made her way to bed and hoped she'd sleep.

In the dim recesses of her mind, Sophia heard pounding. *What on earth?* Snuggling under the covers, she drifted off again.

The pounding continued. A ringing joined in. Sophia recognized the sound of the phone. *Who'd be calling at this hour?*

Struggling out of the cocoon of bedding, she reached for her phone. It wasn't on the nightstand.

Finally disentangling herself from the blankets, she stood. The pounding had stopped but her phone was still ringing. Sophia picked up a robe from the foot of her bed and headed toward the kitchen.

The pounding started again.

Someone was at her front door.

She looked out the security window. Captain Mitchell.

What time was it? Sophia glanced at the security system. That clock said it was eleven thirty.

Unlocking the door, Sophia opened it.

Captain Mitchell stood on the other side of the security screen. Seeing her, he hung up his phone and tucked it into his jacket pocket.

"I see you're okay." His moss green gaze swept over her before settling on her face.

"I am okay. I guess I overslept." Sophia tugged her robe closer and tied the belt.

"Understandable." He remained still. No shuffling for Captain Mitchell.

"I stayed up baking. Would you like a cinnamon roll or perhaps a pecan sticky bun?"

"Fresh from the oven?" His intense gaze fixed on her and he licked his lips.

"Fresh as in a couple of hours ago." Sophia unlocked the security screen and gestured him in.

Cam sat at her kitchen counter while Sophia bustled around heating one of her pecan sticky buns with a pat of melting butter on top.

"I'll be right back." She headed down a hall off the great room to, he figured, the bedrooms. He did time her and realized she was back in less than five minutes. Now wearing a pair of jeans, a multi-colored top and pair of sneakers, with her hair pulled back in a ponytail she looked ten years younger than the age on her driver's license.

"How is it?" She eyed his plate. One, maybe two bites were left of the generous helping.

"Never had better. You could make a fortune selling these." Sophia laughed.

The sound swirled around him. He could eat her cooking and listen to her laugh—nope. Don't go there. He reined himself back.

"I've had people say that before." She leaned on the counter. "But then it would be a business and not something I do for pleasure."

"Or to distract yourself from something unpleasant."

Her brows furrowed. "Or to distract myself, to settle myself down."

She pulled out a roll of aluminum foil and tore off a big piece. Onto it she put another pecan sticky bun and two cinnamon rolls. After folding the foil into a package, she rummaged in a cupboard. When she straightened, she had a brown lunch-sized paper bag. Into it she put cookies.

"These are my peanut butter chocolate chip cookies. I've been told I could purchase my own tropical island if I sold them." She laughed again as she folded the bag, sealing the cookies inside. "Instead of selling them, I feed my soul and gift them to people. Here." She handed Cam the bag and foil package. "You can share them, or not."

"Not likely they'll be shared." He opened the bag and took a deep breath of the peanut buttery chocolate goodness inside. Breaking off a small piece of the top cookie, he popped it into his mouth.

"Definitely no sharing." His eyes closed and a small smile tipped the corners of his mouth as he swallowed.

"I made enough that you could share," Sophia started.

Cam shook his head. "Nope, not gonna happen."

"Do you know how I can thank the 911 operator who stayed on the line with me?"

"I can find out. And, if you want her to have some of your cookies, I can make that happen."

"I've a sugar free recipe I can make if she's diabetic," Sophia offered.

"I'll check that out and let you know. Now, how about getting your car? Or have you made other arrangements?"

"I was going to call a taxi when I got up. I really don't want to put you to any trouble. You've already done so much." Sophia clamped her mouth shut as a flood of words welled up in her throat.

Cam nodded toward the wrapped food. "You've more than paid me for last night. I think I owe you now."

Sophia smiled. "But then I'll owe you if you take me to my car."

"Guess I'll have to follow you back to collect more cinnamon rolls."

"You like them better than the pecan sticky buns?"

"You mean I have to choose one over or the other?"

"No. You don't have to choose. I was just wondering. I might have a fresh batch and be in the neighborhood of the North Precinct. I'd hate to make a mistake and leave something you don't really like."

"Ms. Stewart, there is nothing about you I don't like."

Sophia blushed. "Really, Captain."

"You are brave, generous and the best cook I know. Well, there is one little thing I'm not sure about."

Sophia arched her brow and waited.

"You sleep like the dead. I was getting worried. About ready to call in the fire department and backup. We can't break into a house to check on people without going through the proper procedures.

"Do you set your alarm when you go to bed? Or when you are in the house alone?" His gaze trapped hers.

She shook her head.

He frowned.

"A new habit for you to get into then."

"I've a baseball bat by my bed."

"Good to know. But by then the perp is already in your house."

"Do you think Mr. Brown could find me?" Sophia's knees weakened and her voice quavered.

"Not likely but he isn't the only person out there whose intentions are less than honorable."

"The Safe Elders Program does not give out our personal information. People can leave messages for us through the main office."

"It's better to be safe than—."

"Point taken. I'll read the manual and make sure I know how to set it to arm the perimeter."

"Ready?" Cam stood, gathered up the packaged goodies and offered his free arm.

"I am." Sophia took his arm and, after stopping to pick up her purse, car keys and set the alarm, followed him out to his car. He was a big man. Bigger than Jonathan by several inches in height and several pounds in weight. He was bigger but he was fit. After stowing the packages on the floor in the back seat, he opened her door and waited until she was inside. Closing the door, he rounded the car and slid into the driver's seat.

As Cam drove them to where her car was parked, his mind shifted through various scenarios that would allow him to stay in touch with her. However, when they reached her car, he'd come up with nothing he was willing to act upon. No point in getting involved. No point in finding out she was one of those females who loved the uniform but not the man inside. No point.

When her car started up, he waved and half-saluted before continuing down the street. Last night he'd been on his way home when he'd responded to the call. He'd gone home after dropping her off and filing his report but sleep had not come easily.

Cam filled his lungs with the aroma of freshly baked yeast rolls. Starting his days off with positive thoughts on his mind was a good thing. Maybe he'd head off to the beach for the day. Maybe he'd stop at his favorite bar. Too tired to drive to the beach. Not wise to stop at the bar. *Home, a few beers while watching football.*

4 On My Mind

Sophia shook her head to dislodge the persistent thought. A thought that kept pestering her regardless of her efforts to escape. A picture of Captain Mitchell popped into her mind—again.

He'd seemed weary, not tired but weary as if weighed down by a world of problems. She understood it Saturday night when he'd been on his way home after a long shift. But Sunday morning, he'd still had that aura about him that called to her. All was not right in his world.

What should she do?

That she didn't know. And she questioned whether she should do anything at all.

"I hardly know him," she muttered to herself as she strode to her car at the end of the school day. Somehow, that didn't seem to matter to her inner being. She checked the insulated box in her trunk and knew with the cooler November day, the package of frozen pecan sticky buns and cinnamon rolls were still semi-frozen in the middle.

"Stop second-guessing yourself," she chided as she slid behind the wheel. "After all this time, you know—perhaps not the details but you know you need to see him again."

Sophia drove directly to the North Precinct. Before she'd even gotten out of her car, she saw him leaving the building and heading toward his car.

Rolling down the window, she waved. "Captain Mitchell?"

He turned at the sound of her voice. His gaze narrowed as if he was displeased. And then his expression cleared. He halted, head tilted, waiting.

Sophia put her car in park and got out, heading toward the back. "I brought you something." She'd popped the trunk as she'd exited. Reaching in, she grabbed the foil package. Before she could straighten, she felt his presence, his heat, his energy.

An inner smile wrapped around her heart. She was doing what she was supposed to be doing.

Cam was right behind her when she turned around. Nostrils flared trying to pick up the scent of sweet rolls.

"They are still a bit frozen but 30 seconds in the microwave will take care of that. Or if you live very far from here and keep them in the car with you, they should be thawed by the time you get home."

She shoved the package at him when she realized that she bordered on rambling.

"What would you have done if I wasn't here?" Cam took the package with both hands, hefted it to feel the weight and guess as to how many of the delectable treats she'd brought.

"Oh, I would have left them with the desk sergeant for you."

"Never," he rose on his toes and leaned towards her, "Never leave your rolls or your cookies at the front desk for me."

"Why ever not?"

"Because I'd never get them."

"They'd steal from you?" Sophia knew her jaw dropped and her mouth hung open.

"In a heartbeat."

"So they are—?" Try as she might, Sophia could not say the word.

"Looking for the word "thieves"? I'd trust them with my life and most of my worldly possessions but not with your cooking."

"Oh, well then. I'll just have to bring a box of cookies over so everyone can have some."

"Actually, you do not have to do that. You can bring the box of cookies to me and I'll dole them out as rewards for exemplary behavior."

"Really Captain, I doubt the officers in that building aren't already exemplary."

"That means you don't read the newspapers and watch the news."

"Of course I do."

"Do you not believe that police are corrupt racists who only want to wield power over the less fortunate?"

"Actually, I do not believe that to be true of all officers. However, I'm sure there are some just like there are some teachers who really do not like children.

"If I come by tomorrow at this time, will I see you?"

Cam looked at his watch. "I can make sure you will see me."

"Good, then I'll bring those cookies over. I've several dozen in the freezer. Will that be enough?" During this exchange, Sophia had shut the trunk and moved toward the driver's side door. She was nervous. Her hands were damp, her breathing altered. *He must think me brazen.* Her hand now on the handle, she turned toward him.

He'd followed her and was standing less than two feet away. His Irish moss green eyes held a hint of humor in them, his face held a hint of a dark beard, his mouth held a hint of a smile. She wondered what was going on inside him, if he could tell she was unnerved.

"Between all shifts, we've about 50 people coming and going in there." He nodded toward the precinct building behind him.

"Oh, then I'll make sure there are 100 cookies so everyone can have two."

"Or, a couple dozen will be fine. I'll make sure they are divided between the three shifts."

"Three dozen then, in separate boxes will be easiest for you."

"You trust that I'll pass them out and not just keep them for myself?" Cam leaned in again, caught a whiff of her vanilla scent and almost fell on her.

"Are you okay, Captain?"

Sophia's dark brown eyes were slightly tilted, giving her an exotic look. Right now they searched Cam's eyes, a worried crease pinched her brow.

Cam straightened and stepped back. "If you haven't eaten yet, would you have dinner with me?"

On a darkening November day, after a long and at times difficult shift, Cam's world brightened when a pleased smile lit Sophia's face causing her eyes to tilt a little more.

"I'd love to have dinner with you, Captain."

"Then you need to call me Cam."

"And you need to call me Sophia."

"I hadn't exactly picked where I was going to eat today. Do you have a preference?"

"I've a fondness for Thai and Chinese foods but I can't do MSG." Sophia said, nose wrinkled.

"I know just the place. And, it isn't far from where you live. Why don't I follow you home and we can go in my car."

Sophia drove home with Cam's car in her rearview mirror. *Is this a date?* No, she assured herself. She was following her instincts. Instincts that said Captain Cameron Mitchell needed something she had to give. Instincts that said it was something more than sweet rolls and cookies.

5 Thanksgiving

Over the past two weeks, she'd learned a bit about this intriguing man. They'd had dinner that Monday. His treat at his favorite Chinese restaurant.

The next Saturday, she'd been asked by the Safe Elders Program manager to check on Mr. Stanton. His daytime worker has specifically asked if she'd make the visit because Mr. Stanton had asked about her and commented about her interest in his renovation.

Because Cam went with her, the visit went smoothly.

Sophia laughed as she recalled knocking on Mr. Stanton's door, the leer from Randy as Mr. S called out to come in. When Cam stepped in behind her, Randy's leer abruptly changed to a frown. While she introduced Captain Mitchell to Mr. Stanton, Randy faded from the room.

The visit was short. She asked about the progress on projects the two men had told her about. Mr. Stanton said they'd been busy with other things and would be getting to it this coming week.

Sophia tucked her head down to hide her smile when Cam said he'd worked construction during the summers in high school and college and would be stopping by every now and then to see how things were coming along.

Walking up the dark, slippery path with Cam behind her was very different than her first trek with Randy in the same place. When Cam reached out to steady her over the last mossy spot, her heart skipped a beat. He came alongside her at the top and reached for her hand. In companionable silence they crossed the street to her car.

"Thank you," Sophia said before he spoke. "I've another request." She paused until he nodded.

"I've a big pot of chicken and vegetable soup. I'd like to share it with you. Either with you having dinner at my place or if that's not comfortable for you, I'll send you home with a container. And, if you wait an hour, I'll have freshly baked bread to go with it."

"Not sure what I've done to deserve that invitation but I'm accepting. Be there in an hour."

"Actually, you can come any time. You don't have to wait until the bread is baked. I wouldn't mind the company."

He'd followed her home. Watched some sports program while she busied herself in the kitchen making a tossed green salad and a homemade dressing. He wasn't Jonathan but he was a man and she couldn't remember a time since her husband's death when she had a single man sitting at her table. Of course men had been in her home, but they were all connected to one of her circle sisters.

8 p.m. Thanksgiving Day 2005

During one of their dinners, Cam had told her where he lived. With a large basket containing a full Thanksgiving dinner complete with pumpkin pie and a can of whipped cream on the passenger front seat, Sophia pulled into a parking spot in front of the older apartment building. Cam's car was two spots ahead of hers and that meant he was home. Basket in hand, she made her way up the walkway.

It was an older security system, one where you were buzzed in unless you had a key. She located the button next to his apartment number by setting the basket down and shining a small flashlight she kept on her key ring at the display.

She pressed the button and waited. Pressed it again and waited some more. A third time. *Three is a magickal number.*

"What?" the familiar voice growled.

"I brought you Thanksgiving dinner." The buzzer announcing the door was unlocked didn't sound. Sophia stood in the cold and checked her intuition. *I'm supposed to be here.*

Perhaps she was supposed to bring him dinner but not see him? That idea crossed her mind at the same time the door opened from the inside. Startled, Sophia stepped back and almost tumbled off the one step between the entryway and the sidewalk.

Strong arms grabbed her, steadied her and then hauled her close. The hamper basket was lifted from her hand. She was enveloped by his heat and the odor of whiskey.

"I know this is your time off. I wasn't sure if you'd stopped for dinner some place. Many places are closed today." She rambled trying to fill in the space, the yawning gap between them. Oh, it wasn't physical, Cam's arms banded around her and his chin rested on her crown. *When did he put the basket down?*

"I'm not in very good shape right now." His voice was gruff and low.

"Then a Thanksgiving dinner with your own pumpkin pie and whipped cream should help."

He let her go, stepped back and sighed. Irish moss green eyes, weary with the weight of the world, weary with the weight of something looked her full-on.

"Have you eaten?"

"I have but I saved room for a piece of your pie if you'll share."

"Not sure I have clean plates."

"Let's see." She started down the hall without waiting for him to lead the way. She knew his apartment was on the second floor. No elevator. The stairs started up halfway down the hall.

Cam caught up with her just as she reached the bottom step.

"How do you do that?"

"Walk upstairs or are you talking about something else?"

What to say in answer? Cam didn't want to tell her she'd saved him from a night of drinking himself into a stupor.

Wincing at the sight he knew was on the other side, he opened the door and gestured her through. "Should have told you to come back in a week so I could clean this place up."

Cam set the basket down on a chair after grabbing the pile of clothes on the seat. He made haste to gather clothing he'd tossed right and left, putting it all in his bedroom. A glance in the bathroom and he cringed at the sight before him. He picked up the towels from the floor and tossed them in the tub, pulling the shower curtain closed. It needed a good scrubbing but he was still too tipsy from drink to do more.

When he got back to the living room, Sophia was in the kitchen and the dishwasher was humming. She'd washed up two plates, two cups and some silverware.

"If you clear off the table a bit, I'll dish up your plate. I hope you like turkey with the works."

Smells of the past filled his nostrils as Sophia opened the containers. Turkey, dressing, sweet and mashed potatoes, cranberry sauce and gravy filled the plate she set before him.

"What would you like to drink?" she asked as she bustled about his kitchen.

He didn't answer. Next to his plate was a half empty glass of scotch along with a glass of water.

"I could fix you a pot of coffee," she commented as he took his first bite of heaven.

"Haven't been sleeping all that well." He shook his head and took another bite.

"I can fix you a cup of chamomile tea. It helps one sleep better."

"Don't have anything like that."

"But I do. I always have some tea in my purse. If you'd like me to fix you a cup, I will. But don't think you have to say 'yes'. I know I'm imposing—."

He cut her off with a wave of his hand. "Do Not apologize for being kind to an old reprobate."

Sophia smiled and laughter danced in her eyes. "I'm never kind to an old reprobate. But I'm always kind to my hero."

Cam choked as the last bite of mashed potatoes wasn't quite swallowed.

She was on her feet, pounding on his back before he knew what was happening. Her vanilla scent wreathed around him and he leaned back with a sigh when the spasms abated. Her hands shifted from his back to his shoulders and she gently kneaded the stiffness.

"You, Captain Mitchell, need to take better care of yourself."

If another woman said those same words, he'd have bit her head off. But Sophia was not 'another woman'. Why she saw him as a hero he didn't know. Perhaps he could milk—. Shaking his head, his throat closed in disgust.

"I'm good," he growled.

She backed away and instead of resuming her seat, headed into the kitchen. "Ready for some pie?"

Cam gathered his dishes and took them into the kitchen.

"I'll take those," Sophia said as she lifted the plate and silverware from his hands. "I believe the dishwasher has finished. Why don't we unload it now and then I can put these in to wash?"

It was phrased as a question but in actuality it wasn't one. Sophia opened the door and began handing items to him to put away. Once it was empty, she put his dinner dishes inside along with those that were still on the counter.

Good lord, there's enough for another load. What he couldn't understand was while he was appalled at the state of things, he wasn't embarrassed. He helped Sophia pack up the remaining food and put it in the refrigerator. When she got out the pie, she also pulled out a loaf of bread.

"Do you have a bread knife?"

Did he? Cam rummaged around in a couple of drawers and finally found a serrated knife. Not really a bread knife but Sophia said it would do. She sliced about half the bread, chattering about making turkey sandwiches and how good this bread toasted. The urge to haul her against his chest and kiss her senseless was quickly tamped down.

If he was her hero, she was his angel of mercy.

A large, almost a quarter of the pie, ended up on his plate. A thin slice on hers. She added a hefty squirt of whipped cream to her pie and handed the can to him.

Over pie she asked him about his day. He'd volunteered to trade shifts with the officers who had families so he hadn't been home all that long before she arrived. She listened intently as he described the types of calls they fielded on holidays—domestic violence or domestic disputes. And, yes, alcohol was almost always involved. There were usually a couple of suicide calls but nothing like during the Christmas holidays.

He asked her about her plans since she had a long weekend ahead. Some papers still needed grading, a couple of assignments to finesse for December. She was looking forward to spending the Christmas holidays with friends in Ireland. She'd still decorate with lights and candles but wouldn't have a tree this year.

The evening drew to a close. The pie dishes were added to the dishwasher and it was turned on. In the couple of hours they'd spent together, the disorderly kitchen was orderly. The dining room table cleared off and the mess of papers and magazines strewn helter-skelter around his place neatened. Somehow Sophia brought order to his world without intruding.

Cam walked her out to her car. Smiled to himself as she reminded him to bring his key so he could get back inside. The urge to bend down and kiss her on the lips was stifled but he did kiss her cheek.

She didn't pull away or complain. He imagined he saw a smile, a small secret smile.

He stood on the sidewalk as she drove away. Remained in the cold night air until she'd turned a corner and then waited just inside the apartment building in the hopes she'd come back around.

Of course she didn't. After a few minutes, he trod the stairs to his room.

Thanksgiving dinner aromas still filled the air but overlaying it all was the sweet scent of vanilla. Cam waited until the dishwasher was finished, unloaded it and, instead of stacking things on the counter, took the time to put them away in the cupboard.

He'd never finished his scotch and after a moments debate, tossed the remnants down the drain. After another moment's hesitation, he rinsed out the glass and put it in the dishwasher. Washing up, he padded into his bedroom. The pile of clothes he'd tossed on the bed, spilled onto the floor.

An empty basket sat by the door. Cam sorted through the mound, putting clean clothes away and anything dirty in the basket. The bed cleaned off, he tackled the sheets. He glanced at his watch. It'd taken him less than twenty minutes to straighten his room including changing the sheets.

"Get it together Mitchell. Cut back on the booze and—." Not wanting to confront himself more than that, Cam brushed his teeth. Stripping down, he tossed his clothes in the basket with the rest of his belongings that needed to be washed.

Clean sheets, a full stomach and the faint scent of vanilla reminded him of a soft spoken woman with dark brown eyes.

6 Following Instincts

Monday

If wishes were—Cam couldn't remember the adage but he did know his wish when he went to bed last night had not come true. His sleep was so deep, if he'd had any dreams, he'd no memory of them. Getting up to some semblance of order changed how he viewed his day.

A quick shower, shave and a cup of hot coffee started him off on an upbeat note. He didn't fix a turkey sandwich for work but he did have two pieces of toast with peanut butter along with a piece of pie. A better breakfast than he usually had, he filled his traveling mug with the rest of the pot and actually rinsed the empty pot out and dumped the coffee grounds in the garbage.

When he got to the precinct, a plain white box, twelve inch by twelve inch by four inches deep marked Personal - Captain Mitchell, awaited.

"A Ms. Stewart left it about thirty minutes ago. Said she'd be checking with you and she'd never send cookies to us again if anyone had tampered with it. Gotta tell you Cap, that's the only thing that saved it. That and she left us our own dozen cookies."

Cam grabbed the box and headed to his office. He made himself wait until he'd closed the door and tilted the blinds so no one could see in before he held the container under his nose and sniffed. The weight told him she'd sent him sweet rolls. Could he tell without peeking if they were the pecan sticky buns or the cinnamon rolls?

Instinct told him she'd send both. He put the box aside and booted up his computer, made sure his phone was charging, and looked at messages littering his desk. Littering was a bit of a stretch. He had an order to them. Most important on the left and marching across in descending order with the least important on the right.

Nothing that couldn't wait until he'd had one of Sophia's sweet rolls. His instincts were good. Opening the box, he saw four sweet rolls—two pecan sticky buns and two cinnamon rolls. Not waiting to decide between them, he got out his knife and cut two in half so he had a bit of both.

Sipping his coffee and munching on the gooey treats, Cam started his day. All was not right in the world around him but today his gut didn't tighten as he read reports from last night. The wonders of a good night's sleep spilled over into his day. No matter what came up, his equilibrium remained and his mood never faltered. When he left his office, his awareness of eyes tracking him was acute. *Haven't seen me in such a good mood in a while. More than a while – years more likely.*

Instead of lunch at the diner he preferred, Cam stopped by Stanton's. Randy Brown hadn't seen him coming and he watched for a moment listening to Brown's intimidation of the elderly man. When he stepped to the door and called out, the look on Brown's face was priceless. Anger, frustration, concern as in 'how much had he overheard'. Unfortunately not enough to do anything legal but fortunately enough to make sure he made a stop several times a week.

"Just checking on how things are coming along." Cam stepped further into the room. "Thought I might see some progress." His gaze lasered in on Brown. Stanton started a litany of rambling excuses about all the other things they'd been working on. Brown held his silence. *Smart man.*

"Although it's been a while since I did anything of this magnitude," Cam waved his hand in the general direction of the entire room, "I'd suggest you clean things up first. All this garbage needs to be taken out. The old papers can be recycled."

"Don't get no garbage pickup no more," Mr. Stanton said. "Overdue bill and all."

"Tell you what, Mr. Stanton," Cam said looking the old man in the face. "Let me talk to Senior Services. I'm sure they can put a good word in with the recycling people if not the garbage people. I'll stop by tomorrow and let you know what the deal is. In the meantime," he shifted his gaze to Brown, "you need to supervise Mr. Brown getting things cleaned up and out to the curb.

"I'll swing by later today and see what progress you've made," he said directly to Mr. Brown. "Won't have to come down here because bags and boxes will be at the curb."

As he pulled away in his car, the idea to call and let Sophia know what he'd done had him pulling his cell from his pocket. For a brief moment he thought of driving to Fremont High School and waiting for her classes to end. Instead he left a message updating her on what was going on with Mr. Stanton.

Next he called Senior Services. Because Mr. Stanton's worker was out, he chatted with his supervisor. She wasn't surprised when Cam told her he believed Brown was intimidating Mr. Stanton. They both agreed that until Mr. Stanton said something either to his worker, a Safe Elders Program volunteer or Brown was caught actually doing something, little more could be done than be watchful and visible.

Instinct said to go home when he got off from work. He had food waiting for him along with an open bottle of scotch. While he might prefer someone waiting on him, he wasn't so feeble he couldn't fix a sandwich and a piece of pie. To be on the safe side, he brought the remaining sweet rolls home with him. That ensured he'd have a memorable breakfast.

Relaxed in front of the television, a monster turkey sandwich with all the trimmings in front of him, Cam zoned out watching a sports newscast. When his phone rang he smiled. His instincts told him it wasn't work related. A grin on his face, he saw the caller identification when he answered.

"Because of you, I'm having a great dinner."

"Because of you, I'm baking tonight. I swear the people in your office never have treats."

"Not true. Someone stops and picks up a dozen or two donuts every couple of days. And then we have some who bring in fruit. During the summer we even have fresh fruit and vegetables from the officers who garden."

"When I dropped off the sweet rolls this morning, I thought they would have been gone before I reached my car."

"Oh, that would be true. You have become a legend at the precinct. I expect we'll have officers from other precincts wanting to transfer in and our transfer out requests will cease."

Sophia laughed. "I don't believe that at all, Captain."

"Cam, remember, you're calling me Cam these days."

"I do remember, Cam. And thank you for the message about Mr. Stanton. I'm hopeful that Mr. Brown will take off because so many people are checking in—well, actually my checking won't do anything but your stopping by may have him on his way in no time."

"Hope so." He wanted to ask her if he could come over for the evening. He wanted to ask her to have dinner with him tomorrow night. He wanted to keep her on the phone just so he could hear her voice. "Thanks for calling, Sophia. And thanks for the pecan sticky buns and cinnamon rolls. I've three left. I'm rationing myself to one a day to prolong the gift."

A moment of silence. He almost spoke up but wasn't sure what would come out.

"You're most welcome, Cam. I'll leave you to your evening then. Good night."

7 In the Dark of the Night

December 2005

Sophia checked the pot roast one more time. Cam had been due for dinner an hour ago. He'd called and said something had come up and she'd told him she'd wait—dinner would wait until he got there.

When she thought of him, a darkness enveloped her and her worry meter ticked faster. Something was going on. She banished the idea of turning on the television and watching the news. Whatever Cam was dealing with was bad. Getting sucked into that darkness would not help him.

She lit the candles in her living room, her sacred space, and turned on the rock salt lamp. Standing before her altar, she raised her hands high.

"Great Spirit watch over and guide Cameron Mitchell through the darkness and into the light." She visualized a golden white light surrounding him. Lowering her arms to her side, she closed her eyes and concentrated on the protecting light for a few more minutes before returning to the kitchen.

Cam pulled the gloves from his hands before wiping the sweat from his forehead. It was freezing out but he felt warm. No he felt hot. His mouth was dry, his throat scratchy but worse of all, his eyes were watering.

At one point he'd thought he'd heard Sophia's voice. He shook his head to ward off the unwanted memory of her being at his place two nights ago. He'd made spaghetti—well, he'd opened a jar of sauce and cooked the pasta. A bag of salad greens became a salad. Dessert was comprised of her cookies. It was hard to walk her to her car, to let her leave.

He was drawn to her.

She represents life.

What did she see in him? Today was a prime example of his world and it wasn't pretty.

As he stood with the other officers, the ambulances headed off, sirens blaring, with one child and two adults. Another ambulance loaded the two other children into the back. No need to rush. He'd checked on them himself. Touched their necks in a frantic hope to feel a pulse. Skin was turning cold.

Add this call to the earlier one, the one where the mom was raped while her children were in the next room and any belief, any thread of belief in decency was lost. At least her husband had stepped up, called a grandparent to watch the children and took off to the hospital to be with her. Her assailant had cut her as well as choking and raping her.

The drunk driver who'd caused this head-on collision was injured and also on his way to the hospital. A part of him wanted the guy sent to the morgue. A fitting place for some asshole who destroyed a family.

Processing the scene of an accident, especially where there was a death, took time. Cam looked around, saw everyone was doing their job. He could stay or he could go because he had no active roll. Maybe he'd stop at the hospital and see how everyone was doing. Or maybe he'd just call. Or maybe he'd wait and read the reports in the morning. Or—

He checked his watch. Seven. He'd been due at Sophia's at six. She'd fixed dinner for him and promised him a surprise. He would miss her while she was in Ireland. A mantle of death and darkness enveloped him. Rage boiled from his gut to his mouth. *It's better if I don't see her. Better yet, I should break it off.*

One of the officers waved him over. "They're still looking for him."

"You mean the rapist?"

"Yeah. Thought they had him but he slipped away."

"Thanks for the update." Cam pinched the bridge of his nose hoping the pressure would ease his now pounding head. He massaged the back of his neck. No relief.

"You know how to reach me if you need me," he called over his shoulder on his way to his vehicle. Inside he buckled his seatbelt and eased away from the scene. Sweat beaded on his brow. He opened a window to let in the cool night air. *What in the hell am I doing? It's freezing out there.*

Cam pulled to the curb and got out his phone, dialed the number from memory. "It's better this way," he muttered as the phone rang.

Sophia answered on the second ring. Her voice soothed and he wished he could see her. But, he wasn't fit for human company. He took a deep breath. "Know it's late to call but I won't be coming by."

"It isn't too late, Cam. Dinner is ready and can remain ready for several hours."

"Look, Sophia, I'm dead on my feet."

"You sound like it's been a horrible day. Come by and I'll send dinner with you if you don't want to stay."

Don't want to stay? Cam was afraid that if he stopped at Sophia's he'd never want to leave. But that wasn't going to happen. He was in that dark place. That place where he lashed out at people. He didn't want to lash out at Sophia so he couldn't go.

"I'll bring dinner to your place then, Cam. I can be there in twenty minutes. There's too much food for just me. You know I'm going out of town in two days. I'll set aside some for my dinner and bring you the rest."

He sat in his car at the side of the road and listened to her calm, sane voice.

"Where are you?"

Where was he? He looked around and saw where he was. "Doesn't matter where I am. I'm not coming by and you are not bringing anything to my place."

Why didn't she say something? Argue with him so he could yell at her.

"I'm going to turn off the alarm and unlock the front door so you can just walk in."

The line went dead. She'd hung up. "Stupid bitch!" Cam shouted and pounded the steering wheel. He dialed her number again but she didn't answer. Slamming the car out of park, he peeled away from the curb and swung into her driveway. The car shook when he banged the door shut.

Cam stalked to her front door.

Sure enough, the door was unlocked.

He stormed into the house. "What the hell do you think you're doing?"

"I'm putting your dinner on the table." Sophia placed a full plate of pot roast, carrots and potatoes at one of the place settings. "This is yours."

"Christ, I need a drink."

"Do you want to tell me about your day or would it be better to put it behind you?" Sophia dished up her own dinner and approached the table. "I'm really a good listener."

"My day isn't fit for you to hear about." Cam still stood, his gaze locked on the plate of food.

"You might be surprised what is fit for me to hear. I am not unaware of the worst of human behavior." She sat and motioned for him to do the same.

He remained standing.

"I prefer pot roast warm but it's also good cold. When I've finished my dinner, I can package it up for you to take home."

Cam stared at her. She was dressed in jeans and a teal green top. Her dark brown hair was down but combs held it back from her face. "Why aren't you mad at me?"

"I can be mad at you if you really want me to but you'd have to tell me what I'm to be mad about and then I'd have to agree it was something I could be mad about."

"Sophia, I'm late to dinner, I stormed in here yelling, I've been disrespectful to you. And that's what I've come up with without even thinking about it."

"What I've observed is a weary man who's had a day that has tested even his well-built wall of defense. I've no idea what all has happened but I do know you are well-defended and if the events of the day have broken through—well, all I can say is it must have been a hellishly awful day.

"Why would I want to add to it by fighting with you?"

She pointed to his meal and patted the back of his chair. "Come and eat. If, after you've finished you still want to fight, I'll yell at you."

Cam sat and, after tucking the napkin in his lap, picked up his fork and took a bite. The flavors of the pot roast and seasonings burst on his tongue. The meat almost melted in his mouth it was so tender. The potatoes and carrots—just like his mother used to make except not. There was something different Sophia did to her food that made it extraordinary.

She'd fixed him that chamomile tea with honey. He wasn't ready to admit it soothed. He'd rather have three fingers of scotch but he'd also told her not to go out and buy it if she didn't drink it herself.

They ate in companionable silence. He relished each bite and inwardly thanked his sub-conscious self that knew he needed to be here. Why else would he have been two houses away when he called to cancel?

Sophia offered him second helpings but he declined. He was full and the energy he'd summoned to deal with his day was depleted. The reserves he'd called upon were ebbing. If he left now, he could get to his place before he collapsed.

He picked his plate up and took it to the kitchen. When he turned she was right behind him. Her arms went around his waist and she stepped close. The vanilla scent she favored surrounded him and he sighed.

"Got to go before I drop."

Sophia looked up to assess for herself where he was. "Are you sure you're safe to drive? I can drive you home."

Was he safe to drive? Probably not. The vision of the twisted wreckage flashed in his mind's eye. "Don't want to put you to any trouble."

"Cam, you are not trouble. Come," she tugged on his hand and pulled him into another room. "Sit here," she gestured to a chair. "Now take a deep breath through your nose and let it out through your mouth."

"Are you trying to get me to relax?"

"Of course I am. You'll actually feel more awake, at least for a short period of time."

Sophia led him through the breathing exercise for five minutes. "How do you feel?"

"Like a wet noodle."

"Well, wet noodles can't drive. So here's Plan 'B.'" She led him down the hall, stopping at the first door on the left. "You will sleep here. Bathroom is across the hall. I'm the next room down on the left if you need anything.

"I'm usually up by seven because I have to be at school before eight. I'll make coffee for you and set out a couple of cinnamon buns before I go. All you need to do is lock the front door when you leave."

"Plan B is not gonna happen. Plan C is, I'll nap on the couch in the family room and then leave after waking you so you can set the alarm and lock the door. My car will block yours from leaving in the morning for one thing."

"Don't forget the sack that will be waiting for you in the refrigerator."

"I won't forget it."

Cam stood in the hall, his gaze locked with hers. He wanted to lean down and kiss her but was afraid the friendship they had would be ruined.

Sophia stepped closer and rose on her toes. Leaning in, she kissed his cheek. "Sleep well. I'm right next door if you need something."

He wanted to say he needed her. He wanted to pull her back, press her against him and claim her mouth. He wanted her to invite him into her bed.

Cam squeezed her hand, dropped it and turned into the room. She reached around the door and flipped on the lights. "See you in the morning." Her voice was full of cheer.

He managed to nod.

8 The Morning After

Cam woke to the smell of coffee. He stretched and looked around the room. He'd been too distracted with emotions to take in his surroundings, too distracted by Sophia, if the truth were known.

Pulling on his pants, he trod across the hall to the bathroom. After peeing, he washed his face and hands, drying them on a bright turquoise towel. He finished dressing including his shoes because he heard her moving around. No need to tiptoe out if she was up.

At the end of the hall, his view was of the family room and kitchen. Sophia puttered around, setting out a plate of sweet rolls. Bread was in the toaster and a frying pan was on the stove, eggs next to it.

"You didn't have to make breakfast for me," Cam said leaning against the hall opening. "Coffee would have been more than enough."

"I won't bore you with the importance of breakfast." Sophia cracked eggs into the pan and pushed down the lever to the toaster. "Coffee is ready. Help yourself."

Cam crossed to the kitchen and followed his impulse. Coming up behind her, he circled her waist and breathed in her vanilla scent. A light kiss on her cheek and he moved on to the coffee pot. His first sip of the caffeinated liquid slid down his throat and heated his gut.

The toaster popped up and he reached for the bread just beating Sophia to it. "You finish the eggs and I'll get this." He buttered the toast and grabbed the jar of jam and headed to the table. Turning back, he leaned across the counter for his coffee.

Sophia was easing two eggs onto a plate.

"Take this." She handed him the plate. "I'll bring your coffee."

Moments later Cam sat down to a home cooked breakfast. Eggs, toast, coffee and sweet rolls.

"Do you do this for yourself every morning?" He asked after inhaling his eggs.

"No, usually I have a couple cups of tea and a piece of toast. Sometimes I fix an egg but I don't get the same pleasure if I'm just cooking for myself.

"How did you sleep?" Sophia watched him intently. He put his fork down, sipped his coffee and organized his thoughts before answering.

"Better than usual."

"Better than you usually sleep in general or better than you usually sleep after such a horrible day?"

She'd given him an opening, set it up so he could prevaricate but one of the things he'd noticed about being around Sophia was he didn't lie. He just didn't answer or maybe he was a bit vague but he didn't outright lie.

"Better than I usually sleep in general."

She smiled. The one that telegraphed her genuine pleasure. "I'm so glad. People are more sleep deprived than they realize."

"Don't lecture." He sounded gruff to his own ears.

"You don't have to rebuff someone's concern for you."

Cam sat very still waiting for more. She might be different from any other woman he'd ever known but she was still a woman and couldn't help herself when it came to criticizing or complaining.

"Would you like more coffee?"

His head jerked up so fast, he almost gave himself a whiplash.

"No, I'm good." He stared at her looking for the trick, looking for something.

"Is something wrong?" Sophia's brow furrowed and her face reflected concern.

Cam looked at his watch. "I don't want to make you late for school."

"It's a late opening day and I've a little more time before I have to leave. But, don't let me keep you if you need to go."

He stood and took his dishes to the kitchen, rinsing off his plate and cup and putting them in the dishwasher.

Sophia picked up two grocery sacks and handed one to him. Carrying the other, she started toward the front door.

Cam stopped outside the living room. He'd passed by the opening every time he'd entered the house but he'd never really paid any attention to it. For the first time he really studied the space. "We came in here for a bit last night didn't we?"

Sophia put her sack on the hall table and came to stand next to him. "We did."

"What's all this for? It looks different from formal living rooms I've seen."

"It is different. It's my sacred space. Where I can come and find my peace, my center."

Cam stepped into the room and wandered the perimeter. There was a fireplace with a mantle on which sat some Chinese carving of a woman and dragon and a porcelain blue bird. Throughout the room, rocks and candles covered every flat surface. On a table under the living room window, a black cloth with various rocks and figurines seemed a focal point.

Sophia hadn't followed him physically but he felt her eyes watch him. He reached out a couple of times but something held him back from touching anything.

"What's this for?" He still stood in front of the table with the black cloth.

"It's my altar."

"Like in a church?"

"In some ways it is."

"I've been in Catholic homes and they have a shrine set up. And in some orthodox homes, they've got those icons."

"And Buddhists and Hindus and other religions have altars, a place in their home or business to honor their deities or their gods."

"Is that what this is? Something to honor some god?"

"My altar honors both the Goddess and the God as well as the directions, the seasons, the elements, the whole."

"So you don't go to church."

"I don't go to a church building. I come here to pray, to seek answers to questions, to find peace at the end of a long and challenging day."

"You aren't Christian then." He said the words with little emotion attached to them.

"I do believe that Jesus was the son of God but I also believe you are also—and I am the daughter of God. I believe everything is sacred and part of the divine. I believe that we are all connected and have only to practice in order to feel our connection with each other."

"It brings you peace—what you believe brings you peace of mind?"

"Yes."

Cam had finished his circuit around the room and stood beside her at the entrance. "I can't reconcile God with all the evil in the world. I don't believe in God or Jesus or any of it."

"If it helps you through your days, then that is right for you."

Emotions welled up and he battled them back. He cleared his throat so he could speak, fought the tears brightening his eyes. Two more years and he could retire with full benefits, if he lasted that long. If there was a shred of humanity left. His soul was so dark, he saw death and evil all around him.

Except when he was with Sophia. For some reason, when he was at her house, the darkness lightened and death and evil faded. They weren't gone but they no longer oppressed.

Cam opened the front door, took the offered sack from Sophia and stepped out into the chilly morning. He had a shaving kit at the precinct so he could go right there. It was probably cold enough he didn't need to worry about the food. A wave of exhaustion washed over him and he almost stumbled off the front step.

"Do you need a ride to the airport?"

"No, my friends are picking me up. I hope you have a peaceful holiday, Cam. I'll bring you a treat from Ireland."

"No need. I'm good."

"Everyone needs a treat and Irish treats are the best.

"Oh do you know yet if you are working New Year's Eve?"

"Most likely, why?"

"A friend of mine always has a New Year's Eve party and I thought maybe you'd be free and would like to come."

"Thanks for the invitation but I probably need to pass. Work and all that." He was backing up to his car. He popped the trunk with the key fob and after placing the sacks inside, closed the trunk and got in the car. Backing out of the drive, he put the window down and waved.

Sophia remained on the porch, arms wrapped around her to ward off the cold. When Cam was out of sight, she went back inside. She was attracted to him. A man who courted death, a man who no longer saw the good in people, a man who scoffed at life.

Returning to her sacred space, she stood in front of her altar. Hands, palms up at shoulder height, she sent prayers and protective energy to surround him.

"Blessed Be."

Second guessing herself was never fruitful so she left things as they were and gathered herself to face another day in the classroom. Two more days and they'd leave for Ireland. Two more days—would he call her before she left? Or would she call him?

9 Ireland

December 17, 2005

It was a long flight and less than two months since Sophia had been here for Samhain. Seeing Gabriella with Giovanni warmed her heart.

"Are you okay?" Gabriella enveloped her in a hug of welcome.

"I'm fine. Just a little tired wrapping up school for the holidays and then the flight." Sophia noticed the concerned looks from her Circle sisters but wasn't sure what that was all about. She was doing just fine. Especially now that they were all together and in Ireland.

The Circle had remained intact when Elizabeth married Michael and made her home in Ireland. They would stay together with Gabriella in Italy. Of course it was a bit more difficult to get together flying from Oregon to either Italy or Ireland with babies in tow, but they would manage. Madison

Michelle was an excellent traveler and with so many extra aunties and Ashley's daughter, Rose, to entertain her the trip wasn't so stressful for Diana or Matthew.

The drive to Kinsale was a nice break from the flight. Seeing the green of Ireland's landscape dotted with hedgerows of fuchsias and rock walls called to her. Of course it was stunning in spring and summer with the flowers in bloom but there was something restful about the varied greens in the patchwork quilted land on either side of the road.

She'd enjoyed her time at Giovanni's basking in the Italian sun but being in Ireland felt like coming home. *Maybe I'll do a genealogy search and see if I've Irish ancestors.*

Lunch at The Winner's Circle was welcomed. A chance to stretch, move around and consume Irish stew and a pint of Guinness. Relaxing on the bench, her gaze on the fire, she could see Cam in this place. The idea to invite him the next time they came flitted through her mind. A part of that idea intrigued her and quickened her pulse. Another part frightened her. *I've not been involved with anyone for... . How long has it been?*

Guilt at not instantly remembering how long it'd been since her husband died soured the last bite of her stew.

When his spirit had come to her at their Samhain ceremony three years ago, he'd told her to move on with her life. More recently she'd heard his voice. He'd whispered Cam was, underneath it all, a good man.

She saw that for herself. *He wouldn't be so torn up over what he sees in his work if he didn't still care.*

For another moment she sat still and concentrated on sending him protective energy. And then she turned back to the others who were gathering their things together. A short mile to The Manor was all that was left of their travels today.

Sophia unpacked and, before leaving her room to see how she could help someone else, stood at the window. Every time she'd been here, this had been her room. The view of the drive with the gardens to the left and paddocks to the right never tired. Would Cam see this view as soothing? No, at least not at first. He has so much tension infusing his body it would take a while before he relaxed. It reminded her of Gabriella and Italy. She knew it was right for her Circle sister to remain there because she'd never seen her so comfortable in her own body. Not particularly comfortable with Giovanni but—she smiled. *That has certainly changed. Something permanent? I'm so happy for her.*

That afternoon they met in Elizabeth's study. The men were with Michael and Lily's mother-in-law, Eleanor was monitoring the babies who were both napping. Everyone was participating in the Solstice Ceremony tomorrow except for Ashley's younger son, Anthony, Eleanor, the babies and Seamus, Michael's houseman.

They met at the top of the path leading to the Sacred Grove. Sophia was in the middle of the line, the only one not paired with a man. She'd taken Rose by the hand and invited James but he'd already stood next to Daniel. The path was wide enough that Ashley and Daniel could have James with them but not both children.

Rose held Sophia's hand. "Are you okay, Soph?"

"I'm fine, Rose. Do I look like I'm not?"

"You look like something is wrong but I don't know what it is."

Sophia squeezed Rose's hand. "I'm fine. Perhaps a little tired but that's all."

The little girl was not appeased but she said no more.

Once in the middle of The Sacred Grove the women stood with The Lady and prayed.

"We are The Light

"We are The Source

"Through us Love flows

"Throughout the world."

As was their tradition, the prayer was said times three.

Time to meditate and reflect. Matthew held Diana in his arms. Lily's head rested on Jackson's shoulder. Daniel had one arm around Ashley who held Rose on her lap and his other one draped over James's shoulder. Hunter and Logan were keeping a very close eye on Grant who was kept between them. Michael lounged on one side of the bubbling spring. Elizabeth was next to him, kneeling in the grass, her gaze skyward. Gabriella was seated a little to one side but Giovanni's attention was on her.

Before they left, he approached and knelt before her. Sophia couldn't hear what he said to Gabriella but she thought he was proposing. Her suspicion was confirmed when her Circle sister flung her arms around his neck and nodded her head vigorously.

And then they were on their way back to the house. Food was waiting. Diana and Elizabeth checked on the children while the rest of them made sure there were enough chairs in the dining room for all of them.

They dished up Seamus's split pea soup, sliced his fresh baked bread and set out his deep dish apple pie which would be adorned with sharp cheddar and ice cream when they got to dessert.

Sophia caught a look that passed between Michael and Jackson before Michael spoke up. "Do we have a wedding to plan?"

All heads including hers, swiveled toward Gabriella and Giovanni. Something transpired between them and then Giovanni picked Gabriella up and left the room. They could hear whispered voices but not make out the words. A flushed Gabriella and a satisfied Giovanni finally reappeared.

"Imbolc. We'll marry on Imbolc." Gabriella announced.

"Or, we'll elope," Giovanni added.

Sophia stood followed by Lily, Elizabeth, Diana, Ashley and Hunter. "Six weeks is more than enough time for The Circle to put a wedding together." Sophia said the words with conviction because The Circle had put other weddings together in six weeks. In her heart joy and sadness mixed. The tears in her eyes reflected both happiness and sorrow. On Imbolc she would be the only single woman left.

10 Home Again

December 30, 2005

Sophia shrugged out of her coat and hung it on the hook on the wall just inside the door. The flight back from Ireland seemed longer this time. So many trips this year. Italy in October and then on to Ireland. Home and then back to Ireland for Samhain. And now this trip to Ireland and back. *Already I have tickets to Italy for Gabriella and Giovanni's wedding.*

She didn't begrudge Gabriella her happiness nor did she feel jealousy of her other Circle sisters' lives. She'd known that love with Jonathan, had her years of connubial bliss. The wheel of life turns. Especially after Lily married, she knew the wheel would turn until one-by-one the others would find their soul mate.

However, when Giovanni had picked Gabriella up and carried her from Elizabeth's dining room, an oppressive sadness had settled on her heart. With effort she'd managed a smile, hearty well-wishes and joined in the basics of organizing a wedding.

The Circle knew something was amiss. Gabriella had point blank asked her what was wrong when they'd first met up at the Shannon airport. Lily had tried to talk to her as had Diana. She caught the worried looks from Ashley, Hunter and Elizabeth.

What could she say? She'd told Gabriella that teaching and gardening were no longer enough. And that was true. *Ever since my friend died in October, my life seems to stretch endlessly before me. I'm more at loose ends than when Jonathan died. Then teaching and gardening did fill the emptiness.*

What she didn't say that was also true? The Circle didn't need her as they once had.

"Stop it! This pity party is not like you at all!"

Sophia marched into the third bedroom she used as an office and booted up her computer. If the Goddess was merciful, there would be someone for her to check on tomorrow.

The email from the Safe Elders Program did give her an appointment for tomorrow.

Mr. Stanton.

The Goddess had a strange sense of humor. A shiver of dread traced Sophia's spine and she rubbed against the back of the chair to chase it away. The email gave her a preferred time to drop in and also reminded her to take a police escort.

Was the Goddess giving her an opening to contact Cam Mitchell? Their last parting was awkward and seemed like 'good bye' at least on his side.

And, tomorrow was New Year's Eve. Cam would be working and the timing of the visit was early enough that she could still drop by Jackson's New Year's Eve party. She'd put a pair of nice shoes in the car so she could change after slogging through mud.

A weight of despair pushed her shoulders down and bowed them. *This won't do.* With effort she sat up straight, put her hands behind her back and gripped her wrists. The stretch hurt. *How long have I been hunched over? Time for a cup of tea. Not chamomile but a bracing peppermint.*

Her hands now wrapped around the mug of warm tea, a couple of newly thawed cookies at hand, Sophia tried to relax and sort out her best choice for tomorrow.

One part of her wanted to send a message to Lily saying she was under the weather with jet lag and wouldn't be there. Another believed going to the party would help lift her mood. At no time did she think to cancel the visit to Mr. S's house.

The only decision about the visit was whether to call Cam directly or call the non-emergency number when she was ready to leave.

Actually there was a third option. *I can call Cam at the precinct and leave a message for him about the visit. I can tell him the time and ask him to arrange for someone to meet me. I can do that. I can leave a message on his voice mail.*

That problem solved, Sophia freshened her tea and started unpacking. She'd done this trip enough times she managed with a single carry-on suitcase and a backpack. A chuckle escaped as she put things away—all of her clothes in the laundry, toiletries in the bathroom which left a couple of books for her bedside table. Her first trip to Ireland, she'd taken two full-sized suitcases. Even though she'd brought back souvenirs on that trip and the next couple, she'd always had clothes she'd never worn.

Now? *I just enjoy my time there and store memories instead of stones.*

What am I going to do about tomorrow? It was getting late and she didn't want to wait and call in the morning unless her decision was to call non-emergency when she was leaving.

Unwanted tears tiptoed down her cheeks as Sophia picked up the phone and dialed the number that went to Cam's voice mail. The sound of his voice, so tired and weary, tugged at her heavy heart. She didn't have the will to infuse lightness and energy into her voice. At the end of the message, she left her phone number not sure if he'd kept it or not.

What was it about this dark, weary man that called to her? Jonathan was full of light and joy, his love was tender and yet passionate. She missed curling up with a man, having his arms around her while she read or they watched television. She missed having a man come up behind her in the kitchen, kiss her neck, turn her into his embrace, dance her back to the bedroom. She missed… .

Sophia sat in her sacred space, candles lit, the salt crystal lamp on. The soft glow eased her heavy heart. Was this what her future held? While in Ireland, she'd dreamed of Cam, could see him drinking his scotch in his apartment, see him sitting at his desk at the precinct, see him standing beside his officers at a crime scene.

Because The Lady always hovered nearby, she'd wondered if she was actually seeing Cam or if it was only a dream. He'd seemed enveloped in darkness, no white-gold aura shone around him. She only caught the barest flicker from time to time and believed that was connected to something he was thinking.

Time in her sacred spaced eased the turmoil and lightened the sadness. Sophia went through her normal bedtime routine which included a relaxation exercise that helped her sleep. Lucid dreams were filled with Cam, his hand on her elbow steering her up the path from Mr. Stanton's place. Sophia reached out, took his hand and led him out of the darkness and into the light.

11 New Year's Eve Day

December 30, 2005

Cam sat, his elbows on his desk, his head in his hands, the very picture of despair. He'd seen the light blink, saw caller identification, knew it was Sophia but he'd not answered. The battle raged within him after listening to her message.

He could send another officer to accompany her to Stanton's, keep her safe from Brown who was still lurking around. His gut told him she was in even more danger now that people were dropping in at odd hours and always accompanied by the police.

Stanton was leery now and not as amenable to Brown's braggadocio. Someone showing up every couple of days to see how the project(s) were going demonstrated to the old codger just how useless Brown really was. And Brown knew that one word from Stanton to the police and he'd be evicted. With his record of violence, a case could be made for immediate vacating of the property. Every officer in the precinct would be delighted to provide him an escort off the property.

Sophia had been gone thirteen days. He missed hearing her voice, seeing her putter around her kitchen or organize his. Somehow she managed to leave his place looking like a home without trespassing. She tidied things up instead of moving things around. Newspapers in one pile, magazines in another—both left on the coffee table where he could put his feet up and have the padding under his heels.

He shook his head, threaded his hands through his hair, rubbed his neck and sat back. She'd given him an out. Why did his gut clench tighter than his jaw when he mentally trolled through his list of officers who'd be on duty when she needed someone?

"Because I'm a selfish bastard," Cam muttered to himself. He pushed back from his desk and headed out the door of his office.

"Night Capt." The acknowledgement of the swing shift that he was leaving followed him as he strode to the door. He didn't stop to chat as he sometimes did. Too much blue-deviled to do that but he did nod as he went to let them know he heard them and cared.

When he let himself into his apartment he was resigned to his reality. Of course it would be him who met her and accompanied her to Stanton's. He was a selfish bastard and that's what selfish bastards did. Made decisions based on their own self interests.

December 31, 2005

Sophia was in her car, seatbelt on when she pushed the button that automatically opened her garage door. Waiting in her driveway was Cam's car. Her hand trembled as she unbuckled herself. He'd come. She wasn't sure he would when she called. She blinked back tears of relief and got out of her car. As she started towards him, he got out of his car.

"You didn't have to come here, I planned on meeting you or whomever you sent at Stanton's." It was a cold and blustery day but instead of wrapping her coat closer around her, it hung open and flapped in the breeze.

Cam put his hands on the lapels, pulled her closer and began buttoning it. His intense Irish moss green gaze focused on her. His pupils dilated with desire. When he'd finished with her buttons, his hands rested on her shoulders.

She'd missed him, missed his fresh minty scent, his strength. Missed those moments when the darkness lifted and she saw beneath it to the kind man within.

His hands fisted and relaxed on her coat. Before her eyes, the layers of darkness evaporated and Cam was enveloped in a white light.

Sophia took that as a sign. She leaned into his strength, rose on her tiptoes and slid her arms around his neck. A second passed before she kissed him, pressed her lips to his, poured her longing in to the meeting of their mouths, her fingers massaging his nape.

Cam did not push her away. His arms banded around her and he kissed her back. A kiss filled with passion.

A horn tooting broke them apart.

Sophia saw the apology forming and pressed her fingers to his mouth.

"Do not apologize or I won't give you the sack of cookies in my car."

"You knew I'd come?"

She shook her head and looked away. She'd hoped he'd come but was anything but sure. "I brought them as a "thank you" to whomever escorted me today."

His hands dropped to his side and he stepped back.

She reached out and laced her fingers with his. "I hoped it would be you. Wanted it to be you but the ways things were between us when I last saw you, I wasn't sure you'd come."

"Get your things, we'll take my car." He saw her raised eyebrow. "If you don't mind that is. Thought you could tell me about your trip and all."

"When does your shift end?"

"I'm pulling extra hours. Couple of the guys are really into football so I'm working one of their shifts."

"So when does this guy come on duty?"

Cam fidgeted. "Couple of hours."

Sophia grabbed the sack of cookies, her purse and her notepad from her car, put the shoes she'd planned to wear at the Montgomery House Party by her back door and closed the garage door.

When she looked at this man who intrigued her, the fierce scowl on his face would scare most people away. *I'm not most people.*

She put the bag of cookies on the floor in the back. When she closed the door and turned, Cam was right beside her.

"What's the deal with the shoes?"

"I'm still debating on whether to go to the New Year's Eve party my friends are hosting or not. I'd planned on meeting whomever at Stanton's and I didn't want to go in muddy boots."

"Understandable."

Sophia was chilled to the marrow. The visit with Mr. Stanton hadn't taken that long but she knew with a certainty that if Cam wasn't with her, she'd be dead. Randy Brown's hatred was palpable. He said not a word but she knew when Cam wasn't watching him because she could feel the evil in his stare.

Back in Cam's car, she gave in to the urge to hold herself and rock.

"Tell the Safe Elders Program that you can't go see Stanton any more. And, I'll have a patrol car meet up with whomever else goes so there are two officers. Brown is at the breaking point. I'm not even sure Stanton is safe at this point."

"Has it reached the point where only the police should do the welfare checks?"

"You may be right. I stopped by a couple of times while you were gone—on my own, in addition to the regular checks. Brown's always been dangerous but right now he's on edge and about ready to break. I'll talk to the officers who were out here over the last couple of days. If he's worse now than he was then, I'll talk to the Safe Elders people about the next move."

They didn't even indulge in small talk as Cam drove them back to Sophia's place. During the entire drive, she debated going or not going to Lily and Jackson's. When they pulled into her driveway, she still hadn't made up her mind.

Cam rounded the car and helped her out. Hand on her elbow, he escorted her to her front door. After unlocking it, he ushered her in, turned off her alarm and after divesting her of her coat, gently herded her into her sacred space.

He turned back to the hall and hung her coat on the hall rack before pulling his off and hanging it on another hook.

Sophia hadn't moved. She was exactly where he left her.

"It's me," he said as he came to stand behind her. "Just me." He put his arms around her and pulled her back against his chest.

Her hands came up to cover his and she relaxed against him. "This was even more unnerving than my first visit and that was terrifying. I've never had someone harbor such ugly feelings for me. A part of me wonders how a person turns into a monster like Mr. Brown."

"All through his life, Brown has had choices, Sophia. No one has a perfect road in life. When your husband died, you could have started drinking, you could have become promiscuous, you could have become addicted to prescription drugs."

Sophia stopped his litany of 'could have's'. "No, Cam, I could not. I had my women's circle. They stayed with me. Held me. Listened when I raged. Dried my eyes when I cried. Held me so often I never felt truly alone. And I had this space to come in to. I wrapped myself in a blanket of bluebirds and rocked and cried and railed at the injustice of it all."

She turned to face him. Lifted her head until she saw his Irish moss green eyes. "What's most important is I never had to do any of that alone. Someone was always with me until I regained my balance."

Cam held her with one hand, the other stroked her back. "You were and are always there for them also."

"I try to be."

"Come now, Sophia. You seldom if ever try. You only do."

"Quoting Yoda from Star Wars?" She smiled when his chest shook as he held in a chuckle.

Stepping back, she held his hands. "And you, Cam, you are the same way if not more so. You risk so much for others. If Brown wanted to kill me, and I've no doubt if the opportunity arose he'd do it in a heartbeat, he'd want to torture you."

"Don't underestimate Brown. If he had you in a vulnerable position, he'd rape you first and kill you second."

"But I'm here and safe and the perimeter alarm is on. Isn't it? Oh! You know the code? How?"

"You stand so a person in your front hall can see the code. Now you need to change it."

"So you can't break in?" Sophia turned toward the hall and tugging him along, went in to the kitchen. "Do you want coffee?" She was pulling the pot out as she asked.

"What I want and what I need to do are two different things. I'm still on duty."

"Until?"

He glanced at his watch. "Another forty-five minutes."

"Will you come back when your shift is done?"

"What about the party?"

Sophia stepped toward Cam and leapt into the darkness. "I'd rather spend it with you."

"Are you—?"

"Yes, I am."

"Set the alarm after I leave. I'll bring Chinese takeout. I know this great little place and they're open tonight. You've done enough for the day." He was halfway to the front door when he stopped and turned back. "You're sure?"

Sophia smiled. "I am sure. And, if you're bringing dinner, make sure to include Fried Shrimp and something spicy like General Tsao or Mongolian Beef."

The darkness faded when he smiled and saluted. "Come set the alarm." He waited until she was close, reached for her and pulled her close. His mouth came down on her and he plundered. Sophia's insides heated as his tongue sought entrance and the kiss spiraled from a 'see you soon' goodbye kiss to something much more.

Cam set her aside, opened the door and whistled as he went out. Sophia shut and locked the door. Before she made it the few steps to set the alarm she rested her body against the raised surface.

"Set the alarm."

Sophia turned and looked out the safety hole. Cam was standing there, a grin on his face, waiting.

It occurred to her to open the door and shoo him on his way but she knew he wouldn't leave until he knew the alarm was on. It occurred to her to open the door and give him a goodbye kiss but he still wouldn't leave until he knew the alarm was on. And finally, it occurred to her that he'd be back sooner if she turned the alarm on. So she did.

12 New Year's Eve

While Cam was gone, Sophia puttered in her kitchen whipping up a batch of sweet rolls and chocolate chip cookies. No need to look at recipes, she'd made them for years. Her mind wandered as she set the dough to rise and started on the cookies.

Once they were in the oven, she went to her sacred space. Lighting three candles, she sat and concentrated on the flames. *Here in this sacred space I ask The Goddess to warn me if I'm going astray.*

It was a simple prayer to focus her mind. Eyes closed, she repeated the words.

The darkness turned to a luminous yellow ball with a pulsing white center. Floating across her inner mind the words "Your time has come" undulated in a twisting Mobius thread.

Bringing herself back to the present, Sophia blew out the candles. When she stood, she remained before her altar a few minutes more checking her own body and mind. Nothing seemed amiss although she did sense a change. Her body was—she could be honest with herself in the privacy of her own home, her own sacred space. Her body anticipated being with Cam tonight. Anticipation tinged with longing and a bit of nervousness.

She now lived in an age where people talked openly about safe sex and sexually transmitted disease. She'd never had that conversation except in her classroom. If Cam, who she thought was more experienced in these matters didn't, she was determined to do so.

Back in the kitchen she took the cookies out of the oven and set them on a cooling rack. After cutting the sweet roll dough in half, she rolled it out. One half became pecan sticky buns and the other cinnamon rolls. The dough was rising for a second time when the doorbell rang. Knowing it was Cam, she still checked through the security hole before turning off the perimeter alarm and letting him in the house.

"My goodness, what did you bring?"

Cam sidled in the door, both arms filled with sacks.

Sophia stepped aside to let him in. After he passed her, she closed the door and reset the perimeter alarm.

Strong arms encircled her when she entered the kitchen. Cam pulled her against him and rested his chin on her crown. "You're really sure about this?"

Sophia wrapped her arms around his waist and leaned against him. "Very sure."

He stepped back, put his hands on her shoulders. "Let's see what I brought."

Sophia reached for the closest sack. Before she had a chance to open it, he'd taken it from her. "This is for later. Food is in these sacks."

"Three sacks of Chinese food?"

"Not just Chinese food. I got a dozen eggs," he started unpacking the food from the sacks. "I thought I'd fix you breakfast in the morning." He shifted towards her. "Did I misread the invitation?"

"No, you didn't misread or mishear. I want you to spend the night with me."

Turning back to the sacks, Cam continued. "Eggs, I know you like omelets. Fruit, I know you'd rather have that than bacon. Got some shrimp and an avocado for the omelet."

"You're going to cook for me?"

Cam snugged her against him. "I'm going to cook you breakfast." He bent and kissed her cheek. "Here's the Chinese." He let her go and started unpacking another sack.

Sophia put the eggs and shrimp in the refrigerator and got out plates and silverware. They dished up at the counter and took their plates to the table. Cam held her chair out for her and then sat beside her.

He kept his gaze on his plate when he asked "Do you miss not being with your friends tonight?"

"My New Year's Eve tradition has always been to stay home and reflect on the year past and look forward to the year to come. Do you have a tradition?"

"Work. New Year's Eve means drunk drivers, domestic disputes, bar brawls so I've always worked extra shifts. No family so no reason to stay home. No point in going out and drinking, becoming part of the problem instead of the solution."

"But you were married. You had a family. Even then you worked New Year's?"

"Betsy was pregnant with our first child when we got married. I've never been sure that we'd have gotten to the altar if not for that. Tempestuous would be a good word to describe our marriage. There are those that say make-up sex is the best. Got used to tolerating the arguing, the fighting because of that myth."

"What changed your mind?"

"When," he paused and looked her in the eye. "Are you sure you want to hear the sordid details?"

"Only if you want to tell me."

"I've never hit a woman but there was a time when it took all of my self-control not to haul off and hit Betsy in the mouth to stop her tirade. There was no make-up sex. And then there was no sex at all.

"Heard her on the phone telling one of her girlfriends how she wished she'd never married me. Should have gotten an abortion instead of a wedding ring.

"I packed up my clothes and left that day. Stayed with a friend for a couple of weeks. Considered what to do but options were taken out of my hands. She had me served with divorce papers by the end of the week."

He'd stopped eating and Sophia wasn't sure he'd take another bite.

"Nasty custody and visitation battle ensued. She alleged I'd been screwing around on her. I had had an affair with someone but only the one. My youngest is most likely not my biological kid but it wouldn't serve anything to do DNA tests and all that. She's the one who'd be hurt by it."

"When did you last see your kids?" Sophia put her hand on his.

"Oh I see them all the time. They don't see me. I've never missed a game or performance."

It took a moment before what he said made sense. "You stay in the background so they don't know you're there."

A rueful smile tilted his lips, his eyes remained sad. "They don't want me to come. I keep tabs on the schools' websites to see what's coming up. They never invite me. And, Betsy would just create a scene. She remarried as soon as the divorce was final and seems happy. Probably married to Becca's biological dad."

"If I remember correctly, your oldest is Ben and your middle child is Beverly."

"Bev. She goes by Bev."

"All "B's." She smiled when he grimaced.

"Betsy wanted to do the alphabet. Ben was supposed to be Adam, then her and me. The next kid would have a "D" name, etc."

"And you refused to go along with that idea."

"Yep, and when she proposed the idea of all 'B's', I just didn't want to fight about it." He hadn't taken another bite. "Did Jonathan share your New Year's Eve tradition?"

Sophia squeezed his hand before tucking hers back in her lap. "He did, in part because he came from a family with similar traditions but they did it on Thanksgiving. What they were thankful for that year and what they hoped would come to pass over the next twelve months."

"So what do you want to have happen over the next year?" Cam was again studying his plate.

"The basics. Health and happiness for myself and everyone I care about. Well, actually I'd adore it if that happened for everyone in the world."

He chuckled. "Sort of like the Miss America contest "Peace on Earth.""

"Exactly. And I want to be the best teacher I can be. I want my students to love learning and reading in particular. I want my garden to be plentiful so I can share its largesse with others."

"What about Jonathan's family? What do you wish for them?"

"I don't see them. They live on the east coast and were very angry at me when he died. They blamed me for him moving away from them and they were furious when I had him buried here instead of sending his body to them."

Sophia took a deep breath. She'd been so distraught with grief she'd barely been able to tell her mother-in-law what had happened. Lily had been there and she'd taken the phone and talked to the senior Mrs. Stewart. No one came for the funeral and all communication ceased. At Christmas she'd sent Christmas cards and boxes of evergreens and holly just as she and Jonathan had always done. When the boxes of greens and holly was returned marked 'REFUSED' in red, she'd given up trying to stay connected. And now? When was the last time she'd been to Jonathan's gravesite? Well, she always went around Memorial Day and also on the anniversary of his death. What would it have mattered if she'd sent his body back to his family?

"Whenever I think I've resolved my feelings over his death, something comes up and I realize I've another layer to deal with."

"Sorry if I brought up that other layer."

"I've just not thought about any of this for so long. I wonder what the procedure is to have a grave dug up and the coffin sent elsewhere for burial?"

"Takes attorneys, court orders and costs money."

Sophia smiled. "Of course it does and at this point in time, I'm not sure it would make any difference. I don't need to establish and maintain a relationship with them. If I did it, it would only be to give them some closure, some peace."

Dinner finished they cleared the table. While Cam put leftovers in the refrigerator, Sophia put the sweet rolls in the oven to bake. They started to settle on the couch to wait when Cam motioned Sophia to sit in one corner. He then put her feet up and when he sat, situated them on his lap.

Sophia groaned when he started to massage her instep. "That feels so good," she moaned. "Are you trying to—?"

"Yep, I'm trying to seduce you." A wicked smile twitched his lips as he continued to work his magic on her feet.

"You do know about reflexology."

"Reflex what?"

"The massage technique where you work on the feet and through them every point of the body."

"Nope, I'm just doing what feels right."

"You are doing a perfect job."

In the dim recesses of her mind, Sophia heard the timer on the oven go off. A large warm hand, patted her thigh "I'll get it." She heard the oven door open, pans being shuffled around. Able to finally crack an eye, she saw the time and knew Cam had worked on her feet for thirty minutes or more. *If this is what he can do to me and only touch my feet.* Her nerve endings tingled, her body more aroused.

"Anything else I need to do to them other than take them out of the oven?" He leaned over and his warm breath tickled her ear.

She shook her head.

"Good. I'm interested in seeing Sophia Stewart totally relaxed."

He helped her sit up and then stand. His arm around her waist, her head on his shoulder, they turned off the lights and headed down the hall.

"By the way, I'm clear of STD's and brought a box of condoms. Didn't figure you had any in stock and if you did, they wouldn't be trustworthy."

13 New Year's Night

Sophia leaned into Cam as they walked down the hall, more than glad it was wide enough that they were side-by-side. When they reached her door, he paused for a fraction of a second. She'd taken a half-step before it registered he wasn't right beside her.

"You need to know something else." His voice was low and held a note of sadness or maybe something else dark.

"What?" She turned to face him, her hands now holding his.

"I'll leave your bed before I fall asleep. Sometimes I have nightmares and I could lash out and hurt you."

That note hadn't been sadness exactly. Concern definitely. "Then I have a request." She rose on her toes and kissed his chin.

His hands tightened around hers, his thumb stroking her palm.

"Ask and if it is within my ability, I will."

"Hold me first."

Cam smiled. "You want the cuddling and talking first?"

"I do want that tonight as much as the rest of it."

"Sophia, referring to my sexual prowess as 'the rest of it'. Babe, that hurts."

"I didn't mean to hurt your manly pride, Cam. It's been a very long time since any man has been this near my bed. I'm obviously out of practice."

"I'm teasing, Sophia. I like the holding and cuddling and talking too. Just want you to know when you wake up, I won't be beside you."

"Are you leaving?"

"I'll be in the spare room or out on the couch. I promised you breakfast and I won't leave without saying good bye and claiming a few kisses to tide me over until I can steal a few more."

"You never have to steal a kiss, Cam. I'll give them to you willingly and as often as you want."

"What about wherever I want?"

"I kiss goodbye or hello but your bone melting ones are not for public consumption."

"Got it." He pulled her into his arms and delivered one of those bone melting kisses.

Sophia grabbed hold of his shoulders and held on as his tongue plundered her mouth, hands that still held hers, wrapped around her.

When he raised his head, she was breathless, her body on fire. It would be so easy to jump into the smoldering heat and burst into flames but Sophia wanted to be held. She'd not been held by a man since Jonathan died. Oh there had been hugs from her circle sisters' husbands, but being held was very different. At least for her. Only recently had she admitted to herself that she envied each of her Circle sisters the closeness they had with their men.

Even when Hunter faced the challenges she did with Logan, Grant had been there and he had held her. And now Gabriella had Giovanni to hold her. She, Sophia, was the only one who did not. *We will be lovers before the night is over.*

"I'd like to watch you undress." The words feathered across her finger tips. He'd brought her hands to his lips and was kissing each one.

Her breath hitched. "Does that mean I get to watch you?"

Cam chuckled, that deep naughty intimate one that had always curled her toes. "I'm an equal opportunity kind of guy."

Sophia pulled her hands away and stepped back. She turned and crossed the room to pull the curtains leaving them open a couple of inches. "I like to wake up and see the light."

He'd followed her. At her words, he nodded and toed off his shoes angling them so they were against the wall under the window. He shucked his shirt over his head, taking his undershirt off at the same time. Shaking them out, he folded them and laid them on the back of the chair in the corner.

Sophia's breath hitched at the sight of his naked torso. He was in good shape. Perhaps not the six-pack abs of commercials, but he was fit. A dusting of hair that looked dark in this light but she imagined had hints of red covered his chest, wider across the upper expanse, narrowing as it descended into the waist band of his pants.

"You next." Cam turned toward her, a wicked smile on his face, a twinkle in his eyes.

Sophia slipped her shoes off and put them by the closet. Socks came next and were tucked in her shoes. Turning back to the bed, she unbuttoned her blouse and let it hang open. She shimmied out of her leggings.

Cam's eyes were glued to the slit in her blouse where her turquoise blue bra peeked out. His gaze traveled down and saw the shadow of dark hair at the apex of her thighs. Sophia's face was flushed, more a blush than arousal was his guess. She was so still, if he hadn't seen the beat of her pulse in her throat, he'd be worried about her.

"Sophia, what do we need for you to be comfortable with this?

"I want to be comfortable now."

"But you aren't. Let's take this in stages, okay?" He reached down and flipped back the covers. "Now you turn them back on your side. Then turn the light off. I'm going to open the curtains so there's enough ambient light I can see my way to the bathroom. Speaking of which—." He strode from the room, calling out as he did, "go on and get in bed. I'll be right back."

"Forgot these," Cam brandished the box of condoms when he came back in the room. Setting them on the nightstand on his side of the bed, he took his pants off and crawled under the covers. "Come here, my dear." His arm slid around Sophia's shoulders and he tucked her against his side. "How's this?"

She shifted onto her side, rested her head on his shoulder, and tentatively laid her hand over his heart. "Is this okay?"

"More than okay. Nearly perfect."

"Nearly?"

He put his free hand over hers and pressed it flat against his skin. "Now it is."

The arm around her shoulders moved and his hand began stroking her back. "Do you like this?"

"I like how you touch me but I'm not doing anything for you."

"But you are. You are allowing me into your bed. You are trusting me with your body. You like how I touch you."

"Can we just be like this for a little longer?" Sophia kissed his neck.

"We can be like this for as long as you want if you don't kiss me, stroke me, massage me—"

She laughed a throaty, seductive tone. "I'll just recline here in your arms and count my blessings."

"Am I one of those blessings?"

"Right now you are the first one on my list."

"Are you a list maker?"

"I am. You've seen evidence of that all over the house. I've a list on the refrigerator door, I've a calendar on the counter by the phone—."

"But those things are needed. The list on the fridge is of ingredients. The calendar by the phone shows your availability. That's not the same as a daily or weekly list of tasks."

"I don't really do that except in the spring when I'm planning out my garden. Then I do make lists of what needs to be done when and in what order."

"Will you let me help you with your garden this spring?"

Cam whispered the words and Sophia wondered and not for the first time, what she was doing with this man of darkness who had the aura of death and destruction wrapped around him. She could see the light deep in the darkness and in this moment it felt brighter.

They were such opposites except for this. They were both alone and seeking comfort. His hand continued to stroke her back and her eyes drifted shut.

Only within the last couple of years had she had help with her garden. And would she and Cam even see each other in another month or two. That strange sensation that foretold a message traveled her spine. "Of course you can help with the garden. Seeing new life in the spring gives me hope for all life throughout the year."

His breathing had slowed, his heart beat a steady rhythm while his body relaxed under her hand.

Cam had fallen asleep.

Should she wake him? She'd woken Jonathan up in the morning to begin their day with love. No, her inner voice cautioned her. Instinctively she knew he needed sleep more than a sexual encounter with her. Although she believed it would be more than a meaningless or trivial encounter, she had no illusions this was or ever would be a long term relationship. She was dedicated to life and he may not be dedicated to death but he did not see that all life was sacred and part of the divine.

Sophia slipped her hand out from under his and pulled the covers up before returning her hand to his chest. She'd asked to be held and he was holding her. Lying in his arms was more comforting than she'd thought it would be. His strength even in sleep, his heat, his fresh minty scent surrounded her. She was a strong woman but it was beyond words to just be with someone. *No, not with someone, with Cam.*

14 New Year's Day

January 1, 2006
7 a.m.

"Sophia?" her name was accompanied by a gentle shake. "Sophia, hey, lady, I've got to go."

"Cam?" Sophia struggled to open her eyes. She'd been in such a deep relaxed sleep it was hard to rouse.

"I've got to go. Got called in. Stuff happened and I'm needed at work." He kissed her forehead and tried to straighten but she had her arms around his neck.

"You'll be back."

Cam pulled away and turned to leave.

"Cameron Mitchell, you will come back. Promise me you will be back."

He glanced over his shoulder and saw Sophia sitting up, ire flashed from her brown eyes. She tossed the sheets aside. "You will promise me."

His phone rang. They needed his ETA and expected he'd already be on his way. Weariness warred with duty. Duty won.

"I'll stop by when I'm done."

Sophia's mouth opened to demand more but the look of resignation on his face stopped her. She popped out of bed and wrapped her arms around his waist. "Be safe. But come back regardless of what happens." She kissed his jaw because he'd stiffened at her words. Grabbing her top to cover her nakedness, she padded behind him as he stalked to door to the garage.

She pushed the code that raised the garage door and watched as he got in his car. After what looked like him speaking to someone on the radio, he backed out. The garage door back in place, she walked into her sacred space. A soft glow filled the room when she lit candles and turned on her rock salt lamp. Sophia stood before her altar and manifested a ball of white gold energy.

"Protect him from harm and bring him back to me if it will serve his highest good." Hands held palms up at shoulder height, she waited a moment before focusing on Cam and visualizing the energy surrounding him.

Lily and Diana showed up at one o'clock. They were worried about her.

"I've never been to one of your New Year's Eve parties," she said in response to their query about how she was doing.

"I know," Lily said in reply, setting a kettle of water on the stove to heat before getting out three mugs.

"Make yourself at home." Sophia regretted the words as soon as they were out of her mouth.

Diana stepped beside her, put her arm around her shoulder. "This is why we are here. You are not yourself. Not that you have to always be the same," she added with a side squeeze. "But something seems off."

Lily took the few steps to stand in front of her. "Remember we've all had the opportunity to be hovered over. This seems to be your time."

"You all hovered when Jonathan died and when my friend died a couple of months ago."

"That wasn't hovering in the same sense that this is and you know it. However, you always have the right to remain silent. We can't force you to tell us anything. But don't insult us by saying nothing is going on." After that little sermon, Lily gave her a hug. "You must remember we do this because we love you."

Tea mugs in hand, a plate of peanut butter cookies on the coffee table, they relaxed and talked of other things. Lily shared the highlights of the party. Hunter and Grant were the only ones from The Circle to attend. Of course with Elizabeth and Gabriella in Ireland and Italy respectively, and Diana and Ashley with children it made sense.

"Especially when today is Madison Michelle's birthday," Diana glowed with motherlove.

At forty-five, Sophia knew she'd never have children of her own but her years of teaching had given her strong relationships with some students. And she had good relationships with the children of her circle sisters. Being a well-loved auntie had its benefits.

"Why don't I make a cake this afternoon," Sophia said, getting up and going into the kitchen. "I'm not as good a decorator as professionals but I can manage 'Happy Birthday, Madison Michelle'.

"God Dammit, Sophia," a male voice shouted as the front door slammed.

Before she had a chance to react, Cam was there, pressing her against the refrigerator. His hands gripped her upper arms, his mouth ruthless.

Sophia remained still except for holding his arms.

When he lifted his head, she saw the wildness, the fear in his eyes. She reached up and kissed his cheek. "I've company."

"Fuck!" He dropped his hands from her arms as if she were hot coals.

"Excuse us," Sophia said to Lily and Diana who had risen and started towards her jaws set and eyes blazing. "Help yourselves to more tea and cookies."

Taking Cam by the hand, she jerked and he followed her. Sophia led him into her sacred space knowing her circle sisters would not interrupt them there even if voices were raised.

The rock salt lamp was still lit but she added a bit more candle light. It was important to see his face, see his expression when he talked.

"I gather this was not a good day." She pulled him to sit next to her on the loveseat. Scooting closer she put her arm around his shoulder. "You do need to tell me what you can of what happened so I can understand why you are this way." Her free hand waved vaguely in front of her.

Cam's head was bowed, his arms rested on his thighs hands dangling between his legs.

"I can't talk about it with you."

"Why not?"

"Because you shouldn't be exposed to this ugliness."

"Is it uglier than having a police officer knock on your door and tell you your husband was never coming home because he was on the way to the grocery story by a hit and run driver?

Is it more ugly than seeing your best friend bloody and bruised from her husband's fists, is it more ugly than seeing another friend fight cancer, seeing her children kidnapped by her ex-husband, is it more ugly than seeing a beautiful young girl lured into a life of prostitution? I want to try to understand, Cam. Tell me what happened. I promise you I can handle it and if I find I really can't, I'll ask you to stop."

Sophia waited for him to speak, her hand on his arm.

"The first call was to a rape scene and so was the second and third. When I got there, another call was coming in. This one from an eight year old who said a bad man was hurting her mom.

"The 911 operator stayed on the line and helped the three children get out of the house. We were just pulling up when they emerged, the eight year old holding her six year old brother's hand and carrying her four year old sister. All three children were terrified. The oldest looked at me and asked if I was going to help her mom.

"What do you say to something like that?"

"Knowing you, you said just the right thing. Exactly what she needed to hear."

"The backup units had already deployed around the house and figured out where—where everything was happening. I took the children to my car and had them sit together in the back seat. Told them to wait right there while I went in with the other officers to help their mom.

"He was butchering her using a small razor blade. Blood was everywhere. His pants were down and he was jerking his cock to get it ready to rape her again. Taunting her with how good this was going to be for him and how bad it was going to be for her because he'd cut her again if she didn't show him how much she liked it.

"Her eyes were open but she didn't move. He sliced across her breast and she didn't move. The officer in front of me looked back and I nodded.

"We stepped into the room, guns drawn. She showed no sign of even knowing we were there. Nealy said to raise his hands, he was under arrest. Instead of doing that, he brought the razor blade down as if he was going to slit her neck. We both shot. His brains were all over the bed and the wall.

"An ambulance was already there. I tried to cover her up but there wasn't anything. Took my jacket off and did the best I could with it.

"The EMT's came in and called for the ambulance crew to bring in the gurney. They managed to get her on to a flat board, wrapped her in a sheet and blanket and carried her out of the room.

"I asked them to wait a minute so I could go out ahead of them. Child welfare had been called and they were sending someone right away. The next door neighbor had come out and was standing by my car talking to the children when I got there.

"There was no way to make it better than it was. I crouched down and told them their mom was being taken to the hospital because she'd been hurt. Of course they knew she'd been hurt. The oldest asked if she was going to die.

"What do you say to an eight year old who is hanging on to her brother and sister as if only she could protect them, keep them safe?"

Sophia knew it was a rhetorical question. She rubbed her hand across Cam's back and laid her head on his shoulder. Did he even know she was there? Hard to tell.

"Did you wait until child welfare came?"

He nodded. "The kids seemed to need me right then. Everything was under control at the scene. The neighbor, Mrs. Easter invited the children to come to her house where she had milk and cookies. She whispered to me that their mom was a wonderful woman and would do anything to keep her kids safe."

Cam turned to Sophia. "The mom never responded to anything. Not to her attacker, not to the EMT's, not to the ambulance folks. She didn't even move when the guns fired."

"It's called dissociating. It's when people mentally go away to escape what is happening to them. I've heard where people actually leave their bodies and go up where they witness what is happening to them below."

"Child welfare worker was a pro. Mrs. Easter asked if the children could stay with her for the night and the worker asked her some questions, they filled out some paperwork and that was that. Of course more is to come, I'm sure. But it was obvious that the children knew Mrs. Easter and liked her.

"The worker said there was a file and that the dad was in prison for child sexual abuse."

Sophia had no words. She was grateful she hadn't vomited as Cam recited the last of the day's events in a dispassionate voice.

"Well, that is a good thing because that means they won't have to go live with him."

"But what will happen to them? Mrs. Easter is a nice lady but I don't think she's going to sign up to raise them for the next fourteen or so years." Cam had sat up and his voice was raised.

"Let's ask Lily." She stood and reached out to take his hand.

He looked a question at her.

"Lily worked in child welfare for a long time. She'd also know more about dissociating. I'll fix you a cup of coffee and you can talk to her."

Sophia tugged him to his feet and with her hand still in his, led him back to the kitchen.

"Cam, these are my friends, Lily and Diana." She gestured to each woman as she introduced them. "Ladies, this is Cameron Mitchell, my friend who happens to be a member of the Fremont Police Force.

"Cam has some questions about a situation he was involved in today. Has to do with small children." She looked up at him and squeezed his hand. "They are eight, six and four. Their mother was severely injured in a sexual assault and the dad is in prison. What happens to children in these circumstances?"

Sophia stayed close while she started a pot of coffee. As she moved around the kitchen, she brushed against him or laid her hand on his arm or back. Something to let him know she was there.

Lily and Diana moved from the couch to the stools along the breakfast bar across the counter from where Cam stood. Her intention was to just 'be there' for him but as Lily answered his questions about children and families, she found she was learning even more about what her circle sister had done in her previous life and what had driven her to leave child welfare and focus on vulnerable adults.

"Dissociating is a protective behavior," Lily was saying in answer to his question. "And since this woman has survived horrors before, it is a safe place to be. I'd imagine she did not scream and fight this man because her children were there and if he did something to them it would have been even worse than whatever he did to her.

"I remember a young woman who made that same decision. Her child was in the next room, neighbors on the other side of the bedroom wall. But to summon help from her neighbors, her child would see what was happening to her. In her mind, that was worse than being raped."

Coffee pot gurgled at the end of its routine. Cam moved around the kitchen, fixing his mug just the way he liked it. Sophia saw the look that passed between Lily and Diana. A look that said he was not a stranger to her home.

"Do you have any other questions for me, Captain?"

Somewhere in their discussion, Lily learned his rank. She still had friends on the Fremont police force and Sophia figured she'd know by morning what Cam's reputation on the force was. Or would she?

Diana and Lily had come by today to see how she was. They were worried, but within The Circle they did not go behind another's back to get information. Unless permission was given, Lily would not be making any phone calls. And, Sophia doubted she'd even ask if Sophia wanted her to—but if Sophia asked? Lily's cell phone would be rapidly employed and answers would be swiftly forthcoming.

She felt a shift in the energy, her head swiveled to check Cam. His coffee mug was frozen in midair. Was it on the way up or down? She didn't know.

"I've plans. Didn't mean to interrupt." Cam was putting his mug down and pivoting away.

Her hand on his arm stopped his impending march out the door. "I must have missed something."

"Jackson is fixing his famous spaghetti and tonight is another ice cream contest. Charlie and Jackson against Logan and Grant. I'd hoped the two of you could come."

"Cam and I had made plans for this evening. We need to discuss it and we'll let you know." Sophia had positioned herself so he'd have to step around her in order to leave. It wasn't very fair but she didn't care. He was not charging out the door unless she knew he was okay. And from the waves of discomfort and attitude pouring off him, he was anything but okay.

"If you can't make it tonight," Diana said giving Sophia a hug. "Let me know about the cake. We will be at the spaghetti feed tonight so birthday cake is not in the immediate future. She's not old enough to comprehend birthdays anyway."

Sophia glanced at the clock. There was time to make a sheet cake and decorate it before dinner. But, she only nodded and hugged Diana back. At the door, she hugged Lily. "You'll know one way or the other most likely by the time you get home."

Lily turned back and hugging Sophia again said, "I like him. He's a good man underneath the darkness."

Unshed tears brightened her eyes as Sophia watched her friends get in their car and drive off. They'd parked at the curb, not something they usually did when they stopped by. Cam would have no idea she'd had company.

He was behind her.

She blocked his exit and shut the door. Using her body, she walked into him until he stepped back. After turning on the perimeter alarm, she took his arm and steered him back to the kitchen.

"Sit," she ordered pointing to the stools on the other side of the counter. "And do not apologize." She set the mixing bowl on the counter as she spoke. A hard look in his direction assured her he was paying attention.

"You are a dark and dangerous man but you have a kind and generous heart. We had our plans last night disrupted by sleep. You've had a very rough day." The tears were back. "I absolutely have no idea how you do this day in and day out." She brushed the back of her hand across her eyes, wiping the unfallen tears away.

"You making that cake?"

"I'm thinking about it. But, only if you stay and keep me company and talk to me."

"I'm not—"

"About whatever you want to talk about. You'll have to relive this whole day when you testify in court or wherever else is required in a case like this."

Sophia rounded the counter and wrapped her arms around him from behind. "I am blessed and filled with gratitude that you would trust me with this part of your life." She massaged his neck and then kissed his nape. With a soft pat on his back, she returned to the kitchen side of the counter. "Now are you going to watch me make a cake and talk to me or not?"

"I'll watch and ask you questions."

"That'll work." She bustled around getting out the ingredients for brownies.

"So you're making a chocolate cake?

"No, I changed my mind. I'm making a triple batch of brownies. It will fill this pan and go really well with the ice cream."

"How do you know what ice cream flavor?"

Sophia waved her hand. "The contest is still on vanilla. Best two out of three. They are tied one up."

"So this Jackson is Lily's husband. He's the architect?"

"Correct. And Grant is Hunter's husband. He's a non-practicing attorney right now. Actually he'd have to pass the

Oregon bar to be able to practice here." At his questioning look she added. "He's from Rhode Island."

She measured and mixed while Cam watched. Conversation was non-existent but the silence was comfortable. Once the pan was in the oven, she filled his mug up with the last of his coffee. Picking up her refreshed cup of tea, she joined him at the counter.

"I've been wondering how you slept last night? What woke you up?"

"Had to pee and noticed my phone blinking. When I checked for messages, I knew they'd been trying to reach me. Guess they even sent a car to my place when I didn't respond."

"So they were worried about you?"

"Nah, just shorthanded with so many crime scenes."

"Do you like spaghetti?"

He scowled at her. "If you want to go, go."

Sophia smiled. "Not without you. I'm not leaving you alone tonight. And, although you didn't ask, I'll tell you I haven't slept that well in a very long time."

15 The Contest

Cam berated himself for tagging along. He knew no one and no one knew him. But he owed her. Owed her big time. She never chastised him or criticized him for bursting into her home and attacking her in her own kitchen. Sophia Stewart was a class act, much too classy for him.

He drove in case he was called back in to work. While waiting around, he'd called in his report and also checked with the social worker about the kids. They would stay with Mrs. Easter for a few days until things were sorted out.

Something Lily had said about a series of crimes being committed to cover up the real crime had struck home. The day's earlier victims had all described the perp they'd taken down. And, he'd gone back in his notes realizing there'd been a call in mid-December with a similar MO.

In the end he'd convinced himself he could manage to be social for a couple of hours with Sophia by his side. And she'd assured him, she'd stay by his side and would get a ride home from one of her circle sisters if he was called away. No hassle. No arguing. No nagging.

After helping Sophia from his car, he took the pan of brownies from her and let her lead them to the door. She knocked once and let herself in. He noted there was an alarm system but it wasn't on. He'd have a word with Jackson or Lily. Why have a system if you don't use it?!

Rich aromas of sauce and freshly baked bread greeted him. He followed Sophia into the throng of people of at least a dozen if you counted the kids. Instinctively he knew these people counted the kids equal to the adults.

Sophia made the introductions. The women all welcomed him with an openness that was surreal. The men, however, were more what he'd expected. Outwardly friendly but assessing him, making their own judgement and not relying on the women's take on things.

A stunning auburn haired woman glided toward him. From Sophia's description and recent introduction, this would be Hunter.

"You'd be wise to ignore the gestures of friendship from those two." She pointed at Jackson and Grant. "They will each be attempting all sorts of subtle and not so subtle bribes in order to sway you to their side in the ice cream contest. It's a blind taste test."

"You're serious aren't you?" Cam could hardly believe all this subterfuge over ice cream.

"Good job," A tall blond man eased next to Hunter, his arms around her waist, he gave her a quick kiss on the cheek. "Softening him up for me?"

Hunter laughed. A merry sound and patted his arm. "Not a chance in hell. You are on your own."

"Am not," Grant challenged. "I've got a secret weapon."

"And so does Jackson," Hunter replied, giving him a kiss on the cheek.

"Lily would help Jackson," Grant countered.

"No she wouldn't. We've made a pact. Neither one of us will get involved with this madness. We don't even vote."

Before Cam realized it, he was in the kitchen stirring the pasta while Jackson made a few adjustments in the sauce. The freshly baked bread was cooling on racks and a tossed green salad sat in a large bowl on the counter.

The island held the bar. Whiskey, scotch, beer, wine (red and white) as well as lemonade, soda water, milk. The stove had a tea kettle on and the fixings for various teas were next to it.

Cam waved off an offer of a cold beer or something stronger. He wasn't sure if he'd be called back tonight or not. They were short staffed at his precinct, the flu having decimated their ranks. This time of year, they all got some overtime just because of the extra calls that came in over the holidays. If there was a God, and Cam wasn't betting on it, all would stay quiet and he'd spend the night with Sophia.

She didn't cling but she was never more than an arm's length away. The way she held herself, he could tell she was nervous. What would it be like to be her? To have these women in her life for over ten years. To see them, one-by-one get married until she was the only one left. Technically that wasn't true. The one in Italy would be married February first but for all intents and purposes, she was already.

He thought the kids might eat in the kitchen. There was a table there. But then he looked around. Madison Michelle was too young to be there. The next one in age was Rose and she was eight. Ashley and Daniel's other boys were teenagers or nearly so. That left Diana's Bill and Lily's Charlie – both boys in college and certainly Not eating in the kitchen.

Nothing was said as room was made at the big table and the breakfast bar next to it. Sophia and he ate at the table. Daniel ate at the island with Rose and Diana and Madison Michelle. Cam watched with interest as Rose fed the baby while Diana held her. At one point, Matthew walked over to make sure Diana had everything she needed.

These men were devoted to their wives. Cam knew they would walk through fire and lay down their own lives to make sure their ladies were safe. Under the table, Sophia patted his thigh and took his hand. He rather imagined after remembering how she'd herded him into her sacred space and then backed him away from the door when he tried to leave that all the women were equally fierce and would never walk away from whatever befell their spouses.

No one's life was perfect. From the little Sophia had shared, he could piece together that Ashley was the one who'd had cancer and that would mean it was her kids who were kidnapped by their biological dad. It was hard to tell who might have been the victim of domestic violence. He was positive that was not a part of anyone's life right now.

Appearances could be deceiving. After talking to Lily this afternoon, he knew the deception could work both ways. She'd mentioned it was time to leave child protective service work when she couldn't go to the grocery store without seeing pedophiles down every aisle. He knew what that was like. It was taking a toll to keep his face neutral, to continue to sit with people he didn't know.

A wayward thought popped up. *Wouldn't you like to know them better? Be included, belong?*

Cam couldn't imagine that happening, He couldn't imagine being a part of, or belonging to Sophia's life beyond one day or night at a time.

The woman on his mind squeezed his hand and smiled. Leaning close she whispered, "Now comes the fun part." She helped clear the table, her hand rested on his shoulder when he started to get up. "I'll be right back."

It was obvious they'd done this many times before. Some of the women cleared the table, others put leftovers away and a third group loaded the dishwasher. The men?

Jackson and Grant had risen and were getting out bowls and spoons. Matthew leaned across the table in his direction. "We all use the same type pen and make a small check mark so no one can tell who voted for who." He used his fingernail to show how small the mark was–almost tiny. "This is a formidable competition. Kitchen bragging rights are a big deal." He laughed. "Actually not. Jackson makes the best spaghetti. I make the best chili but Sophia makes the best everything else."

Just then, Sophia called out, "Matthew, you are needed."

Before the ice cream competition formally began, Cam heard the words to the birthday song sung. "Happy Birthday to you." Sophia's pan of brownies were carried to the table where a lone candle burned. She'd used a plastic bag with a hole in one end to write Happy Birthday Madison Michelle.

The little girl did not seem impressed with the brownies but she wanted the candle. Matthew picked her up and walked around the great room pointing things out while Diana confiscated the candle and the brownies were put back in the kitchen.

The men were serious about their ice cream. Two identical containers were on the counter an ice cream scoop in each.

The rules were that everyone had two dishes. A blue one and a green one. The ice cream in one container filled the blue dishes and the other container's contents filled the green.

Jackson's mother, Eleanor had been summoned from her apartment that was attached to the house to serve. She was also the one to collect the votes, tally them, burn the ballots and make the announcement. The announcement was only whether the green or the blue dish contents won.

Who knew which belonged to which man?

Bill had been dragooned into that role this year. He was the one to inscribe a mark on the bottom of each container in such a way it could not be seen from the inside. The ice cream was then secreted in Eleanor's freezer until now.

Cam wore a serious expression as he sampled each ice cream. Both were smooth. Both had vanilla bean flecks in them. Both were creamy in texture. But the green had something that teased his taste buds. Of course he had no idea what that something extra was, but it was enough for him to carefully make a small check mark in the green box.

He handed his ballot to Eleanor, who was circling the table. She went off to her apartment to count. It wouldn't take long but ten minutes later she hadn't reappeared. Cam looked to Sophia. Amusement danced in her eyes. "She's building the suspense. Both Jackson and Grant are very competitive and this part of it drives them nuts."

Thirty minutes passed and Jackson strode to the French doors leading into Eleanor's apartment. He knocked loudly. "Mother?"

Lily sprang to her feet and dashed across the room. She charged past Jackson and through the now open door. "Eleanor, you scared us half to death." Cam heard the scold.

His glance around the table showed him this was not part of the deal.

"I'm alright." Cam heard the irritation in the English accented voice. "I was a bit dizzy and decided to lie down for a few minutes. I must have dozed off."

When Eleanor reappeared she was pale and still a bit unsteady on her feet. She shooed Jackson back to the table but seemed to lean a bit on Lily as she followed.

"The winner is the Green Bowl and by quite a healthy margin." With that announcement she detoured to the fireplace and tossed the ballots on the flames. She said something to Lily, who nodded and walked with her back to her apartment.

Cam watched the herculean effort Jackson made to continue the show but he gave it away with his worried glances at his mother's door every couple of seconds. The party atmosphere had fled.

Sophia whispered, "Eleanor has helped each of us in some way or another. This isn't a good sign that she has sent Jackson away and only wants Lily with her."

Another tense fifteen minutes went by before Lily emerged. She immediately crossed to Jackson. "She's resting now. We'll check in on her from time to time. If she's worse we'll see that she is checked out in the ED but for now our gift to her is to finish our party. She is adamant that her 'little spell' not put a damper on things."

Lily turned to Bill. "So who made the green cup ice cream?"

Cam had missed that someone had put the ice cream back in the freezer which meant Bill had to get them out to check. He struggled to keep the grin off his face.

"The winner of this ice cream challenge is, 'drum roll please.'" Everyone took the cue to drum on the table. "Miss."

He got no further. Logan shrieked and flew into her dad's arms. He fist pumped. They bumped hips and hugged.

Jackson and Bill frowned. They dipped into the green cup's ice cream container. Slowly tasting the blend that beat them, they quirked a brow at each other. "We'll get them next time," Jackson vowed.

"And we won't even break a sweat doing it." Charlie added taking another spoonful of the winning ice cream.

Cam heard him ask Jackson in a low voice. "What did they put in that?"

"Not sure but we'll find out."

Jackson's smile bordered on feral as he approached Sophia. "Could I have a moment of your time?" He held out his hand as if to assist her to stand.

"That wouldn't be sporting, Jackson. If I help you, then I'd have to help Grant and Logan. Remember our rules. We remain neutral. Even your wives can't vote."

Cam wasn't called out. Shortly after the ice cream war ended, for now at least, they left. Sophia spent time talking in a low voice with Lily, Diana at her elbow. He knew she was saying to call if she needed anything, that she'd check in with her in the morning. After hugs and more soft-voice-words, they left.

Sophia was quiet on the way home.

She was still quiet when he pulled into the garage.

Once in the house, she turned and put her arms around him. "Thank you for tonight. I could have missed everything without a problem except what happened to Eleanor... ."

He hugged her tight. "I could use more cuddling and I've been told I'm a decent listener if you want to talk."

"About what?"

He hushed her with a light kiss.

16 Morning Comes Softly

"Phia?" Cam's hand reached across the bed.

Nothing. "Sophia?" He bolted upright, the covers in his hand ready to be tossed aside, when he saw her. She was sitting in the chair in the corner, underneath the windows.

"Did I?"

"No, you did nothing. I had a hot flash." Sophia stayed where she was.

"One of those power surges?" He chuckled.

"Whatever name you put on it." Her voice was soft, she was looking at the floor and pleating her gown.

He swung his legs over the side of the bed and started to stand.

She looked up. "I'm all right, Cam. Just a little more time and my body will have cooled enough for me to come back to bed."

"I'll wait with you." He settled himself back on the bed, leaning against the headboard, covers pooled around his waist. Something was wrong but he had no idea what.

"You don't—"

He waved a hand to interrupt before he spoke. "Yes, I do. I sleep better when you are next to me. I can't remember ever naturally sleeping this well."

"What do you mean by "naturally"?

He heard the curiosity in her voice and relished the reality she was no longer looking at the floor. It was dark but the ambient light coming through the window created a variegated grey palette of the room.

"Well, I sleep well when doped up on pain medications but that isn't exactly a natural sleep." There was more but he hesitated, not sure how much he wanted to share with her.

"So you've been shot?"

"I have and it isn't at all like what they portray on television or in the movies."

"I guess that means you didn't bounce up and continue the chase after the bad guys."

Her voice was soft, thoughtful. He listened for the humor but there was none. Sophia would not see his being hurt or even the fly that gets into the house hurt as something humorous.

"No, I didn't bounce up and go haring off after the dirt bag. I groaned and wanted to cry it hurt so bad."

"But you didn't. Cry that is."

Now he heard a tickle of humor.

"No I didn't cry, I just lay there and cursed. Cursed about all the things that were wrong in my life. I knew I'd survive. The first time, I was shot in the leg but not near the groin so I knew the major artery was not hurt. The second time in the arm.

Neither were life threatening injuries but both hurt like hell and recovery was not pleasant."

"What was the worst part?"

"Being at home and unable to leave. Betsy and I fought continually. She didn't want me there 24/7 but I couldn't leave until I could drive and that was six weeks after I got home. She had to take me to physical therapy, doctor appointments. Bitched the whole time about it."

It struck Cam that he'd recited these facts without even a smidgeon of anger. *What's that about?*

"No one else to help out?"

"My partner had been hit also. We backed each other up but he couldn't show up. Took a couple of weeks before one of the guys came by. Walked in on Betsy chewing me another one. Before he left, he'd made a note of my upcoming appointments. Someone always called and offered to take me if Betsy didn't mind."

"And that helped?"

"Not really. Then she bitched about not being able to talk to the physical therapist or doctor."

"You do know that complaining is one way people show their concern."

"And you do know that complaining is one way people show they despise you."

Silence hung in the air. "I'm sorry Sophia. Didn't need to say that."

"Or maybe you did. I didn't take offense although your tone of voice could have been—no, actually you said what you needed to say exactly how you needed to say it."

"Because?"

"When we are angry or upset or sad or whatever our emotion is at the time and we try to sweeten it up, that isn't helpful. We can't let something go until we face it head on. At the least, you and your wife were not a good match."

"I can agree with that. There was an attraction. I was in the Navy and met her while on leave. We wrote each other and I saw her whenever we were in port. Then she turned up pregnant. I didn't want my child born a bastard so I proposed. I liked her and thought that was enough. Sometimes I wonder if she ever even liked me as a person or if she was only attracted to the uniform."

"And would it make a difference if you knew?"

Cam sat silent for several minutes. *Would it make a difference?* He had stewed and ranted about whether Betsy had ever taken the time to get to know him. But he'd never asked himself why it mattered.

"In some ways it doesn't and in other ways it does."

"If you want to talk, I'll listen."

"When I'm out wearing my uniform, I want to be respected, to be seen as a law enforcement officer. It makes no difference if they know how I like my coffee, etc." He shifted on the bed, pulled the covers up covering his abdomen.

"When I'm off duty, with friends and back then with family, I want to be seen as me, Cameron Trent Mitchell, the man. Does that make sense?"

"Of course it does. At least it does to me. I want my students to respect me as an educator but I want my friends to see me as more than the supplier of goodies and produce."

"And they do."

"Yes, they do. And some of my students see me as more than their teacher. When Jonathan died, most of them came up to me when I came back to school and said words of comfort. Every one of them, even the ones who had given me grief before the accident, were kind and considerate. I don't know how I would have finished the school year if they hadn't all tried to help me through."

"And you had the others. You call yourselves a women's circle, right?"

"We are a sacred women's circle and for short we just say The Circle. Without those women, I probably would still be curled in a ball of hopeless grief right here on this bed."

"They are a formidable lot. I wouldn't want to meet any of them in a dark alley." He chuckled.

Sophia laughed. "You'd never find any of them in a dark alley unless they were coming to rescue one of their own. And their husbands would have something to say about that."

"Would they listen?"

"Of course they would listen. They would pay attention to what he said, any advice he gave, but in the end, if one of us was in trouble there would be nothing the men could say or do to keep us from showing up."

"And the guys are okay with that?"

"I doubt that "okay" is the right word. But they've made peace with it. They've decided that what they gain in the relationship is worth whatever they are concerned about."

"My guess is that they would be right beside their wives or if that wasn't possible, only a step or two behind. I don't see any of them standing back and letting any of you go into danger and doing nothing."

"You see them protecting the other women and not just their own wives?"

"Come on Sophia. You can't have been around them for as long as you have and not seen that each of them have a protective streak a mile wide when it comes to each and every one of the women in The Circle. And that, of course, includes you."

"Do tell."

"You may have stuck close tonight but I know I was being vetted, scrutinized to see if I met the standards they've set as to who would be good enough for you."

"Did you pass?" Sophia leaned forward.

"Not even close."

"I'll —"

"Do absolutely nothing. They have a right to be protective of The Circle. And I feel better knowing they look out for you as well as their wives and children.

"Are you close to coming back to bed?"

Sophia stood and rounded the bed.

Cam held the covers up.

As soon as Sophia was back in bed, Cam scooted down and shifted to his side so he was facing her. His forefinger caressed her cheek. "I missed you. Gave me a start waking up and finding you gone."

"But I wasn't gone."

"You weren't right here." He patted the inches of sheet between them.

Sophia closed the distance between them and wrapped her arm around his neck. Her body warmed, not with hormones but with arousal.

"Are you sure now is the right time?" The breath from Cam's soft growl feathered across her face.

Sophia pulled away, wiggled and squirmed until she had her gown off. "Does that answer your question or do I need to be more explicit?" She slipped back into his arms.

"I will admit I like explicit."

"Cameron Trent Mitchell will you be my lover this morning?"

"Sophia Camila Stewart it will be my pleasure to be your lover this morning if you will be mine." He bent and kissed her ear, her neck. He trailed nibbling kisses along her jaw. His hand made lazy curls from her neck to her lower back.

"Are you taking your time?" Sophia's breathing was rapid and affected her words.

"It's about five and I don't have to leave until seven."

"Oohh, until seven?"

"More like six thirty because I'll need to shower and grab a cup of coffee on my way in."

"While you shower, I'll make your coffee and thaw a pecan sticky bun for you to take. What about some eggs?"

"Coffee and a sticky bun and you. I've a feeling this is going to be a memorable day."

"What—?"

"Shh. No words, just feel my hands and mouth on you." He pulled her to lie across his chest so he had both hands free. One continued to stroke her back the other found her breast and teased the nipple into a hard bud while his mouth rained sweet kisses across her face.

Sophia kissed him back and pressed against him. When she undulated, he slipped his hand between them and found her wet and ready for him.

He'd tucked a condom or two under his pillow. No longer caressing her back, he searched for it. Triumphant when he found the foil package, he shifted so Sophia was beside him.

"What?" Her passion-laced voice was shaky.

"Give me a second, Phia. I'm a bit out of practice." He tore the package open and sheathed himself. "Now where were we?" He kissed her, his hands dancing down her torso to the dark curls at the apex of her thighs. She arched into his hand, her movement bringing his fingers closer to her opening.

Cam kissed her chin, her neck and her collar bone as his fingers delved into her heat.

Sophia's back arched when he took her nipple in his mouth and sucked. Her hips bucked as his fingers thrust in and out.

"Cam, please. I want. I want. I want." One hand clutched his head the other his shoulder.

Her inner muscles clenched around his fingers as her orgasm claimed her. A moan rose from the depths of her soul as waves of pleasure rolled through her.

Cam held her through the turmoil, held her until her body relaxed, held her until she squirmed. Kissed her before she said something.

"Tell me what you liked so I can do it again."

Sophia's startled gaze spoke volumes. She studied his face with her dark brown eyes, darker because of the passion they'd just shared.

He kissed her nose. He held her thus which meant she could only kiss his chin. He smiled when he felt not just a kiss but a nip.

"Again?" He whispered in her ear.

She nodded.

"Am I in the lead again?"

"Do you mind?"

The uncertainty in her voice quelled his arousal.

"I don't mind at all." He didn't pull her back over his chest, instead he laid beside her, his hands toying with her breasts one minute, toying with the curls covering her mons the next, his lips toying with her mouth, her chin, her ears. And when his hand was busy elsewhere, his mouth devoured her breasts, first one and then the other."

Her grip on his shoulders tightened, his fingers dipped into her heat. She was tight and close.

Cam rose above her, positioned his cock at her entrance and eased inside. *Dear God in heaven.* She was so tight, so hot, so perfect.

"Cam?"

He thrust, burying himself to the hilt. Sensations swamped and he rested his forehead against hers gathering himself to continue.

Before he could move, Sophia was shifting underneath him.

"Am I too—?"

"You're not moving." She held his face in her hands. "I've been told that this works better if you move." She stretched up and planted a passionate kiss on his mouth. Her tongue sought entrance and tangled with his.

Cam needed no more encouragement. Mere minutes later he felt her orgasm take hold. He plunged into her heat, withdrawing only to pump deeper. Teetering on the edge, he thrust again and flew into the dark void of bliss.

Before he could withdraw, Sophia's arms and legs had clamped about him. She held him to her as if she was desperate to have him close.

"Do not move." The fierce whisper held him transfixed.

"You just ordered me to move."

"That was before. I want to feel your weight on me. I won't break or suffocate or whatever it is you fear."

Cam obliged checking every few seconds to make sure it wasn't too much. After the fourth check-in, Sophia swatted his buttocks. "I'll let you know when and if it becomes too much."

His plan had been to slowly seduce her and make love to her lasting the better part of an hour or so. That plan had failed because his lady had other ideas. He estimated less than thirty minutes had gone by which meant they had another hour before getting up.

That idea had his cock firming. She must have felt it too because her inner muscles massaged. He was hard again in less than a minute.

"We've got time don't we?" Her hand ruffled his hair back from his forehead. She caressed his neck, her hand trailing down his spine. She didn't move any other part of her body except that one hand and her inner muscles.

"Are you trying to see if you can make me come without overtly moving?" He kissed her, a soft brush of lips upon lips.

"Not really. Just seeing if you're paying attention." She laughed when he withdrew and thrust deep.

"Your turn to concentrate on how your body feels when I do this." He took her nipple in his mouth and sucked. She bucked. He held her down. Raising his head he whispered. "You can't move. Just feel."

She shrank down against the covers, gripping the sheets with both hands. Could she remain still while her body rioted with arousal? Her inner muscles clamped him tight, held on with all their might. She felt the beginnings of another orgasm as Cam thrust deep inside her while suckling her breast. Sophia came apart as the force of her release engulfed her entire body like a tidal wave crashing on an island.

Still floating somewhere on the heated waters of bliss, she was aware when Cam found his own release. He collapsed over her, his head nestled next to hers, his chin on her shoulder. Arms wrapped around him, she held him close as their heartbeats slowed and their shattered breathing eased.

17 And So It Goes

Two weeks later, Sophia stood at the door of her classroom as students filed in. It was her practice to have a smile on her face and a positive word or two for each student. By this time in the year, they expected that from her so filed in one-by-one.

Cam was also back at work. Winter seemed to be a busy time of year for law enforcement officers. He was pulling long shifts because he filled in for officers who were sick. Another bug of some sort had hit his precinct hard. He credited her for his resisting the bug.

"You're just too stubborn to get sick," she'd countered one evening while they were on the phone. Unless he had the next day off or had a later shift, he didn't spend the night with her. Their pattern became one where they talked and cuddled and fell asleep. Most of the time they slept until morning but the agreement was whoever woke up during the night had permission to wake the other.

Not once had Cam had those nightmares he was so concerned about. Not once had Cam left without waking her although he had been called out a couple of nights ago. Not once did Sophia allow her imagination to fly off with a future picture of them together.

It probably helped that Gabriella and Giovanni had had a major crisis. A reminder that nothing was permanent no matter how right it seemed. Still she'd be leaving for Italy in two weeks because they had sorted things out.

As the students settled into their desks, she began the day's lesson. They were talking about 'fairness'. From personal experience she knew life wasn't fair. What she wanted was for her students to think about what that word meant and whether their definition helped them live positive, forward-thinking lives.

Class time was spent in small group discussions. They had a homework assignment to write about their current understanding of the word "fair" and whether the discussion had shown them other ways to interpret the word.

Because she knew her students, she almost always knew what those papers would say but she did the exercise nonetheless because there were always a handful of students during the day who did have an 'aha' moment, who did expand their view of the people and the world around them. Living one's life on the premise that life was fair or should be fair was a guarantee of disappointment at best and disillusionment at worst.

Her other favorite exercise was one she did in May. It was set up in a similar fashion. The topic then was "Choice". 'Do we always have a choice?' 'What are those choices?' And most recently she'd added 'What choice would you make if something you believed in would never come to fruition, would never manifest?' Last year was the first year she'd tried that topic. This year she was having at least one day for discussion and one day for them to write out their thoughts. "Choice" was a hotter topic than "Fair".

Cam's schedule was crazy. He was waiting in the hall when her last class was dismissed. "I've an hour break so stopped by to spend some time with you."

"I need to gather some papers together and then I can leave."

"I'll look around." He strolled to the back of the room where she had a display of books and magazines on different topics.

Sophia had just tapped the papers together into a neat stack when a quiet knock sounded. Looking over she recognized the young woman standing in the doorway.

"Janeen, come in. And who do you have with you?" She smiled at the baby held carefully in her former pupil's arms.

"I hope you don't mind my stopping by." Janeen hesitated before coming all the way into the room.

"Of course not. I'm glad to see you. How are you doing?"

"Okay."

"And who is this little one?"

"My-my daughter."

"She's beautiful. I think she has your nose and chin for sure. What's her name?"

"Sophia."

Her throat clogged with emotions and her eyes filled with tears.

"I named her after you because I want her to have someone to look up to." Earnestness infused Janeen's slim face, her gaze fierce. "I hope you don't mind."

"I'm honored. But she'll have you to look up to. I know you'll be an excellent role model for her."

Janeen teared up. "I want to be but... ."

Sophia pulled out her desk chair and motioned for Janeen to sit down. She perched on the side of the desk and patted the young mother's shoulder. "You'll be a wonderful mother to little Sophia. What she needs most in the world is to know you love her. And it's obvious you adore her.

"Is her father in the picture?"

"Jason's in college back east." Janeen looked up at Sophia, "He wants to be here but it's better that he finish. He's a junior this year so only one more year until he graduates.

"I know he loves me and wants to be with Sophia and me but he also wants his education. I can't afford to go back to see him and he can't get away to come home."

"Spring Break is coming up."

"But he has a job in some big shot law firm. He works there during breaks so I already know he can't be here. His mom says this is for the best. She lets me use her computer every Sunday to email him."

"Where are you staying?" Sophia heard something in this story that just didn't sit right but she couldn't put her finger on it.

"Jason's mom is letting us stay in her RV for now. At least for the next couple of months. I had a hard time delivering her." Janeen hugged the baby and kissed her forehead. "She's so tiny, so precious." She looked over at Sophia. "I'll need to get a job soon. Marla said I should consider putting Sophia up for adoption because I really can't take care of her."

"And Marla is Jason's mom?"

Janeen nodded.

Sophia's memory banks were working full-tilt as she sorted through what she remembered of Janeen. Very dysfunctional family background, drug and alcohol abuse, domestic violence. She'd been friends with a couple of kids and at times had spent the night with one of them. A picture surfaced of Janeen by her locker with a young man, very intense, leaning toward her, shoulders hunched and speaking emphatically.

"Jason Southerland is the baby's father?"

Janeen nodded.

"And he acknowledges that little Sophia is his child?"

Janeen nodded again. "He was so happy when I told him I was pregnant. He wanted us to get married right away but his mom talked to both of us and explained how getting married right then would ruin Jason's plan to go into politics in ten years or so."

"Why are you staying in the RV instead of the house?" This was what had niggled a minute ago. The Southerlands were a wealthy family. Their house had plenty of room for Janeen and the baby.

"Marla is concerned that Sophia's crying will disturb Bart."

"I thought Mr. Southerland worked long hours and was seldom home. Has that changed?"

"I think it's more that she thinks I'm a bad influence."

"What about food? Is there electricity and heat in the RV?"

Janeen's chin dropped to her chest. "I-I-I" She shook her head. "We manage because we've lots of blankets. There is a propane stove so I can heat water. I'm nursing her so I don't need to heat a bottle.

"I'm sorry to bother you, Ms. Stewart. I was riding the bus and it came by the school and I thought-I thought." Janeen stood, picked up the bag she'd carried in.

Sophia saw it had diapers and a blanket. She put her arm around Janeen's shoulder. "You come see me tomorrow. If you don't come here. I'll come to you. We'll talk some more and come up with a plan."

"Jason and I have a plan. It's just going to take us a lot longer than we thought."

"What is your plan?"

"He said if I can make it back there, we can get married and he can increase his student loan so we have a place to live. When the baby is a little older, I can find a job and help support us. But he doesn't have the money to send us right now and I only have food stamps."

"What about WIC? You and the baby are eligible for that?"

"Marla is adamant I'm not to accept charity from anyone but her. If she knew I had food stamps, she'd have a fit."

Sophia pulled her purse from the bottom drawer of her desk. Out of the side pocket she grabbed the cash she kept at hand. "I want you to take this." She folded the bills in Janeen's hand. "You stop on the way home and get something hot to eat. Tomorrow you come back to see me after school. There's enough for a hot meal and bus fare.

"Do you have Jason's email address?"

"It's on the computer but I did write it down just in case—."

"You bring that tomorrow. I'll bring my laptop and we'll email Jason when we have a plan. You won't have to wait until Sunday." Sophia stepped in front of Janeen and rested her hand on Janeen's arm. "I want you to know I'm going to make some calls. I won't mention your name but we both need more information before we can create the best plan for you, Jason and the baby."

"Are you sure?"

"Do I look sure?"

Janeen smiled. "You look like Ms. Stewart when she's determined."

Sophia laughed. "I am Ms. Stewart and I am determined."

Janeen turned back at the door. "I didn't intend to burden you with my problems. I, well, you helped me so much. You believed in me. You encouraged me. You had such faith that I could move past my family background. When she was born, I couldn't think of another name for her. And Jason agreed. It's because of you he stood up to his parents and continued to see me when they told him to stop."

"I will see you both tomorrow.

"By the way, do you have an infant car seat for her?"

Janeen shook her head. "Marla borrowed one when we were discharged from the hospital. We haven't needed one taking the bus."

"I've a friend. I'll borrow one from her so I can take you home tomorrow after we've come up with our plan."

Sophia leaned against her desk listening to Janeen murmur unintelligible words to her baby as she carried her down the hall.

Cam's arms wrapped around her and he pulled her back against his chest. "Southerland, eh?"

"You know the family?"

"Some."

"She's frightened."

"And well she should be. She's living in an unheated RV in the dead of winter. She has no transportation to speak of. I bet it's at least a mile to the nearest bus stop. And she's not exactly dressed for the weather. Those jeans are almost thread bare."

"I'll take her shopping for some clothes. We can go to a thrift shop and get her something warmer to wear. I can take her to apply for WIC. I know Diana will let me borrow the baby's car seat."

"And you'll talk to Lily."

Sophia turned in his arms. "Yes, I will be talking to Lily. And the others."

"You could invite her to stay with you. You have a spare room."

"Before I did that, I'd talk to Jason to make sure he did Not want her with him. He was an excellent student but beyond that, he was a really nice person. Everyone liked him."

"Runs in the family."

"No there's a difference. The Southerlands came to parent teacher meetings so I've met them. People may like their façade but the other students and teachers liked Jason because he was genuine."

"Do you know what school he's attending?"

"I forgot to ask her but I will find out tomorrow. Why?"

"You said Diana's son, Bill is back east and Grant and Hunter are from that part of the country. They may have ideas too."

Sophia kissed his cheek. "Is your break over?"

"If the clock on the wall is right, I've ten more minutes.

"Follow me home and I'll send you off with some cookies."

"I'll follow you home and collect at least a peck on the cheek along with those cookies."

18 Cameron

Cam drove slowly past Sophia's house. It had been a hell of a day and he wanted to see her but—. He turned the corner and drove down another block. "Grow up Mitchell," he growled at himself in the dark. "She's just a woman. Nothing special." The pain that lanced his gut at those words resulted in a string of swear words streaming from his mouth.

"Get a grip." He stopped at the corner, peered down her street, then turning on his blinkers turned the other way and drove off.

Two blocks away his cell phone rang. Pushing the button on his head piece, he answered. "Mitchell."

Inwardly he cursed. He hadn't looked down at the caller id so wasn't expecting her voice in his ear.

"Are you okay, Cam?"

"Yeah." He really wasn't as okay as he wanted her to believe. She was too softhearted to be involved with him. Too softhearted and too nice and too kind and too—just everything good. He didn't deserve someone who represented everything good.

"You were on my mind and I thought you'd be off duty by now. Are you busy?" She laughed. "Of course you are. But do you have time to stop by? I leave for Italy Saturday and I'd like to see you before I go."

He wanted to see her before she went also. He wanted to sink into her heat, feel her orgasm clench his dick, feel her arms tighten around him when he first tried to roll off.

"Don't think I'd be good company tonight." He kept on driving, quelling the urge to turn around. He reached a major intersection, the light green, he cruised through and accelerated.

"Am I bothering you, calling like this?"

Cam inwardly sighed. "No you aren't bothering me. It was a hell of a day and I'm not good company."

"So you think you'd be grumpy or rude or rough or what?"

"Let it go, Sophia. I'll see you before you leave, okay?"

"I didn't mean to upset you, Cam. As I said, you were on my mind and I thought I'd call and see how you're doing."

"Tomorrow night I get off at seven. Is it too late to come by at eight?"

"No, that won't be too late. I'll have dinner—"

"Don't wait for me. If it is another day like today, I'll be calling to say I can't make it."

The silence was unnerving. His hands sweat as the tension in him coiled tighter. "I didn't mean to hurt your feelings."

"My feelings aren't hurt. You told me it'd been a bad day. I didn't realize how much it had taken out of you. Know that I'll hold you in healing light. Goodnight, Cam."

The call ended.

His empty apartment seemed even more so. Turning on every light didn't ease the darkness that surrounded him. In the kitchen he opened the cupboard and stood staring for a long time at the bottle of scotch. If he needed a reason to drink himself into oblivion, the events of today were it.

"Later."

Cam stripped out of his clothes and showered, hot water sluiced over him as he scrubbed desperately wanting the memories, the filth of the day to wash down the drain. Wrapping a towel around his waist he plodded into the bedroom. A faint scent of vanilla teased his nostrils. These sheets had been washed at Sophia's last weekend when he'd spent extra time with her.

He flopped on the bed and hugged a pillow. "I'm pathetic." He needed to get rid of the damn thing but stopped short of throwing it across the room. His eyes drifted close and a white light glowed behind his lids. She was so close. He could feel her arms around him.

The scotch forgotten, Cam fell asleep and dreamed about the woman who embodied life, love and home, everything he'd never have.

Sometime during the night he'd pulled the covers up. And while morning was usually a rough time, today he woke on his own feeling rested. A cup of coffee and he was off to the station. He'd foregone the last cinnamon roll deciding, as he put it back in the freezer, he might need it more on another day.

Going through the motions of the day, he was glad there weren't any murders, rapes, assaults, child endangerment or abuse calls. He was a captain and wasn't a first responder but the flu that had plagued the precinct still did and there just weren't enough people. Most of the day he was on patrol. On a hunch he stopped at the park and asked a group of young men if he could shoot a couple of baskets. He'd made the first one and then ran into a streak of misses.

No one jeered or made comments. He figured that was because they saw the bulge when he made a jump shot that told them he was carrying. Bouncing the ball back to the tallest, he said "Let's see what you can do?"

Smooth moves, a ball handling ease he admired flowed before him as the young men formed their teams and played. Sophia popped into his mind. *What would she do?*

"Good shot!" Cam called out to the guy who'd done a respectable slam-dunk. "Do you guys play here every day?"

One of them nodded. "If I show up with a couple of my buddies will you play with us?"

Cam saw the hesitation, the wary looks flash between them.

The tallest guy stepped forward. "What're you about?"

"A friendly game is all. Not looking to hassle anyone. No talk except about the game."

"Cops can play ball?"

"Off-duty cops can play ball. We'd all be off duty. Nothing official."

"You off duty now?"

"No, I'm not off duty but I was on a break. Need to get back to it." Cam turned, alert to the sound of voices behind him, listening with every fiber of his body for a change in tone that spelled danger.

"Sunday. You be here Sunday and we'll show you how to play ball." He heard the laugher.

Now walking backwards, he grinned. "We'll see who's going to show who how to play ball. Noon?"

As a group they nodded. Clapping each other on the back, they turned back to pass the ball around.

Cam's step was lighter and he whistled as he trekked back to his car. *Now to find four or five or maybe ten more guys to play.* He knew some of the officers were involved with PAL, the Police Athletic League. *A place to start.*

His mood was still high when he pulled into Sophia's garage. She must have heard the door opening and closing because when he got out of his car, she was standing in the doorway to the house.

As he strolled towards her, he took in the sight. Her long dark hair pulled back from her face in a twist that she favored. No make-up except for a neutral lip gloss she wore as a moisturizer. A simple turquoise tunic over a pair of black tights, bare feet. He couldn't see them from here but he knew they would be–and her toes would sport a sparkly polish.

What in heaven's name did she ever see in him? He'd asked her one night when they were cuddling and talking before sleep. She'd used words like 'kind', 'compassionate', 'caring'. Those were not words he'd use to describe himself.

Her warm smile welcomed him. She was glad to see him. And truth be told, he was more than glad to see her. Even when he didn't see her, spend time with her, knowing she was a phone call away helped him set things aside at night, forego the scotch and find sleep without her beside him.

Cam reached for her when he was close enough to snag her into his arms. Her vanilla scent and her arms wrapped around him. His mouth found hers and he kissed her with a tenderness even he didn't recognize. She melted against him and he knew he'd be spending the night. He was a mortal man and he was drawn to this woman like a bee to a flower. He fed from her soft lips and drank of her sweetness.

He pulled back and kissed her forehead and then her nose. "Glad to see me?"

She laughed and gave him a quick peck on the cheek. "What do you think?" She stepped back and taking his hand, led him into the house. "Don't forget to set the perimeter alarm," she said over her shoulder when she dropped his hand and strolled on into the kitchen area.

Cam did set the alarm and then followed her.

"You need to change the code."

"Why?"

"You need to change the code every few months."

"Why?"

"It's the safe thing to do."

"I know the code and so do you. Lily and Diana have it also. If I change it, I'll give the new code to all of you so what's the difference?"

"I shouldn't have the code."

"You'd rather I have to get up and see you out the door when you spend the night and have to leave before I do?"

Cam stepped behind her, drew her back against him. "I want you safe."

Sophia turned in his arms. "And I want you safe too." She pulled away. "I didn't fix you dinner but I do have some snacks if you're hungry."

He eyed the platter of food. Veggies and dip, cheese and crackers, ham and salami were arrayed in a pinwheel pattern. *Of course she'd have food for you. It's part of who she is.*

Picking up a nearby plate, he helped himself. He was hungry, his growling stomach testified to that. "Anything to drink?"

"Cold beer, tea, coffee, juice, lemonade."

"What kind of juice?"

"Tomato and orange."

"A glass of tomato juice sounds good."

"Coming right up."

Ambient light filtered through the partially opened curtains. Enough light for Cam to see Sophia undress and slip into bed. Enough light for her to see the sky when she woke. Small talk was all they'd shared while he ate and she busied herself around the kitchen. He looked forward to their routine of cuddling and talking before sleeping. Tonight they'd headed to bed early enough he thought there might be some love making before they slept. That thought had his dick stirring.

He turned on his side, rested his head on his hand and let his free hand trace circles on her belly. Her muscles twitched under his caress but she didn't push him away or tell him to stop.

"What's going on with Janeen?" He was curious about how Sophia and the others worked.

"She's staying with Hunter and Grant at the Murphy House. She'll house sit for them and check in on Eleanor since both Lily and Jackson will be in Italy."

"How is she getting around? I didn't see a bus stop very close to the Montgomery's."

"Hunter is letting her use her car."

"And?"

She leaned up and kissed his chin. "Mr. Curious." Settling back on the bed, she continued. "She has warm clothes as does the baby. She has a car seat and a bassinette. There is a nanny-type suite of rooms that she and the baby are in. Hunter and Grant are upstairs in the main master bedroom. Before they leave for Italy, the kitchen will be stocked with food for her. She's had her WIC appointment and now has formula. Diana has given her bottles because M2 is starting to drink from sippy cups."

"I thought she was nursing."

"She is but with the stress in her life, her milk isn't as plentiful as the baby needs. She's nursing and then supplementing with a bottle."

"Long term?"

Sophia sighed. "I don't know. I talked to Jason. He is furious with his parents. I assured him Janeen and the baby were okay but he was unable to refocus on them his anger at his parents was so strong.

"Grant said he had some business to take care of in Rhode Island." She smiled. "It just now came up.

"He and Hunter have changed their tickets and will stop in Rhode Island on their way back from Italy. I'm fairly certain, although I've not confirmed it, that Grant will make time to see Jason in person."

"And if Jason doesn't measure up, Janeen has a circle of protection around her."

"I believe Jason will measure up. He has to resolve his feelings about his family first. At least he and Janeen can talk directly to each other. Ashley and Daniel gave her a cell phone to use in exchange for her being home when the children get out of school."

"So she's house sitting, checking in on Eleanor and Ashley and Daniel's kids."

"Not exactly. There actually is a schedule. She'll stop by Eleanor's about ten in the morning to make sure she's up and has what she needs. She'll stop back there around two in the afternoon on her way to Ashley and Daniel's. Daniel is taking off early so Janeen can get to Diana and Matthew's. Matthew will have time to shower and clean-up, even fix dinner without also having to juggle Madison Michele."

"And then she'll go back to the haven of the Murphy House."

"We wanted her to have something to do so she didn't feel beholden. And, her checking on Eleanor eases Lily and Jackson's mind. Her being at Ashley and Daniel's when the children get home from school allows Daniel to work another hour or so. Matthew also gets a break. He's taking Madison Michelle to work with him. Being able to take a shower and clean up, fix a meal without dangling a baby on his hip is a big thing to him."

"You're leaving—?"

"I'm flying out Saturday morning with Lily and Jackson. The others are flying out Sunday night. We're all coming back the next Friday."

"Do you need a ride to or from the airport?"

"My flight leaves at an indecent hour. I'm taking a taxi."

Cam pulled her against him, rained kisses across her face. "I excel at indecent," he whispered in her ear just before he ran his tongue around the rim.

"I'm not imposing on you." Sophia's breathing sped up and she squirmed in his arms.

"Yes, you are. I can stay the night and take you to the airport."

She kissed his neck, her hands gripped his shoulders. "You excel at kissing."

He chuckled. "Let's see if I excel at other things too."

She didn't resist.

Cam paid close attention to her reactions to his touch. He knew what she liked but he wanted to internalize her every movement, her every sound. Never in his life had he wanted to pleasure a woman the way he wanted to pleasure Sophia. When he thrust into her heat, he almost spilled himself. When she arched and cried out with her release, he did.

The next morning, Sophia had his coffee and raisin and nut sweet roll ready when he sauntered into the kitchen. On the counter were three small boxes. "Cookies for you to give away."

He'd told her about the impromptu pick-up game scheduled for noon on Sunday. "This isn't enough. There'll be at least fifteen guys."

"These aren't for them. I'll have something else you can take on Sunday." She busied herself wiping down the counter before putting the boxes in a sack. "Here, I'm sure you know someone who might like cookies.

"I've got to go or I'll be late." Sophia grabbed her purse and car keys. "Be sure to set the alarm when you leave."

Cam stood in the kitchen, the sack with the boxes of cookies on the counter. Without saying anything, she'd given him a reason to stop by Ben's work. He could take his oldest a cup of coffee and a box of cookies.

Emotions he did not want to identify misted his vision. She was going to be gone for seven days. He'd miss her like the devil. Maybe with the space, he'd find the strength to break it off with her.

He was who he was. And he'd hurt her if he stayed in her life.

Cam set the house alarm and climbed in his car. He rested his head on hands that gripped the steering wheel. If he stayed in her life, she'd be hurt. But the idea he'd never see her again? The pain that tore his heart was so strong he grabbed his chest.

19 Cam - 2

Cam picked up a large coffee, black but also grabbed a couple of sugars and cream. He had no idea how his oldest liked his coffee much less if his younger kids even drank it at all. When a parking spot right in front of Ben's office appeared, he grumbled. Sophia would say some god or goddess was with him. "Like hell. They're all against me," he growled as he pulled in.

Debating whether to give Ben the sack with the three boxes or just one, he muttered to himself. "I'll need a few of these for myself after this." With the decision made, Cam carried one box and the coffee with accoutrements to the door. He pressed the handicapped entrance button with his elbow. The swung open.

The look of surprise and suspicion on Ben's face when he saw him nearly had Cam turning around and leaving. "Brought you some coffee." Cam held the cup out as he approached the desk where Ben sat. "You do still drink coffee, don't you?"

"Yeah, I do. With sugar." He didn't stand and he didn't reach out to take the offered cup.

In for a penny, in for a pound. Cam set the coffee and box on the desk, fished the sugar packets from his pocket. "Enjoy." His gut burned and twisted in on itself. He sucked in a deep breath to ease the pain as he turned to leave.

"Dad?"

Cam swiveled back to face Ben. "Yeah?"

"What's this all about?"

Ben had yet to stand. The look of surprise was gone but the look of suspicion was clear.

"Had this extra box of cookies," he gestured, "thought you might like something special this morning. The coffee was an impulse buy."

"Cookies?"

"Believe me, Ben, these are not just 'cookies'. I promise," he crossed his heart with his hand, "they will be some of the best, if not the best, cookies you've ever eaten." He waited to see what his son would do not really surprised when Ben did nothing. "I can take it all back if you don't want it."

"That's all right, Dad." Ben stood. "Just surprised to see you."

In silence they regarded each other for several seconds.

Cam reached out and gripped Ben's shoulder. "Good seeing you."

Ben picked up the box, opened it and breathed in.

"You don't have cookies for Bev and Becca?"

"I do have cookies for them but I don't know where Bev and Becca are."

"You can give them to me."

Cam grinned. "Will there be any cookies left for them?"

Ben took a bite. His whole face smiled as he savored it. "Maybe, maybe not. Where did you get these?"

"Private source."

"I'll see them this weekend."

"I'll bring some by on Friday for them. Appreciate your seeing they get them."

"Won't share where you get these?"

"Nope."

"I'll walk you out." Ben closed the box and put it in a desk drawer. "Be right back," he told his colleague.

So many questions Cam wanted to ask but he kept silent and strolled with his son to the door.

Once outside, he turned to shake hands.

"Everyone is doing okay."

Cam waited for the taste of bile, the spurt of anger but they didn't come. "If it's appropriate, tell them I miss seeing them."

Ben looked beyond Cam's shoulder, stuffed his hands in his pockets. "Miss seeing you too, Dad."

"You'll see me again on Friday with more cookies."

Ben shifted, rose up on his toes and rocked back. "Come around eleven and we can do lunch."

"I will if I can. Some virus is going through the ranks and I'm pulling extra duty."

"Don't get to rest on your laurels?"

Ben smiled and Cam was glad to see it reached his eyes. "Not in this lifetime."

"Gotta…" both spoke at the same time.

"See you Friday, Dad."

Cam waved as he rounded the car and slid behind the wheel. He noticed that Ben waited until he'd pulled away from the curb before he went back in his office.

"Hell," he muttered. "I've just promised Sophia's cookies to my kids without even asking her."

He used the cookies as a bribe to change shifts with someone so he could have Saturday morning off. It meant he'd work Saturday swing, a usually busy shift. The pick-up game on Sunday at noon would come early. But he didn't care. He'd have time with Sophia before she left.

The conundrum that was his relationship with Sophia meandered through his day.

He should break it off.

He couldn't break it off.

He would hurt her.

He'd die before he hurt her.

The other reality was he could be killed and what would that do to her. He knew she cared about him or he wouldn't be sharing her bed. She wouldn't smile with delight when he came in the door.

The cookies and sweet rolls were an added bonus but he knew she baked and gave them away to many people. As he sorted his thoughts he noted she smiled with delight when her circle women came in the door.

Sophia cared about him. She showed it by allowing him in her bed. He was the first man to love her since her husband died. He had a responsibility to protect her.

Cam's brain was still assessing and sorting when he pulled into the garage. He didn't usually come by on nights when they both worked the next day but he had to see her.

She was waiting at the door into the house when he got out of the car.

"Are you okay?" Worry laced her voice and scrunched her brow.

"Yep. Just had to see you." He was so close he could smell her vanilla scent. His hands itched to hold her but he stopped in front of her. "I know I didn't call."

Sophia reached out and took his hand. "Come in. Whatever you have to say can be said inside."

He took her in his arms and held her, breathing in her vanilla scent, sensing her body melt against his, relishing the feel of her arms around his neck, her fingers caressing his nape.

"Cam," she whispered his name. "Are you okay?"

"I am now. Just needed to hold you 'til the ugliness faded." He released her and stepped back. His arms registered the emptiness and he longed to pull her back into his embrace.

"Come and eat. I've homemade soup and some bread."

"It's okay Phia. You don't have to feed me—."

"No, I don't *have* to feed you but I *want* to feed you. Come along." She took his hand and tugged him toward the kitchen.

"I can't stay."

"You can stay long enough to eat."

Sophia dished up the soup and sliced fresh bread still warm from the oven. "I'm really glad you came by, I'll send the rest of this loaf home with you. How did your day go?"

Cam smiled. His Sophia was chattering, a sure sign she was nervous. "Cookies are gone."

She looked his way, eyes narrowed. "Did you eat them all?"

"Nope, I shared."

"May I ask with whom you shared those cookies?"

"You aren't asking if they liked them?"

Sophia laughed. "Did they like them?"

"Of course. Used one box to trade shifts with someone so I can take you to the airport Saturday morning. Gave another box to one of the officers who'd had a really bad day."

She questioned him with a look and handed him his bowl of soup and a plate of bread.

"Gave the other box to my son, Ben."

"Good." Sophia took her bowl of soup and plate of bread to the table and sat.

"You say that now," Cam said sitting across from her.

She arched a brow.

"He's seeing the other two this weekend. If I have more cookies, he'll make sure they get them—if he also gets his own box."

"I don't think that will be a problem. I was thinking of making a sheet cake for the basketball game. I can easily make a batch of cookies too."

"I feel like I'm imposing."

"Helping you reestablish a relationship with your children is not an imposition. And, your reaching out to those young men can only be a good thing going forward. Why would you think you'd be imposing?"

"You've a lot on your plate what with the trip to Italy, the wedding and Janeen."

"Actually, Cam, all of those things are shared. I'm traveling with friends. The wedding is taken care of. And Janeen has been taken in by Hunter and Grant. I can see how important it is for them to help her so I'm not really involved right now."

"Other than talking to Jason."

"True, but unless he calls me, I won't be pursuing that either. Grant and Hunter will."

"Why? They don't even know these two kids."

"It's not my story to tell."

Conversation drifted to inconsequential topics as they finished their dinner, cleared the table and put the dishes in the dishwasher.

"I'm going to make the sheet cake tonight. I'll frost it in the morning and then freeze it. It should thaw before your game is over on Sunday.

"Cookies are on the agenda for tomorrow afternoon when I get home. I can bake, do laundry and decide what I'm taking at the same time."

"How can I help?"

"You can keep me company."

"Nothing more?"

Sophia was already starting on the cake batter. "You can fix me a cup of tea and then you can grease and flour the pan." At his quizzical expression, she instructed, "take a paper towel and put a tablespoon of butter on it. Then wipe that towel over the inside of the pan. Make sure you get the corners. When you've done that, let me know and I'll tell you how to flour it."

It took Sophia less than twenty minutes to get the cake in the oven. An hour later it was done and cooling on a rack on the counter.

Cam had loaded up the dishwasher with the utensils needed to make the cake after licking the beaters and bowl.

"I could get used to being your assistant."

Sophia kissed his cheek. "You're an excellent assistant. I particularly like the mini-neck massage when the cake went in the oven."

"What I wanted to do was a full body massage." He kissed her neck and let his hands knead her shoulders.

"Thank you for your restraint. The cake would have burned and I'd have had to start again." She leaned against him. "I'm not opposed to that massage now."

20 Italy

January 28, 2006
Italy

Sophia met up with Lily and Jackson at the gate just as the plane was ready to board. Cam had spent the night, loved her thoroughly, dropped her off at the terminal and, with cake in his trunk, headed off to his apartment to put it in his freezer.

Stifling a yawn, she hugged Lily and didn't complain when Jackson took charge of her carryon. The obvious reason for the yawning was lack of sleep because Cam stayed over however, it was more than that.

She was worried.

Worried on several levels.

She'd missed more school this year than any previous year since Jonathan died.

Therefore she was less connected with her students.

And she found it hard to stay focused on her class—her attention drifted throughout the day.

But most of all, she was worried about Cam. It was true his was an inherently dangerous job but even after spending time with him for almost eight weeks, the darkness that originally enfolded him was still there. Oh there were flashes of light but they lasted no more than a few hours. He came carrying the dark and at best it faded while he was with her.

In her most vivid imagination, she couldn't picture how someone could survive without the light. Doubt was now a constant companion when it came to him. Doubt that it was good for either of them to continue to see each other. Doubt that she could help him find his own light. Doubt that should something happen to him, she'd be able to find her own light again.

As the plane flew towards Atlanta where they would change planes for the international leg of their journey, Sophia closed her eyes and went through her relaxation process. She needed some sleep so she could readily participate in the festivities.

"Sophia?" Lily gently shook her shoulder. "We're here. Time to change planes."

"Thanks," Sophia said as she gathered her backpack from under the seat.

Jackson had already retrieved her carry-on and held it in the aisle. Grabbing the handle she strode off the plane. Lily and Jackson gained her side. Their next flight left from another terminal.

"Will we make it?" She started to hurry along.

"Wait, Soph," Lily said, reaching for her. "Jackson ordered a tram because the time between flights is short and the distance to the international terminal long."

"Thank you, Jackson. I didn't even think about it."

"Did you get a little rest?" Jackson asked as he looked around for the tram.

"More than I thought I would. I must be even more tired than I realized."

"You've been busy, Soph. We'll all been so busy catching up from when we've been gone, The Circle hasn't even met since Winter Solstice." Lily linked her arm in Sophia's and the two leaned into each other.

"That will change once we are back. We can talk about everyone getting together at Ostera or Beltane. My vote will be that we hold ceremony in Fremont. Even with wee Maeve, it has to be easier for two women and baby to travel to us than all of us travel to them."

"We'll make sure we have a plan before we leave to come home."

"Here's our ride," Jackson announced as the shuttle came to a stop.

Seated together on the flight to Italy, Sophia did not nap. She and Lily speculated on what Hunter and Grant would do about Janeen. Both were very clear that those two would handle everything.

"Logan is coming up for the weekend. She and Janeen were in the same class although they didn't run with the same crowd," Lily shared. "I think that's a good idea because Little Sophia is nowhere near sleeping through the night. Logan can watch her while Janeen takes a nap."

"I'm grateful she came to see me. I don't even want to think about what could have happened if she and the baby had stayed in that RV all winter. I doubt they would have survived. It may be mild in some ways, but we've had well-below freezing nights and not even above freezing during the day.

That place was like a deep freeze when I helped get her belongings."

A car met them at the airport in Florence and within two hours they were at Giovanni's villa. Gabriella dashed out the door and threw her arms around Sophia and Lily. "You're here. You're here. I'm so glad you came today." She bounced up and down on her toes. "Giovanni is out. He'll be back soon. Oh, come in. Come in!" She dashed inside, immediately pivoted and came back out. "Silvio will be here any second and help with your luggage. Soph, you are in the same room as before. Lily and Jackson are next to you."

Silvio gathered up the luggage and headed into the villa.

"Let's go out to the veranda while your things are taken to your room. We'll have something cool to drink and something light to eat. Adolfo is fixing a simple dinner." She turned to Sophia. "You can make your cake in the morning."

"I will talk to Adolfo before I invade his kitchen, Gabby. I don't know that my chocolate cake is appropriate for your Italian wedding."

"But—."

"I will make sure you have your own cake when you come to Fremont. You should not stress out about this. I'll talk to Adolfo and see if it will work out. I'm sure he is fixing a meal fit for a king and queen. He dotes on you."

"He's very sweet."

"And what does Giovanni say to that?"

Gabriella laughed. "You may be right. Talk to Adolfo. I don't want to get on his bad side."

"No you don't because the source of the best tiramisu may dry up."

An hour later, Sophia was in her room. The view looked out over Giovanni's studio to a spit of land dotted with caves. At high tide, she could see the waves entering and retreating from the openings. Regardless of the tide, the play of light on the face of the rocks was ever changing. Light and dark danced across the land. At one point everything dimmed when a large cloud passed overhead.

The scene brought to mind her musing about Cam. She slowed her breathing and went within. Calling his features to mind, she searched for him, searched to make sure he was okay. This time she didn't see him but did feel him. His arms were around her, his chest at her back, she was enveloped in his fresh minty scent and heat. Sensations faded and she was fully back in the room.

A few times she'd tried to be present like this with others but it only seemed to work with Cam. Of course she could 'check in' with The Circle and know in general how things were going in their lives but with Cam? With Cam she was with him. She felt his touch. His scent, his heat were real.

Never would she try to compare Cam and Jonathan. They were so different. Except in some ways they were the same. They were both kind and compassionate men. *Stop now!*

Sophia stood by the window and searched for Cam again. He appeared to be standing in her house, now walking down the hall to her room. He shrugged out of his jacket and shirt, took off his shoes and pants and stretched out on the bed.

On her side of the bed.

She calculated the time difference. It would be dark in Fremont. Cam was staying at her house. A soft smile tipped her lips as she set an energetic circle of protection around her home.

Maybe she was showing him his light more than she realized. Maybe there was more to their relationship than she wanted to see. Maybe they had more time together. *The Goddess will show me the way. I trust in Her guidance.*

The gong that announced dinner, in this case a late supper, sounded. She met Lily and Jackson at the top of the stairs. "How is your room?"

"This place is amazing!" Lily enthused. "I had no idea it was quite this grand."

It was a little chilly this time of year so they ate in the dining room. Sophia ventured into the kitchen between the main and dessert course.

"You make cake?"

Sophia shrugged. "Do you want me to make a cake?"

"Senora Gabriella wants it." He stood, arms folded across his chest, feet set shoulder wide.

"Gabriella will have a whole cake of her own when she travels to Fremont. I will only make a cake if you need me to make it."

He didn't move and Sophia wondered if there was a language barrier.

"Adolfo, this is your kitchen. You are in charge of the wedding feast. If you want me to help, I will. Otherwise, I know you can manage without me and your food will be more than enough without my chocolate cake."

Margretta stepped around her. She spoke in Italian. Adolfo nodded several times.

"It is how you say, I will call if I need you?"

Sophia smiled. "Perfect. If I hear you call, I will come and help however you need me to."

Why didn't she want to bake a cake for Gabriella's wedding? Did she have to have an answer to that question? She shook her head. "No, I don't. It's what feels right."

On her way up the stairs to her room she started to calculate what time it was in Fremont. *Stop. What's important is getting a good night's sleep.* The others would be arriving tomorrow.

Keeping the doors to the balcony off her room ajar, she listened to the rolling waves as she drifted off to sleep. Strong arms held her, warm breath brushed her ear. She was in Cam's arms.

21 The Circle

Giovanni arranged for the men to go into the nearest town to look around. Between the architects, he and Jackson, and the curiosity inbred in Michael and Grant, there were things to see and good wine to drink.

The Circle rearranged furniture in front of the fireplace making sure the low coffee table remained in the center. Gabriella covered the top with a multi-colored silk scarf.

"I chose this because of our diversity." Gabriella put two stones from The Sacred Grove in the West, a pure white stone from the path to the sea wall in the North. In the east she placed a piece of amber Maria Sophia had given her. And in the South, the pine cone she'd found at the cabin less than six months ago.

Lily added an owl figurine in the north, a small red dragon in the south, lapis in the west and citrine in the east.

Diana left a small robin's egg in the east; the Wheel of Fortune tarot card in the south. A thumbnail sized piece of larimar was placed in the west. The Hermit tarot card rested in the North.

Ashley held a silk pouch embroidered with assorted dragonflies. Opening it, she removed four damselflies figurines, delicately rendered in silver wire twisted around semi-precious stones. She placed the green damselfly in the east; the red damselfly in the south, the blue one in the west and the iridescent one in the north.

Elizabeth added a stone from the Sacred Grove to the south, a leaf from one of its trees in the west. A cone from an evergreen tree now sat in the north and last but not least E. set a stone from the spring in the east.

Hunter contributed a dancing ballerina figure in the east, a tiny drum in the south. In the west she added three beach agates and in the north a miniature drumming shaman.

Sophia stood to the side watching the magic as their altar manifested. It never made any difference who brought what or where they placed their offerings, the energy of their gifts transformed the space.

In the east, Sophia placed a small porcelain figurine of a blue bird. An egg, the same shade of blue, went in the south. She pulled out the piece of azurite she kept in her bra and placed it in the west. In the north, she placed a palm-sized snowy owl figurine.

The smudge was lit and passed over and around the altar. Each of them waved the wisps of smoke up, over, around and down their bodies. They stood on one foot and then the other to make sure the soles of their feet were cleansed. When they were done, Gabriella put the abalone shell that held the smoldering sage outside.

Feet set shoulder wide, arms raised palms up, they prayed.

"We are the light

"We are the source

"Through us love flows

"Throughout the world."

As was their tradition they repeated the verse times three.

Silence swirled around them.

Hunter spoke. "God, Goddess, Bless this circle of women. Know that we honor You in all your forms. At this time of our gathering, we ask that You bless and keep our sister, Gabriella. May she know the joys of a loving marriage."

"Blessed Be." They chorused.

"I ask The Lady of The Sacred Grove to be with us this day, to add her blessings, her light to keep any darkness at bay." As Elizabeth spoke, a faint shimmer Sophia associated with The Lady enveloped them all.

"Miracles can and do happen." Ashley's soft drawl drew Sophia's attention. "I ask special blessings for Gabriella and her Giovanni. Their individual paths have brought them to this time and place. All that has come before in each of their lives has led to this joyous time."

Diana's clear voice sang 'she's been waiting' but changed the words and ended with "Giovanni has been waiting for his Gabriella but not in vain."

"This circle of women is strong and has only grown stronger over the years. We ask the spirits of this place to join us in celebrating the love Gabriella and Giovanni share. Watch over them, guide and protect them, this day and forever more."

Sophia had yet to speak. She was still hearing Lily's prayer. They had grown stronger as a circle and as individuals. Each of them had faced trials and tribulations and come through it all with the love and support of one another. What could she add?

"When I look into the eyes of my circle sisters, I see love and commitment. We have become The Circle because of our love and commitment to each other. It makes no difference where one of us is, we remain connected through You, the Goddess in your many forms. We ask that You hold Gabriella and Giovanni in Your light of love as You hold all who recognize Your truth."

"Blessed Be."

Gabriella started the prayer again.

"We are the light

"We are the source

"Through us love flows

"Throughout the world."

As the last refrain ended, they lowered their arms. Holding hands they stood in silence, each within her own thoughts.

When they sat, Gabriella picked up a piece of multi-colored fluorite. "I saw this in a shop in Rome. It reminded me so much of the first talking stone we had all those years ago. I remember, you, Sophia, saying you'd picked it because it represented our diversity. That remains true today.

"I'd like to be last. So who wants to go first?" She held the stone out ready to hand it off to whomever spoke first.

No one spoke for a minute, everyone waiting to see who had something more urgent to say.

Sophia held out her hand. "We are at another turning point in the life of The Circle. We now have two members who live halfway across the world. We know with a certainty that The Circle is unbroken, that our ties are strong.

"We have reached a point in time when our lives are so busy we are not as physically connected as we once were. I would like each of us to consider what we want The Circle to be in our lives. And, I would like to find a few minutes before any one of us leaves to share our thoughts. Is that agreeable?" Her gaze surveyed the group. All she saw were nods.

"Thank you." She took a deep breath and held the piece of fluorite close to her heart. "I also want to thank each and every one of you for all you've done and are doing for Janeen and her baby. I'm actually not sure I could have done it all myself." Her voice caught and tears misted her vision. "I'm struggling with my class this year. My being gone so much has taken a toll and I don't have the connections I've had in the past. How that plays out is I've some discipline problems that drain me dry by the end of the day.

"I'm still planning on putting in my garden this year but the joyous anticipation is missing. I'm doing it because that's what I do. Having these couple of days together with each of you is precious to me." She knew they were curious about Cam but it was not in her to talk about him. Not when she didn't know what their future held. They were attracted to each other and yet, they both looked for ways to distance themselves from each other.

She handed the stone to Lily on her left.

Before she spoke, Lily leaned over, put her arms around Sophia's shoulders and hugged. "I've missed sitting in circle with everyone. This is an extra blessing on top of a plethora of blessings with Gabriella's wedding.

"I've mentioned it before but I can't say it often enough, Ashley is a blessing to both Jackson and me. And when she takes Rose with her to visit clients? You all know that bundle of dynamite and love charms each and every one of them. No matter how curmudgeonly they are at the beginning that has changed by the visit's end.

"What I don't think I've shared is that Charlie has been talking to Jackson. He is really interested in becoming an architect and, of course, Jackson is willing to mentor him. The University of Oregon has a good school of architecture and Eugene is Track Town USA so both of his interests would be served by remaining in Oregon.

"Janeen's situation has also jump-started a conversation between us about children." She waved her hand. "No, I am not pregnant nor will I become pregnant. We have talked about the possibility of turning the little house into a place where young women like Janeen could stay. We'd charge rent commensurate with their income. Why would we charge rent? Because when they move out into the rest of the world, they will have to do so. We thought it would help them learn to budget, etc. I believe Doc S and the Watersons will be here. I hope to chat with them and set up a time to talk to them in more detail when we are back in Fremont."

Next to share was Diana. "I'm so blessed." She laughed. "So far each of us has blessing in our lives. I remember when we were first forming The Circle. "Blessed" or "Blessing" was not on everyone's lips. We've come so far on this spiritual journey together. I also miss our times when we are together. Technology is becoming such that we may be able to use it so that no matter where anyone is, we can see and talk to each other as if in person.

"Now my blessings run in threes: One: Bill is doing well in school and is so excited with his major and the support he is getting from Michael's man-of-business and Giovanni. And, Grant has written letters of introduction to his international contacts.

"Two: Madison Michelle is growing and developing. Of course Matthew sees her as the smartest and best baby in the entire world. She loves him. I think her face lights up more when he comes in the door than when I do.

"And that leads me to my third blessing. Matthew. His face still lights up when I come in the door or even enter the room. I still have my moments, wonder how he can see anything in awkward mousy Diana Louisa Richards that puts that look on his face. Even when I'm bedraggled and exhausted, no make-up and in baby food covered clothes, he still sees me as beautiful.

When I get home, we're making a decision as to whether we are going to try to have another baby. He's been studying things, made an appointment and talked to the doctor because he didn't want to even suggest it if my OB/GYN had reservations. Time will tell."

Ashley ran a hand over her hair. It was almost shoulder length. No longer platinum blond, it was still a pale blond. Her eyes filled with unshed tears as her gaze traveled around the circle. "This summer, if Anthony still wants to go and Art will let him come, my boy is going to Alabama. The agreement is for the summer, but Daniel and I have decided that if he wants to stay for the school year, we will not say 'no'.

"James loves high school. His grades are good. I knew he was smart but I'm sometimes surprised by how smart he really is. He loves math and science. Daniel has started a savings account to help him with college. Especially if he goes to community college the first two years, it will help him with the rest of his college expenses. His teachers say he could get a scholarship if he keeps up the good work. He also loves to work with his hands so he's helping Daniel weekends and breaks if Daniel needs an extra hand.

"My Rose, after what she went through, well I was prepared for her to be scarred for life. But she's stronger for it. Her faith in the Goddess, in The Lady is unwavering. I'd miss her like everything, but when she's older if she could come and stay with you, E, that would be a blessing to her and to me.

"However, the biggest joy or blessing," she smiled, "I used it twice." She paused and then added. "The biggest blessing in my life is Daniel. Y'all know he's home with those kids. He takes care of me, pampers me. I feel precious."

Ashley handed the stone across Gabriella to Hunter.

"Grant and I plan on stopping in Rhode Island on the way back. If you thought he made up an excuse so he could check out Jason, you're right. Both of us feel blessed to be able to help this young woman. And, Lily, let me know about the meeting. I'd like to be there. Grant and I can help with financial support.

"Logan loves school. The University of Oregon is a perfect fit for her. Charlie is there and so are a few of her high school friends but there are so many other people she isn't as afraid someone will find out about what happened to her.

"Grant and I have decided to build a house—at the coast. Lots of bedrooms, big kitchen and great room. He's probably picking Jackson and Giovanni's brains right now. We are also going to buy a place in town. Too many things happened while living over the studio. We want to be away from any reminders of Logan's ordeal.

"However, we aren't sure we want to invest in a big house in the hills when we'll have a big house at the coast. So, we're thinking more about established neighborhoods like Sophia's or Lily's little house. Whether there will be any other little Compton or Parkers running around, we're not sure. We're enjoying the freedom we have right now. Because we're spending time with Janeen, Grant is getting a real sense of what our lives would be like with a new baby."

Elizabeth took the stone. "This is the first time since her birth that Michael and I have been away from Maeve. Shannon adores her and it is mutual. With Seamus to fix meals and Paddy nearby if something comes up—well, I'd be lying if I said I didn't miss her but this is precious time for Michael and me. In fact we are working on adding to the family.

"So blessings. First is The Circle. Without all of you I wouldn't have the life I have with Michael and Maeve. Second is the work I'm blessed to do with The Lady. Third is that Maeve and I will be traveling with Michael when he comes to the states for the Kentucky Derby. Maeve and I'll continue on to Fremont so I know I'll be there for Beltane and Summer Solstice."

Gabriella took the stone. Sophia watched her roll the fluorite from hand-to-hand. A soft smile graced her face. When she lifted her head, tears filled her eyes.

"I'm getting married tomorrow to a man I do not deserve. NO," she raised her hand, "hear me out. I do not deserve his unwavering love and devotion. He waited for me to find my way to him, for me to heal enough that I could even see that there was a path. His patience, his encouragement, his support.

"If he were here, he would agree with you that I do deserve him. Perhaps I do. I know I love him more than I thought I could ever love anyone. I know that being here in Italy has allowed me to feel safe enough to find my way to him. I know that without the behind the scenes machinations of all of you, I most likely would not be marrying Giovanni Migliori tomorrow.

"Sophia contrived for me to stay and write. Elizabeth held my emotional hand when I thought all was lost. Each of you listened and offered your wisdom and support when I asked for it.

"Elizabeth made a friend with an old flame of Michael's and I am doing the same with an important woman in Giovanni's life. Each of you have shown me through your courage that if I was willing to take the risk, I could have what you have—unconditional love.

"Giovanni has said we will come to Fremont so I can pack up my things and find closure where I need to. I want to spend extra time with Doc. S and the Waterson's, go to the homeless youth shelter. If *Holly's Story* sells, I want the proceeds to go to them."

She sat back and let her gaze roam around the circle. "I love you all more than words can express. I'm grateful for every minute of my life spent in this circle."

Gabriella set the stone down on the altar and stood. Reaching out she took Hunter and Ashley's hands. Instantly the others followed. Diana sang "The Circle is open but unbroken." Swaying to and fro they sung the verses times three.

They left the altar in place as they adjourned to the dining room. Adolfo had set out antipasto and a pasta salad. Wine chilled in a bucket, a large pitcher of lemon tea by its side.

Before they had a chance to serve themselves, the men came home.

Sophia watched as like arrows to the target, the men found their wives—or in the case of Giovanni, his almost wife. Would Cam ever fit in to a gathering like this? He'd managed at Lily and Jackson's spaghetti feed. But he'd been uncomfortable and probably would have bolted if she hadn't stayed close.

A picture of him sitting in her sacred space, drawing comfort from the energy in the room popped into her mind. That had been after the time at Lily's.

She shook her head not willing to entertain the idea that she, too, could have what everyone else had. *I had it once with Jonathan and that's enough.*

22 A Wedding and ?

Sophia was the last one down the path before the bride. Giovanni, flanked by Jackson and Michael waited by the sea wall. The backdrop was the bright blue of the Mediterranean Sea and the lighthouse.

Giovanni's mother, his sisters and their families and his friend, Maria Sophia sat on the groom's side. Grant, Doc S and the Watersons were on the bride's side in the second row. Hunter and Elizabeth stayed beside Gabriella. Sophia, Lily, Diana and Ashley took the seats in the front row.

Did the lighthouse beam pause when the groom kissed the bride? Sophia would swear it did.

Instead of the couple leading the way back to the house, they turned, spoke briefly to the priest who'd conducted the ceremony and then their arms around each other's waist they faced the sea.

Sophia rose and led everyone back to the house. It was apparent as she started back up the path that Margretta, Silvio and Adolpho had watched the proceedings. All three staff appeared thrilled Gabriella was now a permanent resident. The room that had been "hers", was now her writing space. The furniture rearranged so a desk with drawers could be brought in. She knew Gabriella loved that space and it brought her creative energy alive.

Of course the food was delicious. Grateful she had declined to bake her cake, Sophia relaxed with a glass of champagne and enjoyed the decadent tiramisu. The thought crossed her mind that she could make that back home. No, she wouldn't do that. This dessert would remain special because she'd only have it here.

It never occurred to her that she would not be back. If they all could travel to Ireland, they could also travel to Italy. *It wouldn't add that much to the total cost to stop both places on the same trip.*

Giovanni's town car took Doc. S and the Waterson's to the Bed & Breakfast just up the road a half-mile. His youngest sister had driven the family up from Rome. They were staying at a small hotel in a nearby town, ten miles away. Doubled up, the rest of them fit in Giovanni's place.

The look on Ashley's face when she was shown to the room with a balcony overlooking the garden and sea was priceless. "I'm not sure how much sleep I'll get." She'd actually twirled, her hands on her cheeks. "But I can always sleep on the plane." She'd headed for the balcony. "See y'all later."

They left in an entourage of vehicles for Rome the next morning. The sumptuous reception was that evening. Gabriella wore her wedding dress and Giovanni a tuxedo. A young woman was drawn into the picture-taking. Sophia learned she was the designer of the dress and all of Gabriella's new wardrobe.

While they all knew Giovanni was a well-known architect, what they didn't know was he was seen as one of Italy's most eligible bachelors. His being taken of the list was a huge society event.

Their plane left just after noon on Friday. The flight was longer what with delays, changing planes and going through customs in Atlanta. Their flight didn't land in Fremont until midnight.

Jackson and Lily insisted she share their taxi. They dropped her off at her home. The cab driver got her suitcase from the trunk.

"I'll take it from here." She took the handle, hefted her backpack over her shoulder and headed to her front door. As she approached the door opened. She didn't see anyone in the doorway but she knew, could feel who it was.

On the porch, she turned back and waved to the taxi, giving Lily and Jackson a thumbs up. As the cab pulled away from the curb, Cam reached out and pulled her into his arms. His mouth came down on hers with a passion that melted her bones. Sophia arched into him as his hands skimmed her sides before gripping her waist.

How long were they there in her shadowed doorway before the kiss broke?

"I'll get it." His words were rough and tossed in her direction as he strode the few steps and retrieved her carry-on. Back in the house, Cam closed the door behind him and secured the lock. Prowling toward her, he reached over her shoulder and reset the alarm.

Taking her hand, he towed her behind him.

A piercing shrill shriek rent the air.

"Fuck!" Cam pushed past her and tapped in the alarm code. The earsplitting sound instantly ceased.

"Sorry. I got it right this time." He held her close and rested his chin on her crown. "A bit rattled."

He kissed her forehead. "Missed you. I didn't want to. I thought I wouldn't see you again. Just stay away."

"I wondered if we'd see each other again. I'd promised myself that I wouldn't call." Her arms around his waist tightened. "I'm so glad you are here because I missed you too."

Sophia tried to stifle her yawn but it overpowered her efforts.

"You must be exhausted. I'll take off and let you get some sleep. "

"Stay. Stay and hold me." She leaned away enough that she could kiss his neck and chin.

"I'll want to do more than hold you."

"We'll set the alarm and you can take a shower with me." At that statement, a ridge now rode her belly. Going on instinct, she shifted, creating friction between them.

"Good God, Phia. I'm a mere mortal man."

"Glad you aren't seeing yourself as immortal. Come to bed Cam. I'm sure you have it in you to show me how mortal you are."

"Are you positive?"

She patted the growing bulge in his pants. "I am."

23 Out of sorts

February always had a couple weeks of warmer weather, something that communicated Spring would arrive soon. Weather-wise this year was no different.

What was different?

Sophia had resigned herself to planting the same garden she had last year. No burst of inspiration struck. She started plants from seed, setting them in rows in her greenhouse. Weeding around shrubs and well-established plants like her roses had her outdoors. Her back ached and the sense of satisfaction at seeing dirt under her finger nails was missing.

Grant and Hunter were back from Rhode Island. She'd been right and they had connected with Jason. Of course, of all of them, Hunter and Grant had been the best people to talk to the young man since both of them had struggles, and that was being polite, with their parents.

Janeen and the baby would be traveling to Rhode Island in March. Logan would go with them during spring break. Jason would remain in school but he would be with Janeen and his daughter. They'd have time to decide what they wanted to do while he finished spring term. Hunter and Grant had insisted the two not marry until June. It had been harder to sell that idea to Jason. Janeen seemed grateful for a chance to spend time with Jason and see what family life with him could be.

She had school. In years past Sophia had joked that teachers looked forward to spring break and the end of the school year more than the students. This year it was no joking matter. Where was the passion, the creativity, the desire to show her students the world around them through books?

Since her return, Cam had been spending time with her every day. Some mornings she woke to him bringing her a cup of tea. Other nights she fell asleep in his arms. And there'd been a few times when he'd been waiting for her when her last class was over. He'd take her out to dinner and follow her home. A kiss goodnight—well, a passionate kiss goodnight—and he'd be off.

Was that what was wrong?

In the quiet of her sacred space, Sophia lit candles, turned on the rock salt lamp and burned smudge. Thoroughly cleansing her space and herself, she stood in front of her altar. With her hands at her side and her head bowed, she listened to the silence.

"Goddess, I am lost. Help me find my way back to my path." Lifting her head, her gaze caught the candle's flickering light. Mesmerized, she remained still. A shimmer of light emanated from a small stone she'd brought home from The Sacred Grove.

"Your old path is gone. A new path awaits." The voice was The Lady's. "Your prayer is always that your highest good be served."

"Will I ever find joy in my life again?"

"Your path is not easy. Darkness will consume you. Remember you are The Source and you'll find joy and love in the end."

"Is Cam a part of my new path?"

"That is for you to determine."

"He's so defended. Darkness is embedded in him. I can't see myself with him in the future but I can't see myself without him now."

"But 'now' is what you have. The future never comes. Remember you are The Source. Through you love and life flows. You have an unending source of love welling up from within. Let it flow." Her voice faded as the light dimmed. "Let it flow." Candle flames flickered. "Let it flow."

The stone turned dark.

The candle flames died.

Sophia stood in front of her altar, her sacred space illuminated by the soft rock salt lamp.

What was she going to do?

"I've asked and been answered. I may not like it or perhaps I don't truly understand the answer." She shifted, moving her feet to shoulder width. Raising her arms she began the prayer.

"I am the light

"I am the source

"Through me love flows

"Throughout the world."

Three times she said the prayer. The heaviness that had weighed her down lessened. She left the rock salt lamp on when she left her sacred space.

In the kitchen she took out her mixing bowl and the ingredients to make peanut butter cookies. "I'll make a triple batch and share them with Janeen, Hunter and Grant." As the cookies baked she cleaned up the kitchen. Still restless, she wandered through her house looking for something to do. "When I get this way, I bake. Kneading the dough helps work off some of this energy." Before measuring out flour and starting the yeast, she paused. "Or I work in the garden." It was dark outside.

"Bread it is. No sweet rolls, just a couple loaves of bread. Maybe Diana would like a loaf." Knowing her circle sister and her husband loved her homemade bread, she greased four pans and increased the ingredients. At the last minute she decided to turn one into a loaf of raisin bread.

Focused on what she was doing, she failed to hear the garage door open. When Cam stepped into the house, Sophia shrieked and picked up a cleaver.

"Hey, sorry I scared you, Phia." Cam stood in the doorway to the garage, hands up in surrender.

"You scared me to death!" Sophia put the cleaver down.

"What's going on? You always hear the garage door open."

"Just lost in thought, meditating as I knead the dough."

"What's in the oven now?"

"Peanut butter cookies—and yes, you can have some but not all even if you are very good."

That boyish, naughty grin that never failed to pump up her heart rate flashed across his features.

"So how many are 'some'?"

"I am not playing that game with you, Cam." She infused her tone with starch.

He laughed. "What game is that?" In a few steps he'd eliminated the space between them. Arms around her waist, he snuggled against her back and nuzzled her neck. Nibbling on her ear, he whispered, "Wanna make a bet you'll agree I can have all the cookies?"

"No, I'm not betting with you."

"You are a wise woman, Phia. You'd lose 'cause I can be Very Persuasive." His hands were roaming, touching her breasts, sliding down her belly, stopping just short of the apex of her thighs. Restless longing for his touch on her bare skin surged.

"I have cookies in the oven and bread to bake. You, Cameron Trent Mitchell, need to take yourself out of my kitchen."

The oven timer said the cookies were done.

"I'll get them out for you." Cam stepped away and pulled the sheets out of the oven.

Sophia fought the sense of loss by jamming the heel of her hands into the dough.

"Now what are you doing?" She glanced over her shoulder to see that Cam had all the cookie sheets on the cooling rack.

"Waiting until you have the bread in the bowl to rise." He started towards her and stopped. That wicked smile was back. "If I remember correctly," the heavy seductive tone sent shivers down her spine, "it takes time for the dough to rise. I've got plans to convince you I need more cookies, maybe even all of them."

Sophia fashioned the dough into a large ball and placed it in a greased bowl. Putting a dish towel over the top, she set it on the counter next to the oven where it was warm.

Cam prowled towards her, his Irish moss green gaze locked on her face.

Sophia's heartbeat rapid, her breath shallow, her insides clenched. She knew exactly what the mouse felt like when it realized the cat had seen it. Unlike the mouse, she stepped across the narrowing space, her arms open in welcome.

24 Valentine's Day

Tuesday isn't a very romantic day but this year that's when Valentine's Day fell. Cam had plans that did not include covering someone else's shift. He had a lady to woo.

He'd loved two dozen cookies from her last week. Those had been distributed among his kids and the officers who'd had the worst shift. Most of the time police work was boring, mundane, driving around and keeping eyes open, awareness heightened. But there were those shifts, and he'd had his fair share of them, when the men and women he worked with saw the worst of humanity.

He knew firsthand the power of Sophia's cookies. And so he shared.

Out the door at four, he headed home to shower, shave and pick up the gift he'd gotten her. On his way he called to see how her day had gone. He had plan A but also plan B in case it had been a bad one.

"Hey, how was your day?" His tone casual, he listened for any sign Plan A wouldn't work.

"Okay."

"Where are you now?"

"Just pulled into the garage. Where are you?"

"I'm brushing my teeth."

"Cam, really, where are you?"

"I'm about thirty minutes from holding you in my arms." The teasing, light tone was gone.

"Cam—."

He interrupted. "Phia, we can talk when I get there. Don't do anything other than take care of yourself. I don't expect or even want you to fix a meal. Maybe a cup of tea but if you can wait, I'll do that for you. See you shortly."

Cam hung up. Not sure if it really was the kids or the fact that it was Valentine's Day and she missed Jonathan, he followed his gut and went to Plan B.

While he dressed, he called the restaurant where he'd made reservations and canceled. She'd sounded exhausted, on the border of tears.

Plan B included take-out from their favorite Chinese restaurant. He made that call, put in the order and then stopped to pick up a bottle of champagne. Because it was Valentine's Day the store had more stock than usual in the refrigerated case. Chilled champagne would be served with dinner.

Everything in hand, Cam got out of his car as the garage door closed. His worry meter notched up. She wasn't waiting in the door for him.

"Phia? I'm here." He called out as he came through the door into the house.

He walked into the kitchen.

Even the tea kettle was cold.

This was not good.

He put his packages on the kitchen counter and headed down the hall to Sophia's room.

As he crossed the threshold, he heard water running. Relief coursed through him. He stepped to the bathroom door. Over the sound of the shower, he heard her tears. He shook his head. "That can't be," he muttered. "Can't hear someone crying when the shower is on." Maybe he couldn't hear with his ears, but his instincts said she was crying. His heart said she was crying but it couldn't tell him why.

His own eyes misting, Cam leaned against the door helpless. Minutes ticked by. He remained standing guard while the woman who meant more to him than anyone else sobbed her heart out.

When the water turned off, he straightened.

"Hey, Phia, I'm here." He pitched his voice loud enough for her to hear through the closed door but just. He didn't want to add to whatever sorrow held her in its grip.

"I've brought us dinner. I'll put the tea kettle on. When you're ready, come on out." It crossed his mind to say something sexy like "come as you are" but he stopped the words before they crossed his lips.

Back in the kitchen he put the tea kettle on, turned the oven on low and set the boxes of Chinese food on a cookie sheet so they'd stay somewhat warm. Champagne was put in the refrigerator. If it was appropriate, he could easily open it.

He heard the tea kettle about to sing so he got up from the couch where he'd been sitting, looking at a book on the coffee table. Sophia's favorite mug was covered with blue birds and she always smiled when she took it out of the cupboard. Cam had watched her fix dozens of cups of tea. He got out the chamomile and after pouring the boiling water over the tea bag, kept an eye on his watch. She liked her tea medium. Not a light discoloring of the water but not so dark it could pass as coffee.

Picking up the mug, he headed back down the hall. Cam stopped at the door to her bedroom which was now shut. He knocked lightly. "Phia, I've got a cup of tea for you."

When she opened the door, the urge to put his foot in the door was strong but he resisted. Her red-rimmed eyes tattled on her. She wasn't dressed but she did have on the oldest rattiest robe he'd ever seen.

Cam handed her the mug. "I just want to hold you. Make whatever it is go away."

Tears spilled down her cheeks. "You'd have to leave then."

Her voice was so soft, he thought he'd misheard her. Her shoulders shook as she valiantly tried to hold back the tears. Cam reached out, took the mug from her hands and stepped close. He wrapped one arm around her, and stepped into her. Stretching, he managed to put the tea on the dresser near the door.

Holding her close while stoking her back, Cam searched for words. All he could come up with was "Why does my being here cause you so much pain?" As that question formed in his own mind, a sharp pain knifed through his chest.

"Phia, I have Chinese staying warm in the oven. I can take it out and put it in the refrigerator and go if that will truly help you." As the seconds passed with no response, Cam's chest tightened and his lungs struggled to bring in air.

Under Sophia's ear, Cam's heart beat a steady rhythm. His arms held her close. She was surrounded by his fresh minty scent and heat. Her conundrum? She didn't want him to leave but dreaded him staying.

A powerful inner knowing that something dire was going to happen to him, something that portended she might lose him had struck her when he'd called. School had not been easy today but it was that darkness, that premonition of death when she answered the phone that had brought her to tears.

One hand stroked a soothing rhythm on her back. His chin rested on her crown. If she didn't want to talk about it, he wouldn't push it. How she wished it was an earlier year, even before Lily met Jackson.

Then Valentine's Day was such fun. She'd make a heart-shaped cake and everyone would show up, usually here because her house was the biggest, but sometimes at Lily's little house. No, not everyone showed up. Diana and Ashley were married and spent those days at home. A few tears leaked at the memory of those dear women and the difficult Valentine's Days they'd had.

But the rest of them? They celebrated. They talked about romance, shared their favorite romance novels and authors, usually Lily brought a bouquet of flowers and Elizabeth brought a plant for her garden. Hunter would get them all up and they'd do a line dance–kids and all. No, in the earlier days, after Jonathan died, there was no dancing.

A chuckle escaped at that picture.

Sophia snuggled against Cam. Her arms tightened around his waist. The darkness, the premonition had not disappeared but it had faded.

She was at a crossroads.

What would she choose?

He would go if she told him to. He would never call or come see her if she asked that of him. But how would that solve anything?

Sophia looked into the dark abyss. No matter her decision, there would be pain. *The Lady said there will be darkness but I am The Source. Love flows through me and I'm to go with the flow.*

She eased her grip around his waist and leaned back. "I'd like you to stay." She touched his cheeks with her hands and rose on her tiptoes to kiss his lips. A bare brushing but the darkness began to fade. "I want you to stay until morning if you can."

25 The Circle

February 19, 2006

Sophia took extra care smudging her sacred space. The room became hazed as every item in the room was engulfed in sage and cedar smoke. A square of red silk marked their altar. The etched green Galway crystal bowl in the center held vials of water from the spring at the sacred grove and the Mediterranean Sea. Two vials held soil from The Sacred Grove and Giovanni's gardens. *I need to find another way of referencing those gardens. Gabriella lives there now.*

Her porcelain bluebird sat in the East. *May I find new beginnings.* She did not say 'easily and effortlessly' as was her habit. 'Resigned' was one word to describe her but she preferred 'Prepared'.

A piece of calcite she'd been blessed to find that blended shades of both red and yellow anchored the South. *May I embrace the present bounty in my life with joy.* 'Resigned' popped into her awareness. She shoved it aside.

In the West she placed her small wand of Kyanite. *May I guard against negativity as I approach The Void.* The sense of something being wrong had not diminished since Cam had spent Valentine's with her. Whatever was going to happen, he was at the center.

Her snowy owl pendant settled against a fold in the silk. *May I know that whatever the future brings, I will not face it alone for you are all with me now and forever more. The Circle was with me when I lost Jonathan. If that is what will happen with Cam, I will not have to bear it alone.*

After adding protective apache tears to each corner, Sophia stepped back. It was a beginning. As each woman added her offerings, her energy, their altar would form into a majestic and beautiful creation of their love and commitment to each other and the world in which they lived.

Before she returned to the kitchen, Sophia lit the bright blue three-wicked candle she'd added between the west and north points of their altar. Today her only contribution to the potluck was to have hot water, mugs and her assortment of teas. Lily and Diana had insisted she not even take something out of her freezer.

Arguments died when Lily had said in a quiet voice, "Let us do this for you, Soph. I can't tell you why this is important for us to do, but we all feel it."

The doorbell rang. Before she reached the hall, the door opened and everyone came in. Her quiet house was full of energy and noise.

For a moment it jarred.

Once coats were hung and food piled on the kitchen counter, Sophia was surrounded by bright smiling faces. The unsettled feeling that scattered her thoughts and sent jitters through her body faded.

The Circle was unbroken even with Elizabeth and now Gabriella half a world away. These women would be by her side in a heartbeat if her worst fears were manifest. Inwardly she visualized her Kyanite wand to ward off the negativity that came roaring to life with those thoughts.

With Lily and Diana on either side of her, she was guided toward her sacred space. Ashley and Hunter had gone ahead and had the smudge going. As she approached she saw Hunter with a small drum. Having the drum beat surround her after walking through the smudge smoke eased the last of her worries. For right now, all was well.

When the altar was complete, she saw Hunter's stork in the South, Lily's lioness alongside it. Diana's Siamese cat figurine was in the East with Ashley's gossamer dragonfly beside it.

"Look what I have with me?" Lily held out a swan and a blue jay feather. "Elizabeth and Gabriella are with us." She put both feathers in the South.

As stones of varying colors were set in the different directions, Sophia saw a shimmer of light from her own altar. Picking up the stone from The Sacred Grove she placed it in the center bowl. A pattern from the etching shadowed the silk.

Her voice barely above a whisper, she said, "The Lady is with us."

"Blessed Be."

Without further words, they circled the altar. Feet spread shoulder wide, they raised their hands palm up.

"We are the light

"We are the source

"Through us Love flows

"Throughout the world."

Three times they said the prayer. With each verse, Sophia's mind cleared as worries, fears and doubts gave way to the light of love The Circle sent out into the world.

Diana sang "The Circle is open" and they all joined in. Joy infused their voices as they repeated the song two more times.

"May we know we are more as The Circle than we are as individuals." Hunter said quietly at the end of the song.

"May we know love's healing power." Ashley lowered her arms.

"May we know with certainty that we can have our heart's desire." Diana's more formal voice contrasted with Ashley's softly accented one. She reached out and held Ash's closest hand.

"May we trust." Lily took Diana's hand. She looked toward Sophia who still stood hands raised, her cheeks wet with tears.

"May we trust all is as it is meant to be." Sophia added before lowering her hands to take hold of Lily and Hunter's.

"Blessed Be."

They held hands while standing. Time passed but still they stood in silence.

Lily squeezed Sophia's. "It's time to connect with E and Gabby." She pulled out her cell phone as everyone shifted and sat around the edges of the red silk scarf.

No one spoke as the phone rang.

"Hello? It's E." They heard the excitement in their circle sister's voice.

"I'm here too," Gabriella chimed in. "We just finished setting up the altar and saying prayers."

"We just finished that too," Hunter replied.

"It won't be a long call because Maeve is due to wake up from her nap. Maybe we can schedule this an hour earlier?"

The Fremont contingent agreed without hesitation.

As if on cue, the sounds of a fussing baby were heard in the background.

"Courtesy of a baby monitor, I know my little girl is awake and needs changing and food. Michael can certainly do the honors with the nappy but he isn't built to do the food part." Elizabeth's voice began to fade. "I'll leave you to talk to Gabby. Love you all. This was fabulous although too short."

"How is everyone?" Gabby asked.

"First and foremost, how are you? How is married life?" Hunter voiced the questions they all had. "We'll share, but you first."

"Being married is—, well, it's —." Gabriella laughed. "It's hard to describe."

"We can hear that," Diana said and chuckled.

"Giovanni is more than I ever thought I deserved to have. At least when we have different opinions, he listens to me. He seems so sensitive to my moods and believe me, here I'm moody."

"That means you feel safe to be yourself," Ashley said her head nodding.

"He's said that I can come see Elizabeth every month until we come to Fremont so we can join you all this way. I-I never even asked."

"He loves you, Gabby. That's what men do when they love you. They look for ways to make your day, your way easier. At least that's been my experience with Jackson."

Sophia saw the other women nod. Jonathan had been that way. He wanted her way in life easier. Even with his death, he'd had affairs like life and mortgage insurance in order so she could just grieve. And Cam? Did he love her? That she wasn't sure of but he did protect and take care of her—she'd had a sense of that on Valentine's Day.

"Gabby?" Sophia's own voice held emotions she was not ready to describe beyond 'like'. "I believe it's mutual. I totally agree with what everyone else has said and am adding 'It's mutual'. You are a safe haven for him. You listen to him. You are responsive to his moods. And, if we were to ask him, he would find it difficult to describe how he feels about you other than with the word "love.""

"I miss you all so much."

"We miss you too," they chorused.

"We'll see you and E soon. April isn't that far away," Hunter added.

"Holding you and Elizabeth in The Light of Love," Diana said. "Let's sing a song."

Elizabeth requested "The circle is open." She and Maeve had come into the room. "My daughter loves that song and E and I can sing it here but let's start it while we are all on the phone together."

They sang the song through once with everyone on the phone. Hanging up, the Fremont circle sisters continued, knowing with certainty Gabriella and Elizabeth were singing as well.

"And merry meet again." As the last notes faded into silence, the women sat.

Lily drew a piece of turquoise from a pocket and after holding it over the lighted candle on the altar, began.

26 The Reckoning

Lily turned to face Sophia. Her friend looked exhausted. They'd been a part of this circle for over ten years and never, except when Jonathan had been killed, had they seen Sophia in such pain. Or at least they all thought it was pain.

Something was terribly wrong with their circle sister. It had started when the friend she'd been helping for a couple of years had died. Now, if even possible, whatever it was, was worse.

Not sure if it had something to do with the man they all knew she was seeing but not talking about, they had decided to do something drastic.

One by one they'd noticed something seemed wrong with Sophia. Quiet conversations, worried looks passed between them. When they checked in with Elizabeth, they learned The Lady had specifically said Sophia's name on two occasions when E and The Lady did their morning prayers.

Lily laid her hand on Sophia's. "We speak with love in our hearts. We are worried for you. Of all of us, you have asked the least from The Circle. Perhaps it's time for us to offer."

Diana, who sat on Sophia's other side, put her hand on her circle sister's shoulder. "We've all felt and now see that all is not right in your life. We do respect your decision not to share your burdens with us. We also can no longer sit and watch as someone we love, who has become a part of each of us, is so troubled."

Sophia wasn't surprised by the words Lily and Diana said. She was surprised they brought it up in circle. So surprised her body surged and she started to rise to leave the room. This was a conversation she expected one or both of them would have with her privately, if at all.

Lily's grasp tightened.

Diana's hand on her shoulder anchored her in place.

Hunter leaned closer. "You will recall each of us has faced a dark time in our lives. You will also recall that in that moment none of us wanted help. You will also recall that we were each reminded there is a gift in receiving.

"Remember how you were a part of each of those moments for us. If you think we will disappear, leave you to battle whatever it is you battle on your own, you are mistaken."

"It's your turn, Soph." Ashley's grey eyes brimmed with tears. "We cannot force you to tell us anything, but we can and will sit here with you and do our best to take some of the obvious pain and worry from your life."

How do you talk when your throat is clogged, your brain is awash with swirling words and emotions run riot throughout your body?

Sophia had no words. The surge of outrage that initially took over her body subsided. She sat, her focus on the pattern the shimmering stone from the sacred grove inside the etched bowl created on the red silk cloth.

With her left hand, Lily picked up Sophia's animal totem, the porcelain bluebird from its place in the East and laid it in her lap. Her right never let go of Sophia's hand.

Diana's left hand was now rubbing her back in a soothing figure eight. She also hummed "We are the light."

Ashley and Hunter joined in.

Sophia was surrounded by the loving energy of these women. On another level she knew The Lady, Gabriella and Elizabeth were with her. *They must be in The Sacred Grove.*

No one left.

No further words were spoken.

True to the words Ashley had spoken, they sat and waited, doing what they could to be with her in her time of trouble.

The clog in Sophia's throat eased, the swirling words in her brain cleared, the emotions faded. She held her bluebird in her hand.

"I seem to be surrounded for much of the day in a grey fog, if not total darkness. What has brought me joy in my life, no longer does. I still bake but not with pleasure or real enjoyment. I've no feeling of delight, of expectation around my garden this year. I'll probably plant some things but the sense of anticipation of seeing plants grow, flowers bloom, produce ripen is missing this year."

No one spoke.

The silence begged to be invaded with words. What more was there to say? To share?

Of course she knew they believed there was more. They wanted to know about Cam but what could she say. Whenever he was near the darkness faded, the grey lifted? Sometimes that was true but other times it was not.

Turning her bluebird over in her hands, she studied the delicate shape, the details of feathers and feet, the exquisite colors. This figurine was a female with the blue on her wings and a reddish hue on her breast. The all blue male was on another altar. *Why don't I keep them together?*

"My personal totem is a sign of happiness. It's a small and unassuming bird in many ways. But when threatened, it can and will defend itself."

"Do you see an answer for yourself in that message?" Lily had removed her hand when Sophia began to handle her totem. Now her right hand rested on her circle sister's shoulder.

"I'm not happy."

"Bluebirds are also about taking care of yourself and finding that happiness if you've lost it." Ashley's soft voice added another layer to her totem's meaning.

"I do know that, it's just—."

"I thought you had two of them?" Hunter said when Sophia paused.

"I do, this is the female. I also have the male."

"Where is he?" Lily asked.

"He's on the altar in my bedroom. Why?"

"Just a flicker of something popped into my head. May I get him?" Lily tensed as if to rise, but remained where she was.

Sophia contemplated Lily's question and request. She lifted her head and looked at Hunter and Ashley across from her. Hunter's turquoise eyes and Ashley's grey ones held loving compassion. How long had everyone sat in silence while she nattered about in her mind?

Words were still difficult to form, to speak out loud so she nodded.

Lily rose and left the circle, walking counter-clockwise. She returned a minute later with the other bluebird in hand. Entering the circle by transiting clockwise, she took her seat next to Sophia.

"Here." Lily handed the mate to Sophia. "Take a minute and tell us how it feels to have them together."

Sophia closed her eyes and looked within. Bluebirds filled her inner vision. They flew with abandonment, their blue wings reflecting the rays of the sun. The sun! But on the horizon, grey hovered.

A tissue was draped across her arm. What?

Her cheeks were wet with tears.

Diana voiced her internal question. "Can you tell us what the tears are for?"

Pictures flew through her mind. The deaths of Jonathan and her friend. The lack of connection with her students this year. The plight of Janeen and Jason. The darkness rushed in, filling her with fear and dread. Out of the darkness emerged Cam. She came face to face with her fear, she could lose him.

Sophia knew in that moment the courage each of her circle sisters had summoned when they shared their fears, hopes and dreams they did not believe could be made manifest. Tears streamed down her face, dampening her blouse. Ashley was right, it was her turn.

Not bothering to wipe her face because she'd have to let go of one of her totems, Sophia sucked in air but kept her head bowed.

"So many confusing pictures. But for a moment, I saw the sun. No darkness, only grey on the horizon. The darkness that seems to consume me was gone—but then it came back with a vengeance.

"Fear and dread—the darkness is my fear, my dread manifest. The Lady came to me after we were back from Italy. She said I would encounter darkness but there was love on the other side.

"There are times when the sense of death surrounding Cam is so strong it terrifies me. I don't want to give him my heart and then lose him." She clutched the figurines to her chest with one arm and grabbed tissues with her hand. Swiping her cheeks to stem the flood did not help. If anything, with her heart so exposed, she cried harder.

Soggy tissues were removed and fresh ones tucked in her hand. Lily and Diana had scooted closer at some point. Lily's arm was around her waist and Diana's around her shoulders. The only sound came from her, deep heartfelt sobs that left her drained.

Sophia rested her head on Diana's shoulder.

"Better?" Lily asked.

"I don't know," Sophia whispered.

"May I offer an observation?" Hunter leaned toward Sophia, her turquoise gaze serious.

Sophia nodded. "We were all with you when you lost Jonathan"

Sophia nodded.

"We are with you today."

Sophia nodded again.

"We will always be with you. And while I know that does not keep bad things from happening, I think every one of us would agree that whatever darkness comes into our lives is easier to face when we are not alone."

"I just don't know if I can do it again."

"Do you regret the time you had with Jonathan or your friend? Knowing now, on this side of everything, would you choose to not have them in your life?" Ashley's soft voice, her southern drawl eased the words she spoke.

Did she regret? Would she have wanted a life without Jonathan, without her friend?

"It's one thing to look back at the past, to the happy memories. It's something else to look to the future and see the darkness just waiting for me."

"You know Soph, all we have is now. We only have today. We can't relive the past and we can't live in the future. All we can do today is make the choices that create the tomorrow we want to experience." Diana rubbed her back.

"I'm not very courageous. I have dreams where I'm sitting in a hospital, holding Cam's hand. He is hooked up to every imaginable machine. I'm so terrified he's going to die."

"Does he?" Lily asked. "In your dream does he die?"

"I don't know. I always wake up when the doctor comes in the room. I think he's going to tell me that Cam is brain dead or will be paralyzed or won't make it."

"But you wake up before you know. Maybe the doctor is going to tell you he's turned a corner and will fully recover." Lily's voice was still soft but it held a note of impatience Sophia hadn't heard in a long time if ever.

"Sophia Camila Denton Stewart listen to yourself. You have talked yourself into this dark place. I'm not saying it isn't a scary place to be because it is. The 'what if's' immobilize us." Lily shifted, her hand on Sophia's chin, she turned her circle sister's head until she could look in her eyes.

Lily's concern softened her tone. "You know every one of us has been where you are. We all know we're hovering. And that won't change. Please do not shut us out. Think about the challenges each of us have faced.

"Speaking for myself, I can honestly say there were times when, if I could have physically done so, I would have tossed you all out along with Jackson. I'm grateful my challenge included my inability to do so.

"You have today and you may have more tomorrows with Cam than you realize. He is obviously important to you or you wouldn't be so concerned about his wellbeing."

"He's a police officer!" Anger infused Sophia's entire body. She sat taller, tears stopped, hardness reflected in her words.

"And you know that Daniel and Matthew work in construction and could be killed any number of ways. You know Jackson flies and is around building sites many times a week. Grant, Michael, Giovanni, anyone of them could be struck down." Sophia turned at Diana's passionate plea. "It isn't that we don't know he's in law enforcement but that, in and of itself is not a death sentence. Hold him in The Light, Soph. Ask him to carry a pouch of protective stones. Do something proactive."

"I do hold him in The Light. And, and I can make up a pouch of protection for him. I just don't know that he'd always carry it with him."

"I firmly believe that if you are doing something, you will feel better. The fear and dread you speak of will lessen. You have the ability to focus on the present, on today, to push back the specter of tomorrow." Diana leaned over and hugged her. "You are stuck with us for now. Expect calls, invitations and help with putting in however much garden you want."

Sophia sighed. "I guess it really is my turn to accept the gift of your hovering." Her gaze rested for just a moment on Hunter and Ashley. Soft smiles lit their faces as they nodded.

"It is indeed," Lily and Diana said in tandem.

"I hope we are through," Sophia said putting her bluebirds together in the East. "I'm dreadfully hungry."

They stood and with arms raised prayed.

"We are the light

"We are the Source

"Through us love flows

"Throughout the World."

After repeating the prayer three times, they remained standing in silence. As one they dropped their arms and after blowing out the candles, exited. *How do we always know when it is time to go?*

With that question still unanswered, she left arm in arm with Lily on one side and Diana on the other. She was ushered to the far side of the kitchen counter, admonished it was the closest she was allowed to get to the inner workings of the kitchen.

Yes, they knew it was 'her kitchen' but today they were taking over.

Food was set out on the counter, a spirit plate fixed with bits of each dish. Hunter led them in prayer.

"Great Spirit, we are grateful for your bounty. We thank each plant and animal who contributed to this feast. We honor their sacrifice and pray they know it was not in vain."

"Blessed Be," they chorused.

Hunter then took the spirit plate out to the garden, placing it within the living circle that held a silver gazing ball. As she set the plate down, she noted that the stand still held the Winter Ball. Soon it would be time to change it out for the green Spring one.

Sophia managed to eat. Of course everyone was totally capable of cooking. She knew great care had been taken in the food brought and shared. Lily brought a pot of Jackson's spaghetti. Diana brought a tossed green salad. Ashley brought a sweet potato casserole that was made from her grandma's recipe. Hunter had brought a loaf of bread, some brie cheese and a chocolate and cream torte. It occurred to her that Grant had done the shopping because of the cheese and torte. Not that Hunter couldn't have, generally her taste went to something simpler – like yoghurt and fruit.

Not only did she not contribute anything except tea but she was denied even cleaning up. "I can at least take my plate to the kitchen," she'd argued when Ashley picked it up.

"Not today," came the firm reply.

"I hate hovering." she'd grumbled.

That only earned her peals of laughter.

Everyone stayed until six before dismantling the altar, gathering leftovers and donning coats. "I'll call" or "I'll be checking in with you" were accompanied with hugs.

Closing the door behind everyone, Sophia turned and set the perimeter alarm. She'd set her pair of bluebirds on the hall table when they'd taken down the altar. Now she carried them into her bedroom and set them together, in the East. The energy did shift when they were together.

Wandering out to the kitchen, she began to fix a cup of tea when she heard the garage door open. A minute later, Cam came in the door. "I thought they'd never leave."

"You could have come in."

He shook his head. He peeled his jacket off and tossed it on the back of the chair by the counter. "Missed you." His arms enveloped her, his lips claimed hers.

I have now and that's all I'll ever have. The truth of those words settled her worry, her fear. She surrendered to the heat and sensations of his expert touch.

27 Acceptance

At the time, Sophia was not happy that her circle sisters had obviously talked about her behind her back. But now? Now as she lay in Cam's arms, replete from their lovemaking, the truth shone bright. Now was all she had, was all she ever had and was all she ever would have.

Life was not fair and those who believed it was or should be lived in a fantasy world. She didn't always like her choices, but choices she did have. The crossroads that determined her future was right in front of her.

One direction led down a grey straight path. Nothing to hurt or disrupt her life was visible. *I'd be safe on this path.*

Bright lights and colors danced along the other path. It wasn't straight but after bending out of sight, bright lights lanced the dark sky between shards of black.

Down which path would she go?

I've thought I wanted the safe life but…Do I really want to live the rest of my life where I am now?

Cam stirred, his bristly chin scratching her shoulder, his hand that had been resting on her belly now stroked her breast. *I have him for as long as I have him. It will be painful if I lose him but I'll have had whatever time we are meant to have.*

Decision made, Sophia started down the brilliantly lit path and into Cam's arms.

Two hours later, Sophia leaned against her desk.

"Class, I'd like your attention, please."

When all eyes were on her, she plunged in.

"You all know I've been gone a lot this year what with one thing and another. And when I've been here, I've not been at my best. I hope to change that for the remainder of the year.

"Starting with right now. Please put your papers away and form into your groups. What I want you to do now is to discuss what the word "fair" means to you? What is "fairness? How do you know when you've been treated "fairly"?

Hands shot up but Sophia waved them down and continued. "I know you had a similar assignment on "fair" a short while ago.

"Now I want you to take a deeper look at this word and how it affects and effects your life. You may want to check the dictionary to remind yourselves of the different meanings on 'affect' and 'effect'.

"For this assignment, I want you to think back to your earlier work. You can write notes from your memory or look back at your previous assignment. I don't expect consensus, I do expect respectful words and voices.

"In addition, I would like you to continue this discussion throughout the day. Ask the adults in your life these questions. Don't forget the importance of follow up questions.

"Tomorrow I would like each of you to give a summary of up to five minutes on what you've learned."

Hands shot up but instead of a dozen or more questions it turned out there was only one:

"Can we just talk or do we have to write something and turn it in?"

Her answer? "No, you do not have to write anything down but you can if you want. You can even write out and read what you want to say tomorrow."

Throughout the day there was at least one student in each class that commented as they passed by "Glad you're back Ms. Stewart".

Sophia was glad she was back also.

Mentally she reviewed her class lesson plans through spring break. The buzz of conversation, the serious looks on students' faces as they grappled with what was 'fair' energized her. This was what she'd intended the past couple of years with this assignment.

Today she was the teacher she'd been in the past. The teacher she'd been at the beginning of the year. The teacher she'd been and would be until she retired.

She hurried home before texting Cam. He always asked where she was and what she was doing. His scolds were legendary—not abusive but she winced at the steely logic he employed. The fact she had a Bluetooth made no difference. It might be safer than holding a phone to her ear, he begrudgingly admitted, but the safest (and he'd emphasized the last word) was to not even be in a moving car.

"I'm home. Please come by no matter how late."

Sophia smiled as she hit send. Of course she'd include punctuation and whole words. After all, she was an English teacher.

That done she took out her baking paraphernalia and got to work. Radio tuned to the "Oldies" station, she sang along as she whipped up cookie dough. A batch of peanut butter and another of peanut butter, chocolate chip. Once those were in the oven, she started on sweet dough for pecan sticky buns, cinnamon rolls and the raisin pecan rolls. Once that triple batch of dough was rising, she made a powdered sugar frosting.

The light on her phone blinked indicating a text message or call. Checking it out, she saw the message from Cam "C U 9ish".

"I'll have dinner and treats for you."

She smiled at the smiley face that came a moment later.

A voice mail message from Lily. "Hi Soph, how is your day going?"

After taking cookies out of the oven and putting them on cooling racks, Sophia fixed a cup of tea, curled on the couch and called her friend.

It wasn't a long conversation. Just checking in with each other. At one point Sophia asked, "Am I getting one call a day from one of you or multiple ones?"

"Depends on what the designated caller thinks."

"I will admit I wasn't grateful at the time, nor was I pleased when you and Diana came back to give me another hug but by this morning I did feel blessed to have you all in my life."

Lily laughed. "I'm sure you weren't at all grateful Diana and I came back and found Cam there." The amusement vanished, replaced by concern. "He needs to come into the light more Soph."

"I know. Right now I think I'm the only light in his life. Although he has recently reached out to his kids, those are very fragile relationships."

"Jackson and I would like to invite the two of you to do something with us. We were thinking maybe just dessert instead of a whole dinner."

"You don't want to be around Cam for that long?" Hurt twisted her belly and tears stung her eyes.

"Oh no, Soph, not that at all. We aren't sure he can tolerate being with us. When he was here before, he was so uncomfortable. If you hadn't been within arm's length, he would have bolted."

"Exactly what are you proposing then?"

"We just thought it would be easier if he got to know us a few at a time. Jackson is the closest in age to him so that's why we thought it would be a place to start. But, this is only a suggestion. You tell us what you think will work best and we'll do it."

"What would work best is for you to come here. But Cam's work schedule hasn't been very consistent because of all the viruses going around the precinct."

"We'll figure out the timing. Jackson is in town for a couple of weeks and will flex around whatever works."

"I'll talk to Cam tonight and see what he says. I'll give him a choice of dinner with you at your place or here."

"Perfect. And if here, what would he want?"

"He's become a fan of Jackson's spaghetti so that would work. And, if you do that, I'll bring brownies to go with his ice cream."

"We've a plan." Lily's pause was a mere second or two. "It's good to have you on your way back. We've missed you. I've missed you. And, just so you know, you've passed today. You've the evening to yourself." She laughed. "Well, mostly to yourself until Cam shows up."

"In love and light," Sophia started the prayer.

"In grace and gratitude," Lily continued.
"In joy and happiness,"
"In peace" they said alternating.
"Blessed Be," they said together.

28 Moving Forward

Sophia wanted to throw the pencil across the room but restrained herself. Her jaw clenched the pencil point broke when she stabbed the paper.

"Hey Phia, what's going on?" Cam lounged on the couch, his feet up on the coffee table, a muted sports program on the television.

"I'm fine." Sophia left the room, coming back a few minutes later.

While she was gone, Cam heard a noise that sounded a lot like a pencil sharpener but he said nothing upon her return. An eraser flew by a few inches from his head.

"I'm sorry, Cam, I wasn't aiming at you."

"Good to know because we'd need to work on your aim if you were." He crossed and recrossed his ankles.

"You could argue with me," Sophia huffed.

"Or you could tell me what's going on." Cam shifted on the couch. His feet were on the floor, he was leaning forward with his elbows on his thighs, his hands dangling between his knees. His Irish moss green gaze zeroed in on her.

"I just can't get the garden right."

"Then don't do it. Let whatever is out there grow but don't add anything."

"But what about tomatoes and peas and basil?"

"What about them?"

"Where should they be planted?" Exasperated she stood and marched to the sliding glass door. "Some of the trees are bigger so the sunlight will be different."

Cam rose and came up behind her. His arms wrapped around her waist, his chin rested on her crown. "It's okay if you don't plant them. You can purchase them at the store." He quickly added when she stiffened in his arms. "They won't be as good, as fresh as yours but you can always buy organic."

"I've had a garden, vegetable garden," she amended, "since I first moved into this house."

"And you can have one next year if you want. Or you can plant things that don't need to go into the ground now."

"The only thing that needs to be planted now are the peas."

"I don't know what the problem is then."

Sophia gestured at the yard beyond the patio and grass. "There's almost a half an acre of land here. It takes planning."

"So where are the peas going?

"Along the fence," she gestured to her left.

"And are the plants over there?" He nodded to his right and the small greenhouse.

"This time of year, you plant the seed in the ground."

"Let's do it." Cam stepped back and reached for the door handle. "We can plant a bunch of peas right now."

"The ground," Sophia started to explain, "the ground needs to be dug up."

"Get a shovel and the seeds, Phia. We can get some of it done." He kept his gaze on her. "Or, let it go. One or the other. Don't twist yourself up like this over peas.

"And do not apologize," he added before she could speak.

"You're sure?"

He nodded.

"I'll get the shovel and seeds. You may want to put shoes on."

The pea garden was about two feet by six feet along a fence. Sophia dug a foot or so while he watched. When she bent to plant the seeds that looked just like dried peas, he took the shovel from her. After a couple of feet were dug, he stopped. Leaning on his shovel, he watched as Sophia dug hole with a finger and shoved a seed in with the other hand. She then carefully covered the spot and tapped it down with the knuckles of the seed carrying hand.

Cam moved on down the space, spading the ground up and chopping it into fine particles with the shovel's edge. He finished and turned back. Sophia was halfway along the row.

"Can I help? I could start at this end—."

She waved him away. "You've done enough. You've done the hard part. Planting is easy."

"You've taken care of this all by yourself?" He looked toward the back of the property seeing several full grown trees that must be twenty feet tall or more.

"When Diana was involved with Matthew, he volunteered to rototiller it. He does that in the fall and spreads mulch to help keep the weeds down come spring."

"Before that?"

"Jonathan and I loved to garden. Between us it was always manageable. But after... ."

"You wanted to keep it going. You are an amazing woman, Phia.

"Anything else I can do other than stand around and watch you work?"

"In the garage, on the other side of your car you'll see some eight foot tall stakes. Bring six of them and a hammer."

"I'll put the shovel away when I do that."

"It needs to be cleaned off."

"I am capable of wiping down a shovel and counting out six eight foot tall stakes."

"And the hammer."

"And a hammer."

Cam dawdled along the way so by the time he reappeared Sophia was planting the last of the peas.

"Now what?"

"Stakes go in the ground every couple of feet. I can usually get the stake in far enough that I can pound it in more firmly by standing on a step stool."

"But you have me so you won't need the step stool."

"The stakes have to be deeper than we've dug."

"Got it." Cam let Sophia put the stakes where she wanted them. He followed her down the line, jabbing the sharp end into the dirt. By standing on his toes and reaching up he could hit the top."

"That's good."

The stake was even with his head. "I'll get the rest of these. You take care of what's next." He'd already started on the second pole when he felt her press against his back, her arms around his waist.

"What?"

"Thank you. You'll get the very first peas."

"That's my reward?"

"Fresh peas are a real treat."

"I'm more of an instant gratification kind of guy. Need something sooner than however long it takes for the peas to grow and ripen."

He was ready to move on to the third post. "I've got an idea."

"What?" She moved back to give him room. His muscles flexed under his shirt as he pounded the wood into the ground.

Cam moved with an innate grace, an economy of movement. No flinging his arms out in a grand gesture. Jonathan had had a dramatic streak, unusual for a math teacher. She smiled at the memory of him bowing with a flourish when he started working on one of their projects.

"Penny for your thoughts?" Cam's voice slipped into her memories.

"Just thinking of gardens past."

"I'm not jealous of him, Phia."

While she was adrift in memories, he had finished with the last of it. Hammer hanging at his side, he watched her.

"You have no need to be jealous of Jonathan, Cam."

"The ghost of him is still with you."

"Not his ghost. His memory, yes, but not his ghost."

He wore his thoughtful, assessing look as he watched her. "Are we done here?"

"Other than putting the hammer away, we are."

"As I was saying, I've an idea."

"And I want to hear what it is. Something about delayed gratification, right?"

He swung his arm around her shoulder as they walked back to the house.

"Totally wrong. It's about instant gratification."

Sophia smiled. She had an idea what Cam's idea might be and if she was off the mark, she'd suggest it herself.

"Are you keeping me in suspense?" She stood in the doorway to the garage as Cam put the hammer away.

"Not any longer," he said as he strode to her. "Your man here has put in a hard day's work. He's hot and sweaty and needs to clean up."

"Are you suggesting a hot shower?"

He gave an exaggerated sniff. "And I shouldn't take it alone."

Sophia laughed. "No you shouldn't and you shan't."

"Shan't?"

"Shan't, it means you shall not take a hot shower alone."

"I think I like that word."

29 Dinner Out or Dinner In

Cam leaned against the bathroom counter as Sophia stepped in. He'd join her but first he wanted to enjoy the sight of her naked body, her dark hair plastered against her back almost to her hips. She wasn't model slim which was just fine with him. He liked something other than skin and bones to hold on to.

When she glanced over her shoulder, her hands raised to wash her hair, he smiled. Even though he couldn't see himself, from her reaction it must be his predatory one. She'd told him there were times she felt like prey when he looked at her a certain way.

First he'd laughed. A moment later he pulled her close. "Not prey as in wanting to hurt you. Certainly prey as in just wanting you."

After that declaration her forehead no longer puckered in a frown. Sometimes she even laughed and crooked her finger inviting him closer. Right now he wondered what she'd do if he just stood there watching her.

The answer was she'd take her shower.

But not the slow, leisurely one he'd envisioned. If he was going to join her before she raced through the fastest shower in history, he'd better get moving.

Shucking his pants, he opened the shower door and stepped inside. "Let me help," he offered, tugging the soap from her hands. "I think you missed a spot here." He rubbed the soap over her belly and down one thigh. "And here." He ran the bar down her spine. "Actually, you missed all of this area." He moved her hair to one side and thoroughly washed her back making sure his movements were slow and that his fingers trailed across her skin along with the soap.

Sophia turned into his arms. "The better to rinse off, don't you think?" She rose on her toes but did not touch him except where her hands held his upper arms. "Don't want to leave any residue."

Cam thought she was going to kiss him, had bent his head in invitation when she slapped the bar of soap in his hand. "Thanks for your help."

"Where do you think you're going?" he growled.

"I'm done so I'm drying off and getting dressed."

"Phia, I thought."

"You Cameron Trent Mitchell dawdled. You will have to wait for another time to shower *with* me."

"You won't stay and watch me?" His invitation was the best he could come up with to salvage the situation because he was not going to press her to stay.

"Perhaps I'll come back once I'm dressed if you aren't done. I wouldn't count on it but you never know."

With that, she stepped out of the shower, shut the door, grabbed a towel and exited the bathroom.

Cam let the hot water sluice over him for a minute before resignation set in. He used the small bottle of shampoo he kept here for just this kind of a situation. If he showed up at the precinct smelling of vanilla, he'd never hear the end of it. With rapid movements he washed himself and rinsed off. His cock wanted her but settled down when the reality she was not coming back in, even to watch him, was clear.

Before turning off the water, Cam took the hand held shower wand and rinsed down the walls, door and floor. That done he turned off the water and stepped out. At the sight just inside the door, he grinned. A set of clean clothes from the inside out, including socks, was on the floor.

I must have been lost in some other dimension to not have noticed her doing that. Wasting no time, Cam dried and dressed. The bedroom was empty. He put his dirty clothes in the bag he brought with him.

Sophia appeared in the doorway.

"You're staying until you have to go back on duty?"

He nodded.

"Then put your clothes by the washing machine. I'm doing a load tonight."

"I can—,"

"Of course you can and if you insist you may. I'm offering to include your clothes in a load of wash I've already planned on doing. Your choice." She turned and walked away.

"Oh hell," Cam muttered as he got the wad of clothing out and stalked to the laundry area. He continued into the kitchen where Sophia was busy fixing tea and a fresh pot of coffee.

"I'm sorry I didn't act grateful for your offer to do my laundry."

"Is it too personal?"

"Something like that." He leaned on the counter. "I'm different when I'm around you for more than a couple of hours. And I don't always know what to do about it."

Sophia mirrored his stance from the opposite side of the breakfast bar. "I know what you mean. At least I think I do. I'm different around you too."

"A good different?" he asked.

"It's becoming a good different. And you? Are the changes you see good changes?"

"When you're with me, I don't see so much evil in the world."

Sophia laughed. "When I'm with you, we are usually in my house. I don't think there is much, if any, evil here."

He reached across, stroked the back of his knuckles down her cheek. "Maybe that's why being here with you feels so good. I leave the evil outside." He sighed. "Well, not always."

"You may bring memories or visions of evil when you come in my door, but no evil comes in with you. There is a difference."

"I didn't mean to upset you by watching you shower."

"I know." She turned and kissed his knuckles. "There'll be other showers."

"Promise?"

"If you continue to help me with the garden, I can guarantee it."

"Deal."

"Your coffee is ready." Sophia stepped away and poured a mug.

"Thanks. What was left in the pot would have been fine but I appreciate your making fresh."

"Let's sit. I've something I want to talk to you about."

A trickle of dread slithered deep in his gut but he remembered the promise of future showers. *She's not going to break it off.*

Sophia sat on the couch, her back to the arm, her feet tucked under her. She held her mug of tea and sipped the steaming liquid while Cam settled on the other end. He positioned himself so he could see her by turning his head but did not mirror her.

"Two things on my agenda," she said holding up two fingers. "One is my garden. I'd like to plant tomatoes and squash, including zucchini and pumpkins when the time comes. I've started many more plants than I want to fuss with this year. I'd appreciate it if you'd see if anyone else at your precinct is interested."

"Will do. I can make a list of what you have and folks can sign up for them."

"It will be easier if I make the list. I was thinking more about sending a flat with starts and people could just pick up what they wanted. They'd all have a sign so people would know what it was."

"That will work. I can let everyone know when the plants will be there so if they want some and are off duty, they still have a chance if they come in."

"We can finalize the details when we get closer to the time which will be late March or April."

"Got it. And the second thing?"

Cam's intense concentration over a conversation about plants struck Sophia as sad. If he was this wound up over plants, what would his reaction be about her next topic? *Only one way to find out.*

"Lily and I were talking the other day." His withdrawal was immediate. How did she know? He relaxed. Not really relaxed, but he leaned back against the couch as if he were relaxing. A wariness was in his eyes and he said nothing.

"You might guess the topic was "us"." She cricked her fingers in quote signs. And still there was no reaction.

"I'd like to invite Lily and Jackson to have dinner with us one night when you're off duty."

"That's it?" His Irish moss green gaze speared her.

"Most of it."

"What's the rest?"

Should she lean forward, reach out and take his hand? Sophia questioned how to say the innocuous rest so he could hear her.

"Lily and Diana are my closest friends of all the women in my circle. It isn't unusual for them to stop by together or individually. It isn't unusual for me to have dinner with Lily and Jackson and Jackson's mother, Eleanor."

"And that has changed because of me."

"Not entirely. I want to spend time with you. It's important to me to spend time with you. What I am proposing is that the two of us spend some time, a few hours one evening, with people who are important to me. They would like to get to know you."

He snorted.

She ignored him.

"And, to be fair, if there are friends of yours you do not see as much because of the time you spend with me, I'm more than willing to reciprocate." Sophia took a sip of her tea, watching him over the rim, trying to read his mood. *Maybe I... .* She stopped that line of destructive self-talk.

Including Cam in her life, beyond her kitchen and bedroom was important. He had already included himself in her sacred space. There were times before he headed out in the morning that he spent a few minutes in there. She wasn't so naïve to think he prayed but she wasn't so unaware she didn't know he felt something that helped him go out the door to his job.

"You have to invite them here?"

"No, the invitation is extended both ways. We can go there. Jackson will make his spaghetti. Lily will put together a salad. I'll bring brownies to go with Jackson's ice cream for dessert."

"We'll go there. Easier to leave than ask someone to leave here."

"That's true." Sophia was proud she'd kept her voice steady when inside she wept.

"I suppose I need to get used to being the specimen under the microscope if I'm going to continue to see you."

"Since you won't fit under a microscope lens, your analogy doesn't work. You have as much power to scrutinize them as they do you. And with your background, you may see something I've missed and you can bring it to my attention."

She leaned forward and tapped his thigh. "You might even find you like Jackson, Lily and Eleanor."

He scowled. "The last time we were there his mom had some spell or something."

"Eleanor had a TIA or a small stroke. She has recovered completely but she is being monitored. This spring when she travels back east to visit her daughters, someone will go with her."

"Not her son?"

"Perhaps. Maybe Jackson and Lily will go. But remember Grant has business interests and property in and around Rhode Island. So maybe he and Hunter will make the trip.

What's important is that she won't be doing those kinds of trips on her own."

"Driving?"

"Driving is under review. Currently she isn't driving. But no one is having her license taken away. She's been perfectly fine since that one episode but everyone, including Eleanor is being cautious."

"You think I can't handle being with the whole bunch of you?"

"Of course you can." Sophia made the change of subject leap easily. "It's just harder to get to know someone when there's a larger group than in a smaller one."

"Larger is better for me."

"Okay." Sophia relaxed. They were now in a negotiation as to how and when this dinner would happen, not if. "If I'm following, you'd prefer the larger group at the Montgomery's than just Lily and Jackson here."

"Let me know when and where and I'll be there." Cam was already up and crossing the room as he spoke. The restless energy he always had when he first stopped by was back.

Sophia put her mug on the table and reached the open area he had to cross to get to the garage just as he did.

"Cam, I don't think this dinner idea is a good one."

"Do not humor me!" His hands fisted on his hips, his stance wide, he glared at her.

"If you do not want to be a part of my extended life, you don't have to. It isn't an edict. An either or. We can continue as we are if that's what works best for you."

"What you mean is if that's all I can handle."

"I made a mistake, come to the bedroom with me."

Cam's chest swelled with indignation. "That's it." He started around her but Sophia matched him step for step.

"I'm not asking you to be intimate. The bedroom is where we have these kinds of conversations. It's where we both know we can talk and be heard." She paused before adding. "I should have had this conversation with you there."

"We talk at night." Cam didn't move.

"We have talked at night. We could start a new tradition and invite the other person to the bedroom to talk." Sophia was aware of every muscle in her body. Even her scalp was tight. There had to be some place where they both knew it was safe to talk.

"I've talked to you about Jonathan, you've talked to me about your kids—those weren't easy conversations yet we managed well because of where we were and our agreement.

"Dinner with my friends isn't so important I want to see you leave."

He rocked back on his heels, jammed his hands in his pockets. "Why is it important at all?"

Sophia touched his upper arm. Muscles were banded steel. Her brown eyes met his moss green ones. *All I'll ever have is now.*

"I want you to experience more of the joy life has to offer. The Circle is made up of women who've had challenges and tragedies in our lives. You already know Lily used to work in child welfare and now works to protect vulnerable adults. We pay attention and work to keep our pasts from darkening our present. They are married to men who support them much in the same ways you support me.

"But underneath all of that it's much much simpler. I want you in my life."

Cam rested his forehead against her own. "My being in your life does not make anything simple."

"Your being in my life makes my life better and I hope my being in your life makes your life better too. That's really all we can manifest."

"My life is better with you," he said pulling her close. "I can't imagine it otherwise."

"Me, too."

He kissed her nose. "Let's give it a try. Dinner at the Montgomery's, ask whomever else. I'll bring some beer if I know what people like."

She wrapped her arms around his waist, rested her head on his chest. "I love you" whirled in her head but was never spoken.

30 Scrutiny and Spaghetti

Cam figured it was better to get this dinner thing over with so he urged Sophia to set it up. A little chagrined when she turned to him and said "Is tonight okay?" he nodded. From the look on her face, she was just as surprised as he was.

And that's how he found himself standing on one side of the kitchen counter watching Jackson stir his sauce. A large bowl of greens sat to his left with three different dressings: bleu cheese, ranch and a vinaigrette of some sort. Sophia's pan of brownies was on the kitchen island. Also on the island was a cauldron of some sort filled with ice. Bottles of beer poked out like bristles or maybe thorns.

Not everyone could make it on such short notice so he wasn't going to be under the lights with all four of the husbands and wives who lived in Fremont. Just two of them. Lily and Jackson who were hosting this affair and Hunter and Grant. The others, Ashley and Daniel, Diana and Matthew had children. He had been warned that Diana and Matthew might show up for dessert with Madison Michelle. Oh, and Eleanor would be joining them. The O'Donnell contingent had three children who all had 'activities'. An awareness that this was an area of his kid's lives he'd missed out on in many ways knifed through him.

"Help yourself," Jackson called out setting a platter of spaghetti with sauce on the counter.

Next to it, he placed a good-sized bowl of grated cheese. *"Nope, freshly grated Parmesan and Romano cheese."* He did remember his first visit and the difference even he could taste in the freshly grated cheeses.

Cam stepped back so others could go ahead of him.

"If you want to wait, step around here," Jackson invited.

From that side of the counter, Cam could see the women all talking with Grant.

"What's that all about?" Cam asked Jackson.

"News about Janeen and Jason."

"Last I heard, she and the baby were probably moving back that way over spring break."

"That's still the plan. But, Grant has talked to some attorneys he knows in Providence about Jason clerking for them. It isn't as prestigious as the clerking position with the judge in Connecticut but he'd be closer to Janeen and his daughter."

"Trade off. Family time versus career move."

"Grant still has contacts and is still respected in that area. He's also put out feelers with a couple of the judges he knows. Jason would like to focus on environmental law and do some pro bono work for non-profits. That's what Grant is looking into. It may not be with a judge, but if it's in the area he wants to practice, then that's good."

"Anyone know what's going on with his parents?"

"Not that I know of."

Cam took a swig of his beer and watched as the small group across the room broke up and started toward the food.

"Bread?" Lily asked as she approached, her brow raised.

"Wanted to get it out at the last minute. It's best warm."

"I can get it." Cam swiveled toward the oven. He picked up an oven mitt, removed the loaf and slid it into the nearby bread basket. Wrapping the linen towel that lined the basket over the bread he placed it on the counter after the salad.

"Thanks." Jackson handed him a plate.

"You're welcome."

"Want another beer?"

Cam paused. "Maybe not. Need to get Sophia home."

"It's up to you. You've had one. We're just starting dinner. It'll be closer to two hours before we're done here."

"Two hours?"

Jackson grinned. "Thinking about making your escape before dessert?"

Cam chuckled. "I'm pleading the fifth."

Grant strode up.

"Cam's pleading the fifth." Jackson announced, stepping back.

"Good for you. I've not been out here that long. Not quite a year since I first showed up and about five months since I moved here. I will tell you that the men are not nearly as intimidating as they are." He motioned with his head at Lily, Hunter and Sophia who were dishing up their plates.

"Good to know."

"I'll also let you in on the secret." Grant leaned closer. "As long as everyone can see you aren't going to hurt her, you're in."

"It may sound easy, but I can guarantee all of us have failed at some point and had to regroup. But," Jackson's gaze rested on Lily who was just sitting down at the table. "Whatever it took to win her, was worth not just the effort but the time and energy.

"Lily love? The cook needs sustenance."

"If the cook wants sustenance, the cook needs to come over here." The laughter in Lily's voice belied the stern words.

Jackson ambled over to her, tipped her back including the chair.

Lily's shriek was short lived because her husband silenced her with a kiss.

"Much better."

"Jackson Montgomery!" Lily sputtered. "You will pay for that scare."

An unrepentant grin on his face, Jackson began filling his plate. "Come on guys, before it gets cold."

"Anyone want a cold beer?" Cam asked, plucking a bottle from the pot.

"Sure, I'll take one." Grant picked up his plate and started down the line.

"Me too," Jackson added now moving to the table.

Cam grabbed two more bottles, opened them and delivered them to their destination before fixing his own plate.

He had no illusions that he'd really be accepted. The deal was he couldn't hurt Sophia. How did anyone ever guarantee that?

31 Not Again

"Not again," Sophia muttered to herself as she sprung up from behind her desk and dashed out into the hall.

"That's enough!" She started toward the two boys who were locked in the classic wrestling stance, hands on each other's upper arms.

"The rest of you go on to your classes," she ordered the group standing around the teens, egging them on. "Now!"

"Stop!" She reached between the two students intent on prying them apart. Her feet flew out from under her and she crashed to the floor. Pain radiated through her head when her skull hit the cement floor.

Darkness.

"Don't move Ms. Stewart. You have to stay still." The urgency, the worry in the young voice was real. Sophia tried to open her eyes but the pain was intense.

"Someone get Ms. Ryder."

Kay Ryder was the health teacher. Why were they sending for Kay?

The bell announced the next period.

"What's going on here?"

Sophia struggled to sit up when she heard the principal's voice.

"Ms. Stewart, don't." Hands held her shoulders, panic streaking through the young voice.

Was that a siren? She prayed to the Goddess it wasn't coming for her. If she could just get up, get to her class, take a couple of aspirin, get through the rest of her day.

"Sophia?"

Kay was here.

Cool hands touched her wrist, her forehead. The young voice said she'd fallen and hit her head.

"She wants to get up but I don't think she should. She was knocked out for a few minutes," the young voice reported to Kay.

"Called 911," another voice said.

"Good job, both of you," Kay said. "Sophia, you must stay as you are until you are checked out. Being unconscious because of a blow to the head can be serious. We don't want you to take any chances."

"Those of you who are in Ms. Stewart's class go on inside." The principal was taking charge of her class?

"I... ."

"You will not be going back in that classroom except to gather your things. Even if it isn't too serious, Sophia, you must go home and rest. And, if you have a headache tomorrow, you must stay home."

"Kay, I'm all right."

"No, Sophia, you aren't.

"I'll stay with Ms. Stewart. Thank you again for coming to get me. Off you go to your class."

"Will she be okay?"

"I'm sure she will be." Kay's false bravado hit Sophia in the gut. *She isn't sure I'll be okay?*

Cam was heading toward Fremont High. His plan was to take Sophia out for a ride, a drink or an early dinner. He was just pulling in the parking lot when the fire truck cruised by him stopping in front of the school.

Out and trotting toward the front door, Cam flashed his badge as he dashed through the front door.

"Upstairs and to the left," the school employee had said.

In that moment he knew it was Sophia who'd been hurt.

Taking the steps two at a time, he reached the top and raced down the hall. The school security officer was standing by the door to her room. But on the floor, with another woman kneeling beside her was Sophia.

"Hey there." He tried for nonchalance but that totally failed. His voice shook.

"Cam?"

"I'm here. EMT's right behind me." He'd bent, taken her hand in his and noticed her eyes were closed.

No sooner were the words out of his mouth than the crew and their equipment arrived.

The other lady stood and talked to one of the team while the others opened boxes and began the process of checking her out.

"Don't leave me." She'd reached out to him.

"I'm right here. You can hear where I am. I won't leave you and if I move from this spot, I'll say something."

"Where?"

"I'm along the wall about four feet from the door to your room." Wrinkles of worry on her forehead eased.

Cam listened as the EMT's talked to her while checking her blood pressure, blood sugar and respiration. "Whatever you are that watches over her, thank you," he prayed under his breath.

Her gasp of pain when asked to open her eyes tore at his heart. His hearing was excellent and his understanding of concussions good enough he knew dilated and unequal pupils was not a good sign. Her confusion as to how many fingers she saw meant she'd be going to the hospital to be checked out further.

Sophia insisted she was okay. It must have been an accident. Even though details were vague, her focus on she was okay and it must have been an accident never wavered.

"Phia, I'm stepping a few feet down the hall to make a couple of calls."

He called the precinct and said he needed a week off due to a family emergency. "I'll check in with you on Monday if I need any more time, otherwise you'll see me next Thursday."

If he had a number, he'd call Lily or Diana or maybe Ashley or Hunter. Someone in The Circle needed to know what was going on. "Hell, what's happening here. I can have it looked up." Making that call almost immediately got him Lily's number.

"Lily, Cam Mitchell here. Sophia's been injured."

"What?"

"She fell and hit her head. Concussion at the least."

"Have her taken to St. Agatha's. I'm with a client but I'll come as soon as I can."

"Sounds good."

"I'm back," he said when he took his place along the wall.

"Cam, tell them I'm okay and can take care of my last class."

"She should be checked out," the nearest EMT said.

"Phia, you need to do what they say. Even I can see you have a concussion. You don't want to mess with that. Can have long term consequences and you know that."

"But,"

"No, buts. I'll come with you."

"My class. What will happen to my class?"

"The principal is in there."

"Oh, Cam, please. You have to go in and do something. It was all an accident. No one… ." She reached for him, tears streaming back into her hair.

"If she's on the gurney, can you take her into the classroom?"

"It's an unusual request, but yes, we can."

On the gurney, the ambulance crew wheeled her into the classroom. Cam remained at her side.

The looks of horror on every students' face reinforced his assumption that Sophia was not just an excellent teacher but well-regarded by her students.

"Ms. Stewart," the principal began, his voice placating.

"I'm being taken to the hospital to be checked out. I'll see you all Monday. Cam will take over the rest of the class."

Cam's head jerked so hard pain radiated up his neck.

"Do you have anything here to take with you?" the closest ambulance attendant asked.

"My purse. Bottom drawer on the right."

Cam retrieved her purse. Kissed her forehead as he placed it next to her. "I'll be along. Lily will be there as soon as she can."

Watching as Sophia was wheeled out, Cam struggled with what to do next.

His attention now on the class, he saw a hand raised.

"Yes."

"Are you Ms. Stewart's boyfriend?"

"That's none of your business." The principal's voice was harsh.

In for a penny, in for a pound. "Why would you think that?"

"You kissed her."

"I kissed her on her forehead."

"But you like her," another student, this time a girl, said.

"And so do all of you."

"Now, what does Ms. Stewart do when there are problems like this?"

"She has us talk about it?"

"Not just talk about it like what happened, but talk about it like what to do so it don't happen again."

Cam decided not to correct the grammar. "Here's what we're going to do. First, I'm Captain Mitchell from the

Fremont Police Department and I am a friend of Ms. Stewart's. And I happen to be of the male gender.

"I'm fairly certain that, if not at this point in your lives, you have had friends who were of the opposite sex."

"You're not going to marry her?"

"Now that question has nothing to do with what happened.

"Second, I want you to count off by fours and then get into groups by your number." Cam waited, watching the process as the students counted to four. The count complete he pointed to sections of the room and assigned the groups to their space.

The principal remained but now stood by the door talking to the school's police liaison.

"As I understand it, three people were involved."

A girl raised her hand. "I was the cause. The fight was over me."

"Punches were thrown?"

"No, almost, but no. Ms. Stewart came out of her room because there were words, you know, yelling."

"Okay, before anyone sits down, you all know who was involved. I don't need to know." He raised his hand to stop the principal from interrupting. "Make sure everyone who was directly involved are in different groups and then sit down."

When everyone had settled and were looking at him, he said, "Now being true to what Ms. Stewart would have you do, I want each group to do the following: from the standpoint of the perp in your group, how could the whole incident have been handled differently. And, the extra group is to discuss how it could be totally avoided."

As voices rose in discussion, Cam took the few steps to where the principal and officer stood. "This is Ms. Stewart's last class of the day, correct?"

The principal nodded.

"If it's okay with you, I can handle this discussion."

"But someone must be punished."

"Let's see what happens. There's only twenty minutes of this class left."

"School rules are that anyone fighting is to be at best suspended and even expelled."

"Good to know. But, I'm sure Ms. Stewart does not want anyone suspended over this. She may be vague about what happened but she was firm it must have been an accident. Again, let's see what happens."

Cam closed the classroom door when the two men left. He had an idea about this group of teens from the looks on everyone's face when Sophia had been brought into the room.

He wandered around the room but kept his distance not wanting anyone's words to be compromised by his appearance.

The bell rang and the clock on the wall said school was out but no one moved to leave.

A hand went up.

"We've figured something out."

"How about the other groups."

"We need another few."

"Sit back in your chairs and stop talking when you've finished the assignment. That way I'll know when everyone is done."

The room quieted.

"Okay, which group wants to start? And just so you know I don't need names."

Bouncing out of her seat to stand was the young girl who had stated the fight was over her.

"We talked about lots of things." Her eyes teared up. "Will Ms. Stewart be okay?"

"I'm sure she will be in time but don't expect her back in school on Monday. She may need to be out all next week."

"Will you be here in her place?"

"Nope, you need a real teacher until she gets back.

"So what all did your group talk about?"

"We talked about the importance of clear communication so no one gets the wrong idea. We talked about why we need to think of how our actions affect others.

"Tell her I'm really sorry," the young girl's voice shook. "I'll be more careful. Tell her I promise I'll be more careful about what I say and do."

"Not a problem. Does your group have anything else to add?" He let his gaze touch on each member of that group.

"Next?"

A young man stood up. His shirt pocket was torn. "You're going to make sure Ms. Stewart knows we're sorry?"

Cam nodded.

"I gotta use my words. Ms. Stewart is always telling us to use our words but sometimes that doesn't work. I mean I told—"

A boy in the next group stood. "He told me he was taking Cassie to the dance but I thought she said she'd go with me."

"Okay, so what did you come up with to help you use words when they don't seem to be working?" Cam asked the first boy.

"It's important to figure out something other than fighting."

Cam nodded to the second boy. "Pretty much the same thing. Sometimes you use your words and they don't work."

"Last group?"

Two people stood, a young man and a young woman began. "Ms. Stewart is always telling us to use our words but she also talks to us about the fact that no one can make another person do something if they really don't want to."

"We think we can change someone's mind, make someone do what we want but that's a myth. We've all been in her classes and know it's what she always says," the young man spoke.

"When we feel ourselves getting frustrated or angry, that's the time to stop and see what's going on. What is it we want to happen that isn't? And if it's important to us, what does she tell us?" The young lady was looking at the class, an expectant look on her face.

The young man raised a hand like a conductor of an orchestra or a choir. "Talk to someone you trust." The entire class recited the five words.

"Okay then, but I've something else to add. You do not have to respond like-to-like. Someone calls you a name, you do not have to shout one back. Someone pushes you, you don't have to push back."

"Yeah, cop talk."

"Do you have any idea how many times I've been cussed at, threatened, called all sorts of names since I've been on the force? Thousands of times.

"Have I been angry, frustrated, at times even furious? You bet.

"How do you think I felt when I saw my friend, Ms. Stewart on the floor?"

Cam waited.

"Worried."

He nodded.

"Upset."

Another nod.

"She's important to you so I bet you wanted someone to pay."

Cam remained still for a moment. "You know I'm a police officer. Do you think I'm armed?"

Heads nodded.

"Did I draw my gun? Did I start throwing people up against the wall? Did I yell orders?"

"No," was a low murmur throughout the room.

"I'll confess, I was beyond worried and upset. I was terrified and angry. So think back to how I was feeling and what my actions were."

"It's 'cause you're a cop."

"It's 'cause I know all actions have consequences and what was most important to me in that moment was to make sure Ms. Stewart was okay.

"Here's an opportunity for you. Any of you want to do a ride-along with a Fremont police officer, get in touch and I'll make it happen. What you'll have to promise is that you'll do exactly what the officer tells you to do. No arguing, no backtalk, etc. When the situation is over, you can ask all the questions you want. And if they aren't answered satisfactorily, you can let me know and I'll do my best to answer them."

Cam checked the time. Class had gone over by almost thirty minutes.

"Everyone here able to get themselves home?" Heads nodded as students gathered their books and backpacks.

"For those of you who were involved, you need to decide what you want to do about it. You know Ms. Stewart has said her falling was an accident and that won't change. Only you who were there know if that is true or not.

"Class dismissed."

When the classroom was cleared, it was obvious to him that three students were lagging behind.

"Anything else you want me to know?"

"Would you go with us to talk to the principal?"

It would delay him getting to the hospital but he knew if Sophia was here, she'd not hesitate.

"If you're sure you want me there, I'll go."

The interview, such as it was, with the principal was short. No punches had been thrown. Harsh words and some wrestling had. The boys were suspended for three days. The girl cried and said she should be suspended also.

The school counselor who'd been called in to the meeting suggested that seeing two boys she liked suspended, having that on their record was its own punishment.

As Cam strode out of the building he wondered what influence the school counselor had over the principal because he'd been sure all three would have been expelled for the remained of the school year.

He called ahead to St. Agatha's. No, no one was there with her. Sophia was being assessed. An MRI or a CatScan would be prescribed once the initial examination was complete.

"Tell her Cam called and everything is good at school and he's on his way."

The urge to put on lights and siren and speed off was strong but being pulled over would only slow things down. He kept to the fast lane, his speed just over the limit and prayed.

32 St. Agatha's

Personal business brought him to St. Agatha's so Cam found a spot in the parking garage. Striding into the Emergency Department, he approached the desk and inquired about a Ms. Stewart.

"Are you family?"

"I'm Captain Cameron Mitchell, Fremont Police. I responded to the situation that brought Ms. Stewart here. I'm here to get her side of the story." Cam held very still not wanting to show how nervous he was. It was a bit tricky being at a hospital outside his jurisdiction as well as not being a legal member of Sophia's family.

The receptionist called back and told whomever answered he was here and asking about Ms. Stewart.

"You can go back now." He started forward, almost tripping over his feet in the process.

"Captain?"

He turned back to see the receptionist holding out a Visitor Badge, a slip of paper with a room number on it. "She's here."

"Thanks. 'Preciate it." Cam was through the doors and searching for A-14 within seconds of slapping the Visitor Badge on.

Stopping at the entrance, Cam's breath caught in his throat. As bad as she looked on the floor, she looked worse in a hospital gown propped up on a gurney. He knocked on the door frame as he stepped inside.

"Phia? I'm here." He took the couple of steps to her bedside and held her hand.

"Cam?" Her grip was strong. "Don't leave me."

"If I'm not here, I won't be far." Tears trickled down her cheeks. He brushed them away with his thumb and kissed her nose. "When you're better, I'll give you a proper kiss."

"Maybe a proper kiss would make me better." Her breathing was shaky and he knew it wasn't from passion.

"Let's see what the doc says." Changing the subject was his next plan but a tall brown haired, blue-eyed man knocked once and came in.

"Ms. Stewart, I'm Doctor Parker, Lily Hughes' friend. She's been delayed and asked me to see you."

"Does that mean my skull is cracked?"

Her grip on his hand tightened.

"Dr. Parker, I'm Cam Mitchell, Ms. Stewart's friend."

"Lily mentioned you'd be here. From what she implied, Ms. Stewart will benefit from your company."

"I'm right here."

Cam smiled at the testy tone. "Yes, you are. Now let's hear what else Dr. Parker has to say."

"Initial examination shows you've been concussed. That means you'll be staying here at least overnight for observation. Your family doctor has been notified and will be kept apprised of any further diagnosis and treatment. There'll be more tests. The recommendation is for a scan of your head. But until that's in place, you need to rest."

"Will she remain here until all the tests are completed?" Cam asked.

"No, I've already admitted her. Someone will be along shortly to take her to her room. You, of course are welcome to accompany her.

"Sophia?" Dr. Parker leaned over the bed, his hand held Sophia's free one. "I'll make sure Lily knows where to find you but in the meantime, Captain Mitchell will keep you company if that's okay."

"He can stay with me?"

"Of course he can. We never kicked Jackson out of Lily's room all those years ago, did we?"

Sophia smiled. "No, you didn't."

"Anything for the pain?" Cam asked knowing the answer was a negative.

"Not at this time. We need to see what happened, see how she's doing before going in that direction."

Cam used his foot to pull a chair closer. At no time as he wrestled things into place did he let go of her hand. Once he sat, he lowered the side rail, leaned over and kissed her fingers. "How many arguments do you break up a week?"

He took the grimace for a pain-filled smile, noted her silence and continued.

"Do you want to know what happened?"

She squeezed his hand.

"You just rest and listen to how brilliant I was."

But before he started on his tale, an orderly came to the cubicle. "I'm here to take her to her room."

Cam let go of her hand but continued to talk to her while the orderly got her ready to transport. Once that was done, he picked up her hand and as they started off, kept up a running commentary. "I've got your purse. I must say I make a rather dashing figure walking through the hospital with a turquoise patchwork purse in hand."

Knowing she kept her eyes closed, Cam gave a running commentary as to where they were and what he saw. In the elevator, he was quiet except for the counting of the floors. They got out on the ninth floor and a short time later, Sophia was wheeled into a room with a westward view.

A nurse bustled in and Cam was ordered out of the room.

"No," Sophia grasped for him. "You can't leave me." Tears ran down her face.

"He'll be right outside the door. As soon as you're settled, he can come back in," the nurse bargained.

"No." Sophia started to sit up. Her cry of pain tore at his heart.

"Phia, I'm right here." He reached past the nurse and patted her leg. "It's all right. I told you I wouldn't go far. Just outside the door isn't that far."

"Please." She struggled to open her eyes, looked frantically for him. Once her gaze caught his, the panic eased. "Please."

"He can stay in the room but not next to the bed until you are settled."

"Thank you, I just can't do this without him here."

"I'm over here by the window, Phia. You've got a west facing view. You'll be able to see the sunset from here."

"Sir, I really do need Ms. Stewart's attention to get her checked in."

Cam wanted to fling a retort but he held his tongue. Hearing her cry out in pain had almost brought him to his knees. Being strong for someone else was a great idea in theory but lacked something in practice.

Everyone seemed very efficient and it didn't take long for Sophia to be transferred into the hospital bed, vitals checked and pain level determined.

"I'm sorry I can't give you something right now, but we need to wait and see what the test results show and how you're doing in the morning." On that final note, she made sure the rails were up and left the room.

As soon as she'd left, Cam crossed to close the door. He left it open a crack so Lily would know to come in. Pulling a chair next to the bed, he sat down. This time he did not lower the railing but stuck his hand between the lower and middle rail to hold Sophia's hand.

"I'm here." He stroked the back of her hand with his thumb. "You need to rest now. I'm not leaving. If I can, I'll go with you when you have the tests, but, Phia, you know they may have rules that say I can't."

She squeezed his hand.

It wasn't long before an orderly was back to take her to imaging. Cam could walk through the halls with her but he could not be in the room while the testing was done.

Lily was waiting when they returned to 9-14.

"Do you know how she fell?" Lily asked when the three of them were alone.

"Two boys were tussling over a girl. Sophia went out to break it up. If she got hit, that was an accident. The looks on the faces of her class when they saw her strapped in the gurney? Even the boys were shook and the girls, well, some of them were crying.

"Before we were interrupted I'd asked Sophia how many arguments she broke up a week. Never got an answer." He squeezed Sophia's hand. "Care to answer that now?"

"They don't happen every week and not even every other week."

"But they happen often enough that your class knows what you do to sort it out."

Sophia didn't respond.

"I've let everyone know you were brought here but I also said you might be released. I can see that won't be happening tonight and most likely not in the morning." Lily spoke in a matter-of-fact way. "You will recall my time here for a concussion and injuries. You don't look like anything more is wrong than the concussion. That's bad enough but, when you get frustrated, remember you don't have to wear the immobilizers."

"Immobilizers?"

"I was in an accident several years ago and in addition to a concussion when my head came up close and personal with the pavement, I also sustained injures so I could not use my arms."

Sophia grimaced. "I have that to be thankful for."

"So, how many of those situations do you deal with a year?"

"Too many." Sophia, eyes still closed, winced as she turned toward his voice. "What happened after I left?"

Cam repeated how devastated her students were by what had happened. "I had them count to four and divide into groups with three of the groups having one of the perps." He patted her hand when she looked to protest. "It's my story, I get to choose the terminology.

"Your principal was there but he stayed by the door. The school police liaison had been called and he was in the hall.

"Three of the groups' assignments were to figure out how things could have been handled differently. The fourth group was to come up with a plan to prevent incidents like this from happening again.

"That turned into a conversation about how to handle situations that don't go the way you want."

Sophia was not following the conversation. Cam figured that between the pain and the fuzzy mental functioning, she'd lost track. But Lily was listening and nodded for him to continue.

"Long story short, I invited any of the students who want to go on a ride-a-long to let me know. The three kids who were directly involved decided to talk to the principal. The school counselor was there so instead of being expelled, the boys were given a three day suspension. The girl just has to live with the consequences for her choices.

"Oh yeah, there was that exchange about my being your boyfriend." He grinned at Lily's arched brow. "We had a short discussion about friends who are of a different sex not necessarily being romantically involved. Well, we never really used the term 'romantically involved' but it was implied."

"An adventurous day." Lily's phone rang and she stepped out to answer it.

"I'm still here, Phia."

"Don't leave me," her voice was slurred.

"I won't leave you but you have to tell me what you remember of my story."

"You lied." Those two words were clearer.

"I lied? What did I say that was a lie?"

"You said you're not my boyfriend."

"I'm your friend, your lover, your admirer. I might also admit to being your gentleman friend, but I'm not and never will be your boyfriend."

"Don't leave me." A stronger voice enunciated the words.

"I'm right here."

Lily returned. "That was Diana. She'll let everyone know. She had two emails, one from Elizabeth and one from Gabriella asking about you, Soph. Seems they felt something was wrong. She's assured them you'll be okay."

Cam took that information in. Elizabeth in Ireland and Gabriella in Italy sensed something was wrong with Sophia. Sensed something strong enough that they sent an email to everyone in The Circle to check it out?

"Had they checked with each other first?"

"I don't think so."

Lily leaned over the bed, one hand held Sophia's free hand, the other stroked her forehead. "I'm going now. Cam is here. You won't be alone."

She straightened. "If something comes up and you need to leave or need anything else, you've got my number. My phone is by the bed so it makes no difference what time it is if you need to call."

"Food?"

Lily chuckled. "I'll get you something from the cafeteria before I go. Anything in particular?"

"Doubt they'd have a stiff drink or even a beer so I'll settle for a hamburger with the works, fries and a chocolate milkshake. And if they don't have milkshakes, a bottle of seltzer water will do."

"I'll make sure I have a chocolate milkshake with me when I come by tomorrow," Lily said and smiled. "I'm off to the cafeteria." Stopping at the door, she turned back. "They'll have tea, coffee, juice here on the floor."

Cam took his time eating the food Lily brought back. No milkshakes but there was a tall glass of Arnold Palmer she thought he might like.

She also brought the fixings for hot tea and made the first cup for Sophia making sure Cam saw what she did. "The proportions are different because these are smaller cups."

Evening came. Sophia was checked and rechecked. There were times her words slurred but when he talked to her she responded. That was a good sign. The slurred words weren't.

After the last check, when the lights were out, Cam toed his shoes off and lowered the rail. He stretched out beside Sophia and she snuggled into his arms with only a whimper of pain. He dozed off and on but when roused, he'd whisper to her. She always answered and although some of those answers were a bit off, she'd not lost consciousness.

Cam was awake when the nurse came in to check on the morning shift. She frowned finding him in the bed. Her look softened upon seeing Sophia relaxed in his arms. "Phia, I have to get out of the bed now. Need to use the john."

Sophia winced when he shifted away from her.

Grateful there was no cry of pain, he headed down the hall to the public restrooms. He'd thought at one point his bladder was going to break but his training had seen him through that crisis.

Padding back into 9-14, he heard the nurse asking Sophia questions. Her answers were hesitant as if she had to search her memory for them.

"What's your husband's name?" the nurse asked.

"Jonathan. He's dead."

Cam's throat clogged as his guts seized. It was true, Jonathan was her husband and he was dead.

"Who's staying with you?" the nurse asked.

"Cam. My friend, Cam, is. He makes everything better."

"Then it's a good thing he can spend this time with you," the nurse said.

Grateful she hadn't said her lover, Cam stopped short just as he started in the door. Why would he be grateful she hadn't said they were lovers? Was he afraid or ashamed of that reality? It would be beyond believable that her friends and their husbands didn't at least think they were intimate. Especially after the last fifteen hours or so.

"I'm back," Cam said, stepping into the room. He crossed to the bed and bent to kiss Sophia's forehead. "Feeling any better?"

"A little. Right now I just want to go home."

"Let's see what the doctor says."

Doctor Parker and Lily arrived at the same time. Lily had a large insulated mug in one hand. "Made with real ice cream. Jackson's own homemade chocolate made into a milkshake."

Cam accepted the vessel and accompanying straw. "Can I share it with Sophia?" he asked Doctor Parker.

"If she wants some. There aren't any dietary restrictions." After asking Sophia questions and checking her eyes, he remarked, "I'm having a neurologist come by this morning. If she says it's okay, you'll be discharged. The biggest thing will be that someone will need to be with you for a few days."

"That won't be a problem, doc. I've time off for as long as Sophia needs someone. I'm not the best cook but we won't starve. And if there's anything she's uncomfortable with me helping her do, I'm sure Lily or one of her other friends will be available."

Lily hung out with them until the neurologist came by. She confirmed the diagnosis of concussion. The MRI from last night did not show a brain bleed or a cracked skull. But the headaches and slowed cognition meant she should not be left alone.

No driving for at least 24 – 48 hours.

Immediate return to ED if there is:

Loss of consciousness

Increase in headache

Vomiting

Decrease in cognitive functioning

"This is more than doable." Cam said looking over the sheet of instruction before handing it to Lily.

Lily nodded.

Lily stayed with Sophia while he got his car. By the time she was belted in to his car, her head was pounding. The acetaminophen with codeine worked if she was quiet but didn't take care of the more severe pain when she was up.

Driving into her garage, besides getting the prescription filled, he saw another problem—Sophia's car was still at school.

"Let's get you inside."

He'd just gotten out and turned off the alarm when Diana and Hunter pulled in the driveway.

"Just in case we can help with something," Hunter said.

With both women there, it was easy enough for him to carry Sophia into the house and stand her up in the hall. "Bed or recliner?"

"Bed."

Hunter scooted around them and disappeared into Sophia's bedroom before he could pick her up.

"Let me walk."

He steadied her while she shuffled down the hall. Hunter had pulled the covers down, had a gown out and stacked pillows along the headboard.

"If you can help her into bed, I'll reposition my car."

"Where's her car?" Diana asked.

"Still at the school."

"When we get Sophia settled, we'll go get it. Are the keys in her purse?"

"Yes, in a side pocket." Sophia wobbled, held up by Diana and Hunter.

"Great and maybe you can pick up her prescription?"

"Not a problem. I'll drop Hunter off to get the car while I go by the pharmacy."

Cam strode across the room and picked up the chair that usually sat in the corner. Positioning it next to the bed, he helped Sophia to sit. "Once you're set, I can move it back or we can leave it here until you're steadier on your feet."

Moving his car took a few minutes. Not enough time to find his own emotional equilibrium. He was supposed to see his oldest son on Sunday. *I'll wait to cancel that until I know how she's doing. Maybe she'll be okay with one of her friends being with her.* He stood out in front and looked around the neighborhood, breathing in the chilly February air. *So normal. I'd never fit in here.*

33 This and That and Ceremony

Saturday

"Cam?"

He turned away from the sliding door leading into the backyard at the sound of Lily's voice.

"You've been a blessing in so many ways, I hardly know how to say this to you.

"Just spit it out then."

"We had planned, that is, the others and I had planned on a gathering tomorrow. After Soph's accident, we believe it would be good for all of us if we kept to our plan."

Here was his out, a way to keep his date with his son. They were on rocky ground and Cam cancelling because of a woman would be a significant setback. *Will I ever get past the lies she told about me?*

"Not a problem. I just don't want her alone yet. She's still a bit off."

"Yes, she is and someone would stay here until you returned. One of the things we're going to discuss is how we can be here with her."

"Do you think I'm not capable of taking care of her?"

"You are more than capable. We also know you have a job and other people who depend on you. Hunter can stay with her and so can I. Ashley and Diana can check on her during the day. We just have to figure out the details."

"I've taken time off. Will let them know Monday if I'll be in on Thursday or not until next week."

"Do you have any appointments or other commitments to keep? I'm sure one of us can be here."

"I'll check the refrigerator and cupboards, pick up groceries when I'm out tomorrow."

"And if you are running low on something later in the week, one of us can pick it up on our way over to visit. We may not stay with Soph, but we will be stopping by. She tracks better when we talk face-to-face than over the phone. I'm still not clear how the two of you met or even when that was but I remain grateful for it." Lily turned away and headed toward the hall.

Cam remained by the door his unseeing gaze drifting around the garden. His focus sharpened on a bit of green poking through the dirt.

Opening the door, he went out to investigate. Something was growing. As he got closer he saw the green shoots poking up throughout the garden. Racking his brain for what grew in late February he came up with what his mother planted. Crocus, and later, daffodils and tulips, not that he was sure any of these shoots were them.

He wandered over to where he'd helped Sophia plant peas. No sign of life—yet.

Rubbing the spot on his chest where an odd pressure built, Cam returned to the patio area. What was happening? He wasn't having a heart attack and it wasn't indigestion but the pressure weighed heavy. "Get a grip!" He muttered the stern admonishment.

The pressure, now edged with panic, grew.

"I need to get out of here."

He grabbed his car keys and strode down the hall to Sophia's bedroom door. "Anyone want a latte?"

Lily and Diana declined. Sophia looked startled.

"I'm just going to the coffee shop down the street. Be right back." He controlled the impulse to run to his car. Once out of the garage, the pressure eased.

A part of him wanted to keep on driving but he'd given his word.

A part of him wanted to believe he could belong but that would never happen. He was too deep into the darkness. Sophia was the light. It would never work.

The tightness was back but it was different this time. This tightness held pain. This tightness led even further into the place with no light.

Sunday

Lily and Hunter arrived a little early with a grocery list for Cam that he took before he left. They brought larger than normal portions of their contributions for their potluck. There would be enough food for Sophia and Cam this evening and maybe even for tomorrow.

Ashley and Diana escorted Sophia to her sacred space because she wasn't as steady on her feet as they'd like. And, because the constant headache became excruciating if she leaned over, they'd rearranged the furniture so everyone could sit on a loveseat or chair. A low table in the center served as their altar.

Hunter had the smudge ready and did the honors as everyone came into the room. Tendrils of smoke lingered near the ceiling. A lit candle provided light and heat to cleanse their offerings.

A healing altar appeared as each of them set stones in each direction: malachite, moonstone, crystal, amethyst, lapis lazuli, turquoise, amber and copper balls graced each direction.

Elizabeth's green Galway crystal etched bowl in the center with a vial of water from The Sacred Grove almost completed their creation. Around the outside, they placed stones from Giovanni's garden path that Gabriella had picked out for them. Actually, they'd learned as they'd each picked out stones that spoke them, what they'd been drawn to was rubble from the original building...parts that had already crumbled in ruin before Giovanni restored it.

Without consulting Sophia, they'd decided ahead of time to do their ceremony sitting unless Sophia was steady on her feet. Because of the seating, they were too far apart to hold hands. Setting an energetic circle, with elbows close to their sides, they turned their hands, palms up toward the circle sister on each side. Focusing their minds, they sent energy out through their fingers to each other.

"We are the light

"We are the source

"Through us love flows

"Throughout the world."

Three times the prayer was said.

Diana's soprano voice started to sing "The River" and they all joined in. As the song came to an end, Diana picked up the rose quartz talking stone.

"I'm so glad we are gathered here today. It isn't that I've anything really to share other than I've missed this, missed us. And I can feel Elizabeth and Gabriella's energy. We've come a long way along our spiritual path and I look forward to continuing this journey with each and every one of you."

Hunter took the stone. "Grant and I are so very blessed to have this opportunity to support Janeen. Neither of us believe we could have done this way back when because we were so young and even more important, because of family pressures. We've forgiven ourselves and each other and rejoice in not only this opportunity but also a chance to build a life together.

"Because of our time with Janeen and Mary Sophia, we do want a child to raise. We are still discussing how to make that happen." She laughed at the raised eyebrows. "Well we know *that* part of it. But," a seriousness invaded her tone, "I'm at the age where things can get iffy with a pregnancy but we aren't sure if we want to adopt.

"We're exploring options including buying Lily's little house and setting it up as a transition home for homeless young women who are pregnant. If we do that, we'd buy a house nearby. We've also talked about buying a duplex and having the other side available for young homeless moms. As you can see, we've lots of ideas but no decisions."

She started to hand the stone to Ashley but pulled it back. "We've also been looking at houses on the coast. I know we talked about building a house but that takes much longer. We'd like a place before Elizabeth and Michael are here in late April." She then handed the stone to Ashley.

"My last check-up shows me still cancer free. I may not have breasts but I do have other body parts cancer likes. I'm getting used to my 'new normal'," she crooked her fingers. "You might wonder what that is."

Heads nodded.

"I'm recovered from the mastectomy and reconstructive surgery. I've settled into the house and no longer think of it as 'Daniel's House'." Again the finger movement. "I've a lifestyle I never even allowed myself to dream of. I can just go grocery shopping and buy foods that aren't even on sale. For me, that's a luxury. I've a loving husband who fully supports me in all ways. He's loved by my children to the point where Rose and James are totally 'our children'." Another finger crook.

"Even the idea that Anthony will spend time with Art this summer isn't as frightening because when he comes back, I won't be alone. Daniel and I've talked about varying scenarios and have ideas about how to handle it. With Lily's help, we've found a counselor we really like. She's trained with Dr. William Glasser and we've read his books. Lots of good ideas that we're already implementing. Life is good."

Sophia was next but she handed the stone on to Lily after receiving it.

"I know what you mean, Diana. I've made a vow to not let my life get so busy I lose this time sitting in circle with you. Or, if it is busy, still taking the time to gather in ceremony. What I want is to add to our time. I don't mean meeting more often unless that works out for everyone, but what I've noticed over this past year is we tend to not meet so soon after our time in Ireland.

"Our ceremonies there are so intense, I do understand why we skip a month, but I'd like to suggest that we reconsider and, instead, build upon that intensity and see what happens."

She laughed. "Of course I bring that suggestion up when we do not have any travel plans to The Sacred Grove in place. But it is something to think about because we may want to have a longer retreat, just the seven of us this spring or summer when we are all together in Fremont.

"I know what you mean, Ashley. Compare my little house to Jackson's? I do think of it as my home but usually refer to it as Jackson's. Need to spend some time thinking about where that comes from.

"If you want to use the little house as you described, Hunter, let's talk. It might work best to set up a non-profit or charitable trust or something that can continue after we are gone. Perhaps talking to Grant about that would give us more information and a direction to pursue."

Lily shifted so she looked at Sophia. "Do you want to talk? You do know you don't have to."

"I don't know what to say." Sophia did not reach for the stone.

"Whatever comes to mind, Soph."

"Head hurts too much. It gibberish. Better here."

"Is the pain less when you're in here?" Diana leaned forward.

Sophia nodded and then winced, raising her hand to rub her forehead.

"Y'all, I believe we need to just stay here for now. Nothing says we can't close the circle and still stay here, even bring our food here." Ashley paused, her gaze rested on Sophia's face. "If that's okay with you."

Her brain whirled with words peppered with red pain filled dots. She'd read somewhere about manifesting pain into something solid so it could be better managed. There were times when she had more clarity. Cam holding her was the one that always seemed to work. Worry, fear, problems faded when he wrapped his arms around her, whispered in her hair and relaxed.

For such an active man, she wondered how he could be so still. When she had the words and asked, he reminded her that a lot of police work involved waiting.

Somewhere in the last minute or so, the whirling words had strung together into sentences. Part of the fear was she never knew when that would happen and when they'd stir up again.

"I'd like to stay here."

"Then, Lily will stay with you and the rest of us will put the food together and fix you a plate." Diana stood and motioned to Hunter and Ashley.

"Spirit plate?" Sophia queried.

"We'll bring it in here for prayers before taking it outside," Diana said.

"Did we close the circle?"

"Not yet, Soph. We'll do it when we all are ready to leave. I think it's helpful to you to have this energy surround you."

"You may be right, Lily. I think I've a piece of malachite on the table under the window."

"I'll get it for you." Lily returned with the stone. "Do you want to hold it or do you want it on the altar?"

"Please hold it over the candle. I'll tuck it in my—, oh, I'm not wearing a bra. Where will I put it?"

Lily returned to the table and opened a drawer. Extracting a small pouch, she handed it and the malachite to Sophia.

"Thank you, I hate to be such a bother but even little things seem overwhelming some of the time and then at others, the haze clears and I think I've turned a corner and will be able to go to school tomorrow."

"I think you need to plan on this week and maybe even next being home. Your brain had a nasty jolt and it takes time for the brain to regain its equilibrium."

"I've missed so much school this year."

Lily filled the slight pause. "And that's okay. You've had a lot happen this year. Some painful and some joyful. Focus on what brings you joy and you'll heal faster."

"Words of experience?"

"Words of experience and hindsight. If Mark and the rest of you hadn't known me so well and if Jackson hadn't been willing to entertain me in the evenings, I wouldn't have been home as early as I was. My resentment and obstinacy interfered with my own recovery."

"And you might not have Jackson in your life in the same way," Diana said coming into the room.

Hunter followed with a spirit plate. She set it on Sophia's lap and nudged one of her hands to hold it.

"We give thanks to the plants and animals who have sacrificed for our benefit. We are grateful for every bite we take. We honor your part in the circle of life.

"Blessed Be." They chorused.

"There's plenty more where that comes from," Hunter said when they were seated with full plates on their laps.

As the meal came to an end, Lily said, "We've yet to talk about who will visit when. I think, unless Soph disagrees, it is probably best if we stop by at different times."

They looked at Sophia who looked back, a blank look on her face.

"We don't need to do this now," Hunter said. "I vote we enjoy ourselves and have some dessert. I brought a lovely cheesecake and I have cherry, strawberry or Marionberry toppings."

She took orders and Ashley went with her to help carry the plates back.

Lily took the few steps to Sophia. Kneeling in front of her she asked "Do you need to rest?"

"Brain tired, too much."

"Do you want to go back to your room now?"

Sophia's brow wrinkled. "Where's Cam?"

"Cam's not here but he'll be back soon."

"Wait."

Lily looked at her circle sisters who were standing in the entryway. Diana had joined them while she was talking to Sophia.

Their worried looks mirrored her own. Now she wondered why she hadn't asked Cam about how long he'd be gone. She did have his cell number but since she had no idea where he was or what he was doing, she wouldn't call. Both she and Hunter could stay as late as necessary.

A glance at the clock on the mantle showed Diana and Ashley would be leaving within the hour. Still more than enough time for him to return so they could leave together and plan on who would stop by tomorrow.

Hunter handed Sophia a plate with a slice of cheesecake with a Marionberry topping. "Your favorite, Soph."

Ashley followed with napkins and forks for everyone.

Conversation was stilted at times as they steered around normal topics about her students, classes and garden. Thankfully Diana had Madison Michelle stories and Ashley added some about her children.

Dessert finished, Diana and Ashley gathered dishes and took them to the kitchen. Sounds of the dishwasher being loaded and then turned on drifted into the other room.

When they returned, they told Sophia that leftovers were in the refrigerator and confirmed the dishwasher was running.

"Let's formally close the circle now," Diana said. "Ash and I need to get going in a little bit."

Again they reached out and formed an energetic circle. Again they said their prayer three times. They circled around Sophia's chair and hugged her lightly although holding her hands tightly.

Hunter stayed with Sophia as Lily walked out with Diana and Ashley. Out on the front porch, they verbally signed up for a day of the week to check on Sophia.

Diana and Ashley picked days and Lily assured them that between them, Hunter and she would have things covered. "Remember, Cam is still staying here so this is more a casual visit. Time for him to have a break, take a shower or whatever else he needs to do to take care of himself."

Less than ten minutes after Ashley and Diana left, Cam returned.

Sophia perked up at the sound of the garage door opening.

Hunter met him as he came in from the garage and gave him a brief rundown of the food available. "You can call any of us to pick something up, or come and stay while you run errands," she'd added.

Cam refused their help to get Sophia back to her room. "She's comfortable where she is for now. When that changes, I can manage."

Leaving, Lily and Hunter stopped beside Lily's car. "I'm worried about her dependence on him, his influence over her but on the other hand, I can't ascertain anything concrete to be worried about." Lily glanced toward the house as she spoke.

"It's because Soph has always been the one helping us. We've never seen her dependent. Even when Jonathan died, she had her mental faculties, could take care of herself."

"I know Hunter. They are just such opposites. When you look at Cam, his aura of darkness, the sense of death surrounds him. Sophia has always been about life, about living and growing and giving."

"That hasn't changed. I see her befuddled but that's the concussion. And, think about it, Lily. I don't think Cam looks as dark now as when I first met him in January."

"You may be right, Hunt. I just have this uneasy feeling."

"We'll be stopping by every day. I'm planning on two visits and a phone call."

"That may be overkill."

"You have an uneasy feeling. I'd rather be safe than sorry. If Cam doesn't like it, he'll have to learn to deal with it.

34 Dealing With It

Why he was letting this bother him? *Who the hell knows?*

Except he did. They didn't trust him and that stung. He allowed they didn't really know him but that didn't help.

How he wanted to tell them to stay away but he clenched his jaw against spewing accusations at them. When he cleared his head of the red haze, he knew all of it, his part and theirs came from a concern for Sophia.

If his visit Sunday with Ben had gone better that would have helped but Ben had a bug up his ass and wouldn't let the past rest. Why, his son, asked, did he cheat on Betsy? How could he do that to her?

And what to say when you'd promised yourself you'd never say anything about the parentage of your youngest child? She didn't even look like him although there were traces of Betsy, there were also traces of their neighbor at the time now Betsy's husband.

In the end, he'd told Ben he had to get back because his friend couldn't be left alone for very long yet—a concussion. But he didn't go right back. He'd driven around aimlessly.

Except it wasn't aimless.

Down memory lane he went, driving past the house he and Betsy had first lived in and where Ben had been born. Then the house where the-oh-so-nice and helpful neighbor was next door. They'd moved when he learned she was pregnant. Somehow he'd known this child was not his.

Cam shook his head to chase the past away. Filling the void were pictures from work. He'd seen a couple of officers he knew on break and stopped to catch up. Things were fairly quiet except for some guy who was grabbing women off the streets. He didn't rape them, just cut them up and left them bleeding in a gutter.

The lightness he'd felt on Saturday was gone, replaced with the heaviness, the darkness of his job. Death was the ultimate darkness. Was that what that sense of impending doom was about? If it was his death, that was one thing. God forbid it was Sophia's or even one of his kids. Knowing her had given him hope that maybe the chasm between he and his kids could be bridged.

As the week progressed, being with her hour after hour was torture.

Wednesday

"What are you doing?" Cam leaned against the door frame into the bedroom watching Sophia rummage through drawers.

"Finding something to wear to school tomorrow."

Even though he'd expected this confrontation, he wasn't really prepared for it.

"You have an appointment with the neurologist on Friday. You can talk to her then about being released to return to work."

"I don't want to wait."

"Any reason why?" Cam made an effort to keep his voice calm, his tone easy and his posture relaxed.

"I've been gone too long. Missed too much school this year."

Mentally he mouthed the often said words. Sophia was obsessed about the amount of time she'd missed this year.

"You have missed a lot but you do know that until your brain is healed, you won't be at your best in the classroom." He repeated the response he'd come up with that usually halted this thread.

Not today.

"My brain is just fine. I'm tracking better."

She was firing up as only a person with a head injury could—her anger control mechanism still out of commission.

"I agree you are better. The question is whether you are better enough that you can teach six class periods." He straightened and took the two steps to stand in front of her. "I've an idea." He stepped closer, his hands on her shoulders. "I think you need to see your students in the last class. And, I know it's important for them to see you.

"Why don't we go over to the school this afternoon and you can stop in and see how they're doing. Let them know how you are. Then we can see how you fare. It will give you ammunition if the doctor wants you to take another week off."

"But I don't know what to wear."

Cam helped her pick out a pair of dark slacks and a brightly patterned top. She brushed her hair and he helped her put the turquoise clips on each side to hold it back. "It's because it's backward in the mirror," Sophia had explained when she raised her hand to throw the clip.

"That's why I'll help. It isn't backwards in the mirror for me."

They stopped in the school's office. Cam was grateful the principal was out of the building. He signed in and picked up a visitor pass.

He didn't offer to help Sophia up the flights of stairs but he did keep pace beside her. She was a bit winded and using the handrail by the time they reached the top. Determined woman that she was, she marched down the hall to her room.

They'd time things so she was there just before the ending of the fifth period. She wanted to talk to her substitute before sixth period began.

Cam stood beside her along the hall blocking her from view as the bell rang. Students dashed out. When the last were out of the class, he took her arm and escorted her inside.

"Ms. Stewart!" the substitute said coming to her feet. "I didn't expect you. No one said."

When Sophia said nothing, Cam assured her they'd stopped by so her sixth period students could see she was recovering well.

On the ride over, Cam had asked Sophia what she wanted to say to the students. She wanted to know how they were, what they were studying and, with his prompting, to let them know she was okay.

Sixth period students were arriving. As they saw their Ms. Stewart, they detoured from their desks and crowded around her. The substitute attempted to have them sit in their seats but her voice was drowned out by the excited babble at seeing Sophia.

Cam waited a few minutes before stepping in. "Take your seats!" His louder, unaccustomed male voice got their attention.

"Okay, Sophia, you can tell them what you came to say." He was watching her and saw her eyes dart around the room. She had a death grip on his hand.

"Do any of you have any questions for Ms. Stewart?" Cam spoke into the silence.

One of the boys who'd been in the tussle raised his hand. "Will she be okay?"

"Ms. Stewart was concussed when her head hit the floor. She's improving but it may be a while before she's back in the classroom."

That remark was greeted with frowning pinched faces and eyes filled with worry.

"Ms. Stewart has friends who are helping her if she needs it."

All eyes shifted from him to her.

"It was important to her to come by school today," he added not knowing what else to say.

"I wanted to see you." Sophia found her voice. Her hand clutched his like a vice. "I am better. I miss you all so much." She looked over at Cam. "Captain Mitchell said some of you were worried about me and I wanted you all to see that I'm okay.

"I know you're in good hands. You've got the best substitute teacher in Fremont." She smiled at the substitute teacher, took her hand in her free one and whispered. "My memory needs more time."

Cam didn't hear the other teacher's reply but saw compassion and the glint of tears when she leaned close and said something in Sophia's ears.

Sophia turned at the door and waved before, head high, she strode out into the hall. She held onto his arm as they descended the stairs. Exchanged pleasantries for the minute it took him to turn in his Visitor's badge and sign out.

Tears were free flowing by the time they reached his car. Grateful for an automatic, Cam held her hand as he drove them back to her house.

Lily's car was at the curb. She was waiting as they came in from the garage. Sophia saw her and collapsed sobbing in Lily's arms.

"Tea," Lily mouthed guiding Sophia to the couch in the family room.

Cam put the tea kettle on and got out the fixings for a pot. The pain in his gut was not a heart attack—too low. Not indigestion—he hadn't eaten. He knew it was caused by caring too much for someone. Someone who brought light into the world. Someone he had no right to.

35 Not Yet

"Not yet, Ms. Stewart."

While she didn't like the news, Sophia appreciated the matter-of-fact way the neurologist communicated.

"Your reaction time is too slow for you to be safe driving. By your own account your cognition is unreliable. It is obvious you are better than when I first saw you."

Sophia waved her hand, "But, I still have a ways to go before I'm driving or back in the classroom."

"You are correct. And, no, I can't give you a time frame other than to say, 'not next week'.

"Are there other tasks Sophia and her friends need to be wary of?" Lily and Cam had come with her and she was glad for Lily's input. Grateful for Cam's support.

"The obvious ones are anything that means the stove or oven are turned on or water is running."

"I'm sure we can take care of any concerns in those areas," Lily assured the doctor.

When they left the doctor's office, they chatted on the way to the parking lot. Cam had brought Sophia and Lily had met them there.

"Cam?"

He turned toward Lily, "Yes?"

"If you have something you want to do, I've cleared my calendar for the remainder of the day and can take Sophia home."

"I'll stop at the grocery store and get a couple of items we're low on and pick up deli sandwiches. What do you like?"

"Veggie if they have avocado on it or roast beef with a white cheese."

"Phia, you want your standard peanut butter and jelly?"

"Only if you join me."

Cam laughed and put his arm around her. "I'll get the salt and vinegar chips you like, too."

Sophia turned her face up for a kiss, but Cam squeezed her shoulder before, with a wave in their direction, he headed to his car.

Lily linked her arm in Sophia's and they started walking to her car. "I know you wanted the appointment to end differently."

"Anyone would. But I'm realistic enough to know that if I drove off and killed or even injured someone or something because my brain took too long to figure out what to do, I'd be devastated.

"You know how awful it was for me not to remember the names of the students or the substitute. I don't want to experience that again. So, if I need to stay home for another week, I'll manage."

They'd reached Lily's car and got in. Lily turned on the ignition and backed out of the slot.

"What's hard is one minute everything seems to be working just fine and the next my brain is awhirl, confused and I can't think or talk."

"You're doing just fine."

"Right now I am but in another minute I could be rambling nonsense instead of making sense. I don't think I can handle doing that in front of a class."

"And you don't have to. When we get to your place, we'll talk more and set things up so you are safe and as independent as you can be right now."

"I've kept Cam away from his job and—,"

Lily interrupted. "I don't see Cam as someone anyone can make do anything. He's there with you because that's where he wants to be. Both Hunter and I've told him we can come if he needs to go somewhere. He's not taken us up on that offer."

When they got to Sophia's, Lily parked at the curb.

Sophia easily got out of the car and walked to the house, her steps steady. After resetting the alarm once they were inside, she put the kettle on for tea.

Lily got mugs out and Sophia brought out her assortment of teas. Fixing their drinks when the water boiled, they took their cups to the couch and sat.

"The main thing I see that needs a reminder is your tea kettle. It isn't a problem when you put it on because its whistle lets you know the water is boiling. But when you have the heat turned down and leave the pot on, it could boil dry if you are distracted."

"You think that's a problem?"

"I think it could be. However, there are strategies we can put in place to prevent that from happening."

"What else?"

"You take showers so I don't see water running as being a danger. The worse that would happen is your water bill will go up because you forget to turn it off. If you took baths, then the tub could overflow. Same thing if you washed dishes by hand but you have the dishwasher."

"Reading is hard because of the constant headache and then sometimes I can't remember what I've read."

"You can't let that bother you or you'll drive yourself crazy. Plan on rereading those books when this is behind you.

"One of us can stop by every day or even twice a day until you are fully recovered if Cam can't be here."

The outer garage door lifted. A few minutes later Cam came into the house carrying a sack of groceries and another one from the deli about a mile away.

As he put the packages on the kitchen counter, a knock sounded on the front door. Sophia got up to answer it. The alarm sounded when she opened the front door.

Cam was there in a flash, punching in the code so the shrieking noise stopped.

Frozen in place, Sophia stood with the door open, her hand on the doorknob.

Cam's hands on her shoulders, his heat and fresh scent reassured and she shook off the terror.

Lily had come to see what was happening.

"Hunter and Grant, come in." Lily motioned them in the door and towards the kitchen.

"It's all right, Phia." Cam pried her hand from the knob and closed the door. He left the alarm off and, arm around her shoulder, led her back to where everyone had gathered.

Sophia's cell phone rang and Lily handed it to her. The alarm company checking in. Tears threatened as she tried to make sense of what they were asking.

Cam whispered in her ear. "Tell them it was an accident and you are okay."

Her voice shaky, Sophia managed "Accident. Opened door by mistake.

"Yes, I'm okay. I've friends with me right now."

"A bit of excitement to whet the appetite," Grant said, pulling sandwiches and chips out of their deli bag.

Hunter had plates out and Lily was refilling the tea kettle.

Cam, his arm around Sophia's shoulders, guided her to the sliding glass doors. "After lunch we'll take a walk through your garden. Looks like things are beginning to grow. We can check on the peas we planted."

"Lunch is served," Grant announced.

Her breathing had returned to normal and so had her heart rate but her heart that was not a body organ bled with sorrow. When the alarm had gone off, she'd frozen. Did Hunter have the code? She thought Lily did but right now wasn't sure of anything.

Sophia turned when Lily touched her arm. "It's going to be okay. These things are going to happen but it will pass. A week ago you couldn't have gone to the front door on your own you were so shaky. To get through this, you have to look at what you've accomplished not how far you have to go."

"Is that how you did it?"

Lily smiled. "I had a lot of hovering that also helped."

Hunter grinned. "I know it's not nice of me to smile and I wish you didn't have to deal with this." Her turquoise gaze locked with Sophia's chocolate brown one. "It does no good to fight it or rail at the injustice. What works best is to surrender to the flow and trust all of this is in some way serving your highest good.

"Hovering saved my sanity so know we will hover as much as needed so you are whole and sane and well when this passes."

"Phia talks about gifts in bad things." The thought popped out of Cam's mouth.

"We all know that even in the darkness there is a gift of light. We can't always see it at the time and it may be years or decades later before we do," Hunter said.

"For some, they never seek the message or the lesson that all of life's experiences give us," Lily added. "We are blessed to be in The Circle because if we can't see it, one of us can and our agreement is to help each other on our journey."

Sophia relaxed as the messages resonated. It didn't matter if she remembered them or even recalled this time and place. What mattered was, in that moment, the words soothed and the bleeding in her heart stopped.

36 I Can Do This

Sophia watched Lily talk to Cam. He didn't like what she was saying. He scowled but that was all. When Lily, Hunter and Grant left thirty minutes later, signs were on all the doors to the outside reminding her to turn off the alarm. The sliding door to the backyard had a plastic encased sign reminder to turn it back on. Another series was in the kitchen and focused on making tea, specifically to turn the burner off and to put the milk back in the refrigerator between each cup.

Hunter and Grant would stop by in the morning, bringing pastries from their favorite bakery.

Diana and Matthew along with Madison Michelle would be by in the afternoon. Matthew would check out her garden and write out a list of what he saw needed to be done to keep it up. Weeding was always needed.

Sunday she and Cam were invited to Lily and Jackson's. Everyone was getting together, including Janeen and little

Sophia. Having met Maria Sophia in Italy, Sophia was astonished that there were so many Sophias in the world.

There was a time when she knew no one with her name. If that baby grew up to be as elegant as the former model, she'd...she'd what? A frown creased her forehead as the thought slipped away. Sophia breathed in through her nose and out through her mouth. The tension eased and her headache throbbed instead of pounded.

After living so many years by herself, Sophia longed for the quiet and solitude. As her gaze registered the notes, a sadness crept into her heart.

"Not yet." The doctor's words whispered through her mind. "Soon."

Sunday night

Snuggled against Cam, Sophia rested her head on his shoulder. The past two days she'd seen an improvement. When she took her time and remained calm, she did better. Her memory responded and her headache faded. Instead of occupying her primary thoughts, the pain was a drumbeat in the background.

It was time to let him go. With the notes to remind her, she'd managed an entire day not putting herself or anyone else in danger. She'd enjoyed their time at the Montgomery's and she'd remembered where things were kept in their kitchen. That was a good sign as was her ability to follow conversations. Participating was another thing but Sophia took heart that she was following the back and forth and remembering most of it.

Tipping her head back, she kissed his jaw and stretched to nibble his ear. They'd not been intimate since her accident. If she had her way, tonight would change that.

Cam kissed her brow and tightened his arms around her. From the very beginning she'd felt the luxury of being safe when in his arms. Lily had talked about Jackson being the first person to stand up for her, to put himself between her and danger. While what she had with Cam wasn't the same, there were elements that mirrored Lily's experiences.

Seeing Lily now, one would never know what she'd been through. That she'd had a concussion and worse, serious injuries. *I've no better role model than Lily.*

"Can we talk?"

"What's on your mind, babe?"

Anyone else calling her 'babe' would raise her hackles. Somehow, coming from Cam, it was an endearment but she admitted to preferring his 'Phia' to 'babe'.

"Two things."

She felt him smile when his jaw shifted on her head.

"I want to know when you plan on going back to work. I'm doing well enough I don't need someone here with me all day long."

This time when his arms tightened around her, they telegraphed his upset.

"I'm not sending you away. And I'm not telling you to leave. I'm saying I think I'm doing well enough I can be on my own for a few hours at a time. Someone is coming by at least once every day as it is in case you want a break."

"That's not why they come by."

Sophia heard the gruffness but said no more. Cam had his loquacious moments but she'd noticed there were distinct times when he used few words. Instinctively she knew this was one of the latter.

"They worry about you and want to make sure I'm taking care of you the way they think you should be cared for."

"They do worry about me but not about you taking care of me. If that was why they came by, you'd find them camped out 24/7 and their husbands would have had many talks with you to warn you away."

"As if—." He waved his hand in dismissal.

"Don't underestimate them. What they did when Lily, Diana, and Ashley were threatened? I'm not saying you'd be intimidated but you would be impressed. They aren't wimps who back down when people they care about are in danger."

"So, let me get this straight. You want me to clear out?"

"No, I want you to resume your normal life. Get up, go to work, etc. If not every day, then at least start back. Before I was hurt, you stayed with me a couple of nights a week and then we had more time on weekends."

Sophia levered up and looked him in the eye. "I'm better and I'll be okay if you go back to work. I will be back in the classroom in another week or so if I keep improving. Maybe not all day, every day but at least part of the time.

"I feel like I'm monopolizing you and there are other things you need to be doing."

"Such as?"

"Spending time with your kids. Seeing who needs your support at the precinct. Making sure everything is okay at your apartment."

"Are you done?"

"I am if you are at least thinking about what I've said."

"And the second item on your agenda?"

Sophia scooted so she was sprawled half on and half off him before holding his head between her hands and kissing him with longing, yearning and passion. "I've missed you," she whispered before nibbling his ear.

"You're sure?"

"Yes. I probably couldn't deal with making love against a wall but here in a soft bed, I'll be fine."

"Do you fantasize about the wall?"

She laughed and curled her tongue around the outside of his ear. "Not really. But I know about that position from some of the romance novels I've read. It doesn't seem too comfortable."

One hand stroked her back while the other played with her breast. "We could probably manage if you want to try."

"What I want is to not try but do, right here in this bed with you."

"I don't want to hurt you, Phia, so you'll need to take the lead."

"I can do that." She caressed his chest, flicking her nails over his flat nipples on her way to his penis. A light raking of her nails from base to tip created just the reaction she wanted. "I think you like my second agenda item better than the first."

"You must be psychic." His mouth fused with her and Sophia relaxed even as her body heated with arousal. The condom was part of their foreplay. When he was sheathed, she straddled him. Taking him into her body, at first she rode him slowly but as passion ruled, she was swept away. His hands and mouth on her breasts shot her into a climax that rocked her soul.

Breathing ragged she slowed but continued moving until his hands clutched her hips and he surged.

Sophia sank onto his chest. His arms wrapped around her. As their breathing and heart rate slowed, she acknowledged she needed him to go because she wanted too much for him to stay.

"Am I too heavy?" Sophia asked when he shifted.

His arms tightened. "No, covers."

She reached behind her and after groping around gripped a corner of a blanket. There was a sheet but she didn't want to leave the haven of his arms to find it.

"Is this enough?"

"Perfect." Cam fussed with the blanket until it was wrapped around them.

Sophia kissed his chest and then his jaw. "One of my favorite words."

37 Normal: An Ever Changing State

It was Tuesday before things changed. Monday morning, Cam's hands and mouth teased her awake with an orgasm that left her weak and sated, a smile of satisfaction curving her lips. Together they went grocery shopping. Once home she made a double batch of cookies. With her recipe book, she had no problems.

After a lunch that consisted of sandwiches and a pasta salad from the deli, they strolled through her garden. "Baby steps" she reminded herself when frustration bubbled at her brain balking at a plant's name.

But Tuesday morning, Sophia woke to Cam's leaning over her kissing her goodbye. He would check in with her later and see her tonight.

After a hot shower, she dressed and headed to the kitchen to fix tea. It occurred to her to take all the notes down but this was her first day alone and she didn't want to blow it. Caution prevailed.

Ashley stopped by around ten and together they made a batch of pecan sticky buns. She dozed once they were in the oven and was very grateful her circle sister was there to take them out. *I'm better but... .*

Diana and Madison Michelle stopped by around four. She'd come across her master plan just before they arrived. Watching M2 toddle along the pathways distracted her from identifying plants whose names she couldn't recall.

When they left, she was tired. When she heard the sound of the garage door opening, she was resting on the couch watching the Home and Garden Channel. *Cam.*

Sophia turned the television off and met him as he came in the door to the house. He looked tired. "Hard day?"

A quick kiss on the cheek and he headed to the bedroom. At first her instinct was to follow him but she waited. Instead she turned back to the kitchen where a pot of homemade soup warmed on the stove. Glad she and Diana had found it tucked in the back of the freezer, it meant dinner was waiting for them.

There was store bought bread from yesterday when they'd stopped at a bakery on the way home from grocery shopping. Normally she'd have baked bread last night but her day had been full and while her brain was working better, she still tired easily.

"How was your day?" Cam asked as he came into the family room area.

"Good. Ashley and I made pecan sticky buns and Diana and the baby were here." She pointed to the large piece of paper on the coffee table. "I found my master plan for the garden. All the plants are labeled on it. Tomorrow I plan on taking it with me when I walk through the garden."

"Something smells good." Cam sniffed the air.

"Dinner. Diana and I went through the freezer and I found a container of homemade soup. That and the bread we bought yesterday is dinner."

"I can make a salad."

"If you want to, okay, but I'm good with soup and bread. It's comfort food." Sophia took bowls from the cupboard and set them on the counter, a large ladle was already in the pot.

Cam did not talk about his day so much of the meal passed in silence. From earlier times spent with him, she knew it had not been a good day. Something dark and dangerous had happened. She shivered and questioned her decision to avoid watching the news today. *No, it was right for me. I'm better but being calm helps my brain work better.*

Even when they went to bed Cam was quiet. He held her but they did not make love. Another morning kiss woke her—he was leaving.

With Lily keeping her company, Sophia made a double batch of bread. "I fell asleep when the pecan sticky buns were baking yesterday. I'm grateful Ash was here to save them."

"Are you going to bribe me to stay until they're done by sending a loaf home with me?"

Sophia laughed. "If that's all it takes, consider yourself bribed."

Cam did not come to dinner or to stay the night. He did call but was vague about what was going on. Sophia did not sleep well that night. Even though she clutched his pillow and his fresh minty scent surrounded her, his heat and his arms were missing.

Thursday marked two weeks since the accident. Today when she strolled through her garden, it looked more familiar. She knew the names of almost all of the plants. Could she manage a classroom?

Leery she could make it through an entire day, she called and spoke with personnel. After explaining her predicament, they agreed she'd try her first period class next Monday and see how it went.

Personnel already had a statement from the neurologist that she was to return to work in increments.

It crossed her mind to leave a message for Cam but she hoped to see him that evening.

She didn't so before she went to bed, she did call and when she got voice mail, told him she'd be starting back to work with first period only on Monday.

Friday when Ashley stopped by, she and Cam were invited to "grill night" Saturday. When Cam called Friday evening to tell her he couldn't make it that night either, she told him about the invitation and explained 'grill night' was usually hamburgers, hot dogs and sometimes steak. They also grilled vegetables and had a fantastic potato thing they did.

"I'll try to make it but don't wait for me."

She gave him Ashley and Daniel's address. "Take care of yourself."

"I am."

"If I could drive, I'd bring you cookies and sweet rolls."

"Don't overdo, Phia," he'd cautioned.

"I'm not Cam. And I don't do any serious baking unless someone is here with me.

"I've been spending time getting reacquainted with my garden. The peas we planted are about ready to sprout. I'm still not sure what I'm going to do about planting this year. I don't feel the excitement or anticipation that I have in years past."

"If I don't make it Saturday, I'll come see you on Sunday."

Sophia wanted to tell him she missed him that she hadn't meant for him to be so distant but she didn't. He had a difficult job and his absence, his distance was what he did to protect her from the death and darkness that was part of his life.

"I'll make a meatloaf and then you can take a meatloaf sandwich to work on Monday."

Several seconds of silence passed but Sophia refused to break it.

"Looks like we've got a plan."

There was a note of resignation in that sentence but Sophia ignored it. She'd see him on Sunday. Monday they'd get up together and she'd go off to school and he would travel to the precinct.

That's when it hit her, she still couldn't drive. *How am I going to get to "Grill Night" much less school if I'm not released to drive?*

Diana and Matthew lived closest. She asked them to take her. When they arrived, she asked Diana to ride with her while she tried to drive to the school. "It's less than a mile away and I can take residential streets to avoid Monday traffic.

"This way, if I can't do it, I'll pull over. Diana can drive my car home and I'll ride with you. I know it's a—."

"It's a reasonable plan," Matthew interrupted.

Sophia backed out of the garage and waited until the door closed before continuing into the street. Matthew followed in his extended cab truck as she took the familiar route to school.

"How do you feel?" Diana asked.

"I see you aren't a white knuckled passenger." Sophia joked.

"And you are avoiding my question."

"Nervous. And, I'm tired and my head is pounding."

"Then driving Monday isn't an option. You want to be at your best when you are with your class. Expending all your energy on the drive here, isn't your best plan."

"Are we trading places?" Sophia asked.

"We are because, while I'm sure you can tough it out and get us safely to Ashley's, I want you able to enjoy yourself."

"How are you getting to school?" Cam asked over dinner on Sunday.

"Matthew will stop in the morning and take me on his way to a job site. Lily or Diana will pick me up and bring me home. I tried driving—don't Cam. Listen to what I have to say before you challenge me.

"Diana and Matthew came to pick me up for Grill Night, you missed great food by the way. Diana was with me while I tried driving. I made it to school but it wiped me out. It doesn't make sense for me to drive to school and then not be able to go in or get myself home."

"Call and tell them I'll drop you off. No point in Matthew going out of his way."

"Your precinct is in the opposite direction of school, Cam."

"Less than a mile." His Irish moss green gaze stared. "Dropping you off at school on my way in is not a hardship. That is unless you don't want me to do this?"

"No, wherever did that come from?"

He didn't answer and in reality she didn't expect him to. They got through dinner and watched a travelogue together.

"With Mitchell as a last name, you must have some Irish heritage."

"Somewhere in the past."

"Do you know when your ancestors immigrated here?"

"No, do you?"

"Way back when, the forbearers of the Denton family were the Rawsons and Edward Rawson was on the second boat—right behind the Mayflower.

"Have you ever thought of doing a genealogy search?"

"Not really."

They watched the rest of the show in silence. One of the many things she liked about Cam was the comfortable silence. His arm was around her shoulder and her head rested in the crook of his arm. Her hand was on his thigh and his free hand lightly held it. From time to time he absently rubbed his thumb on her palm. She knew when he realized it because he stopped.

Her heart ached for the closeness she used to feel with him, for the confidences he shared about his work and his children. She wanted to ask but he was almost as defended against her as he'd been in the very beginning two months ago.

Two months. She'd known him longer because he'd come into her life in November but it was the end of December when she'd returned from Ireland that they really began to create a relationship.

All I'll ever have is now. And to have now, it must be enough.

The program over, they retired. She would not let him leave without making love. With Jonathan she seldom initiated their love making.

With Cam it was different. He didn't have to have that level of physical intimacy. He enjoyed their cuddling and talking—well, lately the talking was nonexistent. But he held her and allowed her to hold him. They might fall asleep with her head on his chest but the last couple of times he'd been here, she'd awakened and found their positions changed.

What was making him so distant? Try as she might, nothing that came to mind that made sense to her.

In truth what really mattered was he was here—now.

Sophia slipped off her robe and gown and climbed into bed. His brow arched.

"Unless you're too tired, I plan on seducing you." She inwardly cringed at her bossy, challenging voice.

"If you did a really good job, I wouldn't be too tired."

"I'm not sure what that means, Cam." Sophia sat back on her heels.

"It means, Phia, that while I may not be aroused at this moment, I'm sure your seducing me will correct that almost immediately."

She curled up next to him, her hands wandering. Torso muscles twitched under her touch. Movement under the sheet—his penis did too.

"Are you going to tell me what you'd like me to do?" Her hand was mere inches away from her eventual destination.

"Not tonight," Cam's voice was gravelly.

Sophia stopped and pulled away.

Cam stared at her, his mouth open in protest.

"Condom," she said as she rubbed against him while leaning over to the nightstand.

"You know they have special treatment for torturers," he growled.

Sophia laughed as she settled down next to him. The condom in her hand, she traced patterns with its edge. "How am I doing? Are you feeling sleepy?"

"Tease."

"Not for much longer." Her hand wrapped around him and he grew larger, hotter, harder. "Do men ever?"

"You talk too much," Cam tipped her face up and sealed his lips over her mouth.

Sophia let her passion and longing flow into that kiss. He didn't object when she continued to kiss and fondle him until he took the condom from her and rolled it over his burgeoning erection.

Cam surged inside her.

Sophia relished the fullness, the heightened sensations as he plunged faster and faster.

Together they plunged into the abyss of bliss.

38 Too Much

Cam sat at his desk supposedly writing a report except his fingers didn't move across the keyboard. He stared at the still blank form. This morning he'd dropped Sophia off at school. She'd leaned over and kissed his cheek. Her breath as she said "Thank You" tickled his ear and his cock twitched.

"Not a problem." Nothing more than those three words. Not call if you need something much less "see you later".

Scrubbing his hands over his face, he pulled his concentration back to the screen. A few filled in blanks later, his mind wandered. Or maybe it strayed. Perhaps jigged. *Whatever.*

It took effort to bring his attention back to the task at hand.

"Hey Captain."

Grateful for the interruption, Cam clicked 'save' and turned to Officer Smith, who'd recently transferred to this precinct.

"Heard you're getting cookies from the Stewart woman."

"The Stewart woman?" A warning simmered beneath the simple question.

"Yeah, Sophia Stewart. Met her in conjunction with another case I was on last year. Nope it was November, I think the year before. Custodial interference, child endangerment."

"Ms. Stewart endangered a child?"

"Are you kidding? You must not know her very well. She and Lily Hughes are formidable. Well the other women are also except for the mother. She was battling breast cancer."

"Ah," Cam found his footing as bits and pieces of conversations popped into his mind. *Ashley's ex kidnapped the kids.* "Didn't know you'd been on that case."

"First responder. Ms. Hughes would have battered the door to the house down if I hadn't been there."

"And Ms. Stewart?"

"She sent me my own personal box of a dozen pecan sticky buns and cinnamon rolls along with a dozen of those fabulous peanut butter cookies." She flashed a cheeky grin. "It's all over the force that she's been sending treats here. It's why I put in a transfer. Those cookies are addictive."

"Not sure there'll be many more treats sent here, Smith. Ms. Stewart has more things to do than supply North Precinct with food."

"Then you must have a private agreement with her."

"Out-of-line, Smith."

Officer Smith straightened but didn't salute. "Yes, sir." She pivoted and strode away but not before Cam saw the cheeky grin reappear on her face.

"Hell!"

Thirty minutes later, Cam had finished filling out the fifteen minute report. He perused it one more time before clicking send and speeding it on its way.

Next on his list was to sort out the requests from Sophia's sixth period class and assign them to different officers for 'ride-alongs'. Because he didn't want to assign anyone on a Friday or Saturday night nor did he want to have them out too late, he listed all the Wednesdays and Sundays until Spring Break. *They probably wouldn't mind Spring Break but more work for me because families may have plans.*

He sent the list to the various officers who had volunteered for this project as well as the school counselor who would coordinate that end.

Checking the clock, he sent a text message to Ben confirming their dinner plans. It was slow going but he hoped he was making some progress with his eldest. At least Ben had good memories of family time when Cam had been around.

Twitchy, Cam got up and paced through the building. When there was an opportunity he had a few words with the different members of the staff. After fifteen minutes or so, he stopped chatting and just waved. The most persistent comment had to do with those damn cookies. He couldn't bring himself to say there'd be no more cookies coming their way because he wouldn't be seeing Ms. Stewart.

Checking out on the big board, Cam strode outside needing to stretch his legs and work out the mess his life had become. He chided himself for allowing Sophia to become so important in his life. He berated himself for spending so much time with her. He shoved his hands deep in his pockets and cursed under his breath. People were giving him a wide-berth as he strode—*Not even, I'm stomping and scowling. Get a grip, Mitchell.*

There was nothing else for him to do. He had to break it off. He knew she cared about him. Sophia wasn't the kind of woman who had just anyone in her bed. And she talked to him. Although lately some of it was gibberish because of the concussion, last night wasn't gibberish. Last night had been the best sex he'd probably ever had. *You're a bastard, Mitchell. It wasn't sex. She made love to you and you loved her back.*

Disgusted with himself, Cam returned to the precinct building and by sheer force of will, dedicated the remainder of the day to work.

That night he stretched out on his couch, some sports talk show on the television but Cam had the sound muted. Dinner with Ben had ended badly. He saw his son's clenched jaw that mirrored his own. Pushing Ben to set something up or even talk to the other two had not been his best move.

Why had he done it?

Cam reached for the glass with three fingers of scotch. He shifted so his head now rested on the arm and he could more easily take a drink. Somehow he never seemed to need a drink when he was at Sophia's.

Here it was different.

Here he always needed a drink to relax enough to sleep.

Turning the television off, Cam got ready for bed sipping his scotch as he readied his automatic coffee pot for morning, washed up and set out clothes. He added another finger of the amber colored liquor to his glass before shucking off his clothes and, after setting the glass on the night stand, flopping on the bed.

In the dark he assessed his day.

High point was dropping Sophia off at work, her kiss and Thank You.

Low point was dropping Sophia off at work, her kiss and Thank You.

It would be so easy to stay with her longer, to make that a morning habit but he cared about her too much to do that to her. Sophia Camila Denton Stewart was made for sunshine not shadows, for laughter not tears, for life not death.

Cam reached for the glass and finished it off. Grabbing a pillow he held it close and wished it was a warm, soft woman who smelled like vanilla.

39 He's Gone

March 12, 2006

Sophia knocked on the door of the Murphy House. Hunter answered. When she walked inside, Lily, Diana and Ashley were already there. The low table in front of the brightly burning fireplace showcased the beginnings of an altar.

They were meeting at the Murphy House because Sophia asked that someone else host today's meeting of The Circle. Hunter volunteered.

Cam had not been back to spend the night since Sunday. He'd called her Wednesday to see how things were going. He'd also come for dinner on Friday but left after less than two hours. It was a busy night in the world of crime.

Later Sophia noticed the few personal items he'd left there were gone. *While I was fixing dinner, he must have packed them up and put them in his car.* She was so used to his moving around the house, it never occurred to her he was leaving.

The Circle's business side was The Golden Cauldron. Today's agenda included an update on their house totem business, review bank balances, etc. Sophia knew everyone was excited about the prospect of turning Lily's little house into a safe haven for young mothers escaping abusive situations. They also had an idea of buying some land where they could hold classes and retreats. Purchasing land was a long term goal. The idea about the little house? That could be set in place rather quickly.

As always, the house had been smudged before the rest of them arrived. Hunter was supplying the food so they only had themselves to bring along with their ideas. Sophia struggled out of her coat, struggled to put a smile on her face and even struggled to make her feet move across the room to where the others gathered.

Her skirt pockets held her altar offerings. Her power animal, the bluebird she put in the west, the void. Her prayer as she set it on the bright multi-colored silk surface, "Show me the way to the light." Her bluebird was accompanied by lapis lazuli, sodalite, blue calcite, and turquoise.

In the north she added a small selenite wand to a piece of snowflake obsidian, blue lace agate, a plinth of selenite and a crystal cluster.

Continuing around the altar to the East, Sophia laughed. They'd all brought robins in various poses. She added hers to the four others. "Guess who wants spring to arrive and soon," she quipped.

Her red faceted glass heart along with one made of rose quartz joined a piece of carnelian, yellow calcite, red jasper and yellow fluorite in the South.

The center held a handmade pottery bowl Hunter had found in one of the Kinsale shops. Of course the silk scarves had been purchased while they were in Italy for Gabriella's wedding.

Everyone was represented here and the energy was warm and welcoming.

Hunter had a laptop with her and clicked around. She heard a phone ringing and then the screen showed Elizabeth and Gabriella waving at them.

Technology was rapidly invading their lives. A part of her was distressed at handwritten letters being replaced by emails and now this?

But this allowed her to see her circle sisters, allowed them to participate in real time. Maybe technology had its benefits. *I'm just out of sorts.*

Together they raised their arms and prayed.

"We are the light

"We are the source

"Through us love flows

"Throughout the world."

Elizabeth started their business meeting.

"With Gabby so close and Shannon also available, I'm scheduling retreats on the Sabbats and workshops on the months in between. If I'm not here, Shannon will lead them. Of course she'll be paid for her time. One reason Shannon is so excited is that she would like to transition to another job but feels the need to take at least a month off. By committing to support the Retreats and Workshops for this next year, that will allow her to manifest that dream."

"I'm doing house totems for Giovanni," Gabriella's grin filled the screen. "I love being so close to E and Maeve. I'm going to learn to ride a horse! Can you imagine that! Dickens has assured me that I'm a natural because the horses all seem to like me.

"I'm so excited I'll be able to see you all soon. Less than two months until I can give you all a real-time hug instead of a virtual one."

"I totally agree," Elizabeth added. "Now what's going on with everyone else?"

"I took your advice, Gabby and talked to Doc S. She's agreed we can use her cabin for small retreats if we clear the dates with her and accept one young woman she refers to us." Diana's excitement radiated and enveloped them all.

"We are going to talk about how to set up Lily's little house as a haven for young mothers escaping abusive relationships. Grant's helping us with the paperwork and whatever other legal stuff we might need. If he can't do it because he hasn't taken the bar in Oregon, Ms. Lawford will." Hunter's grinned and turned the laptop screen so E and Gabby could see Ashley.

"I'm talking to Ms. Muir, the social worker who helped us so much when the children were taken." Ashley no longer wrung her hands or cried when she talked about that terrifying time. "We thought she'd be a good resource because we'll need to have professionals available. And, she knows the child welfare system."

"I'm doing house totems for Jackson. We had talked at one time about creating a pamphlet for the home owners, something beyond the Certificate we agreed on. I'm toying with the idea of putting something like that together. We'd send the people we've already worked with complimentary copies. I want to make them compelling because that will support the homeowner staying respectful of their house totem but it may also generate interest."

"And," Lily continued, "Our bank account is healthy even though we've had many expenses these past twelve months with so many trips to Ireland and Italy."

Sophia had listened to what everyone else was contributing. In the past she'd always had her garden and her baking but these days? "I don't know what to do. I don't seem to have much energy for anything yet. I don't even know if I'll put in a garden this year. Of course what's already there will bloom and produce fruit. P-p-peas were planted. C-C-Cam helped me with those."

Lily appeared beside her, wrapped her arms around her and held her tight. "You deserve a break, Soph. We've each had our times when we felt, probably, pretty much as you do. That maybe we weren't pulling our weight. Time does heal us and time can brings us new opportunities."

"I know that in my head but my heart struggles."

"And that's because you are a loving, caring, compassionate woman who is loved by many."

"Soph?" Gabriella called to her.

She looked at the laptop screen at Gabriella's serious face, mirrored by Elizabeth's who was still next to her.

"Your room is always ready at the villa."

"And here," Elizabeth added. "You only have to let us know which airport, which airline and what date and time and we'll pick you up.

"Seamus loves cooking for you."

"And Adolfo loves trying to get your recipes from you. You'd do me a favor by worming his tiramisu recipe from him so I can have it when I'm in Fremont."

"Thank you both," Sophia's voice was shaky as was her smile. "I know I'm loved by everyone in The Circle."

"And your students past and present," Diana added.

"And our children regardless of their ages," Hunter now stood on Sophia's other side. "Without you in their lives, well, I know you've made a big difference to more than just my Logan."

"But neither our children nor any of us are Cam." Diana's formal voice held a sad, soft note.

Sophia shook her head. "No, you aren't," she whispered. "He's gone. Physically that is. I can still feel him. It's more what he hasn't said than what he has said that I know he has this idea that he'll hurt me if he stays, that he isn't good enough for me."

"And that means he's terrified of his feeling for you," Lily's arm around Sophia's waist squeezed her closer. "And, while I'm sure he knows his not being around hurts, he thinks it doesn't or won't hurt as much as whatever he thinks he might do in the future."

"It's the darkness, the sense of death he brings into my life that he worries about." Sophia managed the words through the pain of the truth of them. When she'd first met him, he was her savior. The light at the top of the dark path. As time passed she wondered if she might be his savior. A beacon of light to guide him out of the dark abyss.

"Do you think the light frightens him?" Sophia asked the others. "Do you think he's so accustomed to the dark, the feel of death that light and love scare him?"

"It's possible," Diana spoke up. "I know there was a time when I didn't feel worthy of Matthew's love. My world was pretty dark. Not in any way like Cam's but there are similarities."

"What helped you then?"

"Two things. One he loved me unconditionally. Even when he turned away after Dennis's accident, he never stopped loving me. And, eventually I found the courage to accept his love, to trust in it, to claim my happiness."

"If you don't want to put a label on your feelings, Soph. Don't." Ashley's grey gaze focused on Sophia. "Keep sending him light, keep him in your prayers, stay with him energetically for now. As time passes, you'll know how to proceed. At least that's my advice. I'm doing some version of that with Anthony. 'Course I love him, but he's still insisting on going to live with Art. All I can do right now is love him and hold him in the light, trust that in the end all will turn out as it should."

"Lily's reminded me that all I-I ever had or wi-will have is the present."

"And missing him tells me those times when the two of you were in the present—well, they were special times." Lily let her gaze travel around the room. "I suppose for a penance—that is if you feel the need to offer one—not that a penance is expected but the one I have in mind would be welcomed when next we meet."

"Lily," Elizabeth warned. "If you are going to suggest the decadent chocolate cake, you had better change the timeline."

"You will have very disappointed, bordering on angry circle sisters," Gabriella added.

Lily leaned close. "They are psychic because that was what I was going to suggest. Ashley and Jackson are dying to learn the recipe and I know would gladly be your sous chefs."

Sophia couldn't remember the last time she'd made the six layer cake. Seeing everyone's looks of anticipation teased a smile from the brooding frown.

"If I feel the need for penance, I would not need any help, especially if it was something as simple as a chocolate cake." She could make six of them and send one complete cake home with each of them. Maybe a seventh so she could have a piece and share it with everyone. *They'd be so surprised if I trotted out six extra tall cake boxes.* Imagining the looks on her face eased the darkness sitting on her chest.

"I'll think about it."

A song and their prayer ended their time with Elizabeth and Gabriella.

"That was awesome," Ashley said while Hunter put the laptop away.

"It was. And I've a suggestion," Diana said, still standing. "I'd like to eat next. We can leave the circle intact and decide what we want to do after food."

"An excellent suggestion. We should act on it." Hunter was already gliding across the floor to the kitchen area.

Sophia noticed a pot on the stove and the makings for tea as well as plates and bowls on the counter. As she approached, the aroma of warm bread wafted toward her.

"We're having a homemade vegetable soup, bread, organic salad greens with a vinaigrette dressing and Grant and Logan's ice cream for dessert. Help yourselves." She waved her hand across the counter.

"I've got the spirit plate ready." Hunter picked the small plate up from beside the stove and drizzled a teaspoon of soup over the bread and salad. Opening the freezer, she used a clean spoon to nip a bit of the ice cream from the carton and tapped it on top.

Raising the plate shoulder high she held Sophia's hand with the other. When everyone was connected Hunter prayed.

"Great Spirit, Goddess, Gaia we give thanks to the plants that make up this meal, to the animals who provided the milk and cream and butter. We honor all life and are grateful for their sacrifice so that we may live."

"Blessed Be," they chorused.

Sophia was included in the conversations but was drawn away from them to wherever Cam was. If she closed her eyes, she could see him. *He's safe. That's what counts. He's safe.* Was it wrong to hold someone in protective light if they didn't know? This was the place to find out.

At a lull in the conversation she asked the question foremost in her mind.

"We've been doing energetic work for some time now. We've practiced gathering the energy from the light of love and sending it out to the world, first with The Lady and then here in Fremont and most likely individually.

"If you hold your husbands in protective light, did you talk to them beforehand? In other words, do you have their agreement? Is it wrong or unethical to do that without their consent?"

The chatter died down as each of them pondered the question.

Lily was the first to speak. "I don't know that I've asked Jackson but he knows when he travels, I always hold him in white light while he is gone."

"I've not done that with Grant because we're together on any real trips, but I do know," she quirked her fingers, "when something is going on. I'm talking about something bothering him. He's had years of practice in keeping a neutral face, covering up his emotions but on some level I know when something has happened and when it's just him being him."

"So you're connected to him energetically," Sophia clarified.

Hunter nodded.

"There was an accident on a worksite last month. I didn't know what had happened, but I had a gut feeling that something was wrong." Ashley took a deep breath and sighed. "It's a blessing and a curse to be that tied together. I debated for thirty minutes before I called. Actually tortured myself for thirty minutes. I knew something had happened. Knew it as clear as anything.

"Daniel wasn't involved. He was next to his guy when the saw bounced and almost cut a finger off. Thankfully he was wearing protective gloves and glasses so no severe damage was done." Ashley shook her hands and shivered at the memory.

"I haven't had that experience." Diana gave Ashley a sympathetic look. "I have that connection with Madison Michelle. Sometimes I can hear her talking to me in my mind. She's staring at me and I can just hear her.

"I do know when Matthew walks in the house, even when the first thing he does is give me a kiss." She blushed and cleared her throat. "I know if something happened during the day. I've not thought that much about why I know but I do."

"Does this help, Soph?" Lily's blue-eyed gaze searched Sophia's brown one.

"When we were in Italy, I could see Cam here in Fremont. There are times I feel his presence even though I'm alone. I've thought I was crazy when I smelled his fresh minty scent when standing on my patio."

"The connection with him is strong." Lily held Sophia's hand. "Trust, Sophia. Trust that what happens is what needs to be. And always remember you are held by all of us in The Light of Love.

"I know we didn't actually answer part of your question, the one about whether we've talked to our husbands. I'd venture to guess that none of us have had an outright conversation with them but because they know us, have been in ceremony with us, they would also know on some level—know that we do all we can to make sure they are safe and return to us."

40 Trust

Sophia's life had had a pattern that was now disrupted. She had starts of tomatoes and other vegetables. She'd left a message for Cam about the starts but had not heard back. When Diana stopped by Sunday evening, she'd left with a flat of plants: zucchini, tomato, pumpkin, three different kinds of lettuce, radishes and cucumbers. She just trusted that keeping the spaghetti, acorn and butternut squash was the right decision.

"I'm sharing this largesse with Ashley," Diana said putting the plants in the trunk of her car while Sophia held M2.

"Good idea. All of the kids will enjoy watching them grow." Sophia handed the baby to Diana who expertly settled her into the car seat.

"Take care of yourself, Soph," Diana said and hugged her.

"I've worked my way back to working full time this week but I'm exhausted by the time I get home. Something light to eat and I'm ready to call it a day."

"Matthew has his pot of chili on the stove. I'll bring a container by tomorrow. He'll be thrilled with these plants and that way you don't have to cook."

"I'll welcome Matthew's chili tomorrow. I can swing by on my way home from school."

"You just get yourself home. M2 and I'll come by around four o'clock with chili and cornbread."

Sophia waved as Diana pulled away from the curb. None of her circle sisters pulled into the driveway any more. *Still holding out hope Cam will come by.*

Back in the house, she pulled out her mixer and the ingredients to make bread. Unseeing she watched programs on television while it raised and raised again. Setting the timer for one hour, she placed the contraption next to her when the bread went in the oven.

At least I get some pleasure from my baking. Not the anticipation of creating something good to eat I used to have. But I do have a sense of accomplishment when I see the results on the counter.

It crossed her mind to make a batch of cookies. A fleeting thought she pushed away in favor of taking a nap. The timer woke her. Bread on the counter to cool, Sophia shuffled back to the bedroom and bed.

Full darkness awaited her when she woke. Sophia staggered into the bathroom to wash her face and brush her teeth before crawling under the covers. In the twilight between wakefulness and sleep, she mentally sought Cam. He was 'there' but far away. *Tired.* Wrapping her arms around his pillow, she drifted into a deep sleep where dreams were lost.

True to her word, Diana and M2 knocked on her door at four on Monday. The cornbread was still warm. Sophia put the container of chili in a pot to reheat it. "Chili is one of those dishes that's always better the next day. Be sure and thank Matthew for me."

"Have you had time to check your email?" Diana sat on the couch watching M2 explore the bag of toys Sophia had put aside for her.

"No, should I check now?"

"Email from Hunter. They arrived safely. And she thanked you in all caps for the double batch of cookies you made for Janeen as well as the batch for them.

"Jason met them at the airport. Today Grant drove him into Providence to the law firm he'll be clerking at this week. This week they are all staying at Grant's place on the shore. Hunt said Grant was dropping by a couple of friends who are faculty at Yale. Doesn't hurt for them to know Grant is mentoring Jason.

"Final details aren't confirmed. The biggest drawback is transportation. Grant's place isn't exactly close to shops. And if Jason is commuting to school every day that leaves Janeen and the baby alone."

"What about Martha? I thought she was living there."

"She has been but has offered to move out. And, she didn't sign on to help a teen mom. But, if she remained there, Hunt said something about she was visiting family this week, that would solve the transportation problem—or it could."

"Do you really think Grant and Hunter will come back here without setting them up with some form of transportation?"

Diana laughed. "Not likely."

Relief that her former student had a chance to make a life for herself clouded Sophia's eyes with tears. Everywhere she looked, she saw couples. And not just couples but happy couples.

Trust. Stay in trust. But it was a constant battle to stay in trust that all was as it should be.

Tuesday

Sixth period was finally over. These students were still walking on tiptoes around her. Even though it was her easiest class because no one was disruptive and everyone was prepared, it was still the hardest class of the day.

Unnatural. They were teenagers, seniors and trying so hard to be perfect. "Talk about senioritis and perfection." She jotted the note to herself for Friday on the monthly calendar on her desk.

Friday

Sophia had planned a shortened class today because she still wanted to talk about perfection and the need for these students to be themselves. While many thoughts had come and gone over the past three days, she'd written nothing down because this was part of her "trusting" all was as it should be.

"Before I dismiss you," she began not sure what the next words would be, "there is something important I want to talk with you about." Sophia leaned back against her desk. Every student sat tall in their seats, eyes trained on her, eager expressions on their faces. She took a calming breath before continuing.

"First I want to thank you for helping me get back to teaching a full class load. Your efforts to be on time, cooperative, prepared, your self-control has made a big difference in my taking on all six classes. I will be grading papers over Spring Break and hope to have everything returned to you on Monday.

"However, there is more I want to say.

"While you are on Spring Break, take care of yourselves. Use your new-found skills to keep yourselves safe. Spend some time considering how you've been able to accomplish everything you have in this class over the past three weeks. The time you spend reviewing how you've handled yourselves is key to your future.

"It isn't about being perfect. None of us are. So, what is it about?

"I think it has to do with focus, or focus on priorities. However, that would be true for me. There are other perspectives. I look forward to further discussions with you on this topic."

A hand shot up before she dismissed the class.

"Ms. Stewart, we missed you being our teacher."

"And we wanted you to come back sooner rather than later."

"We talked and looked up concussions and knew what we needed to do to… ."

"To set the environment that was best for you so you could be here."

Through eyes misted with tears, Sophia saw heads nodding. "Thank You. You've done an incredible job." Her voice shook with those same tears.

"Class dismissed."

Sophia had stayed in trust these past few weeks at school. Now it was time to take her own advice. How had she managed at school but not at home? *I've stayed in trust I could do it and I did. So my question is not about school but about what I need to do to stay in trust when I'm home.*

Home is where my memories of Cam are strongest. How can I turn those memories into a strength?

41 Shot

To celebrate finishing the grading of all class papers, Sophia had invited Lily and Diana over for the evening. Jackson was hanging out with Matthew and M2. Daniel had taken Ashley and the kids to Bend for the weekend to celebrate their first anniversary. And Hunter and Grant were still in Rhode Island making sure everything was in place before they returned.

She'd heard from Janeen who'd asked her advice on how to make Grant, especially, stop buying things. "In many ways, Janeen, it isn't about you or little Sophia or even Jason. He's doing it for himself." In the end she'd explained, "He missed out on this part of his daughter's life. I know he enjoys shopping and it's a new experience for him to shop in baby stores."

To prepare for the celebration, she'd searched her recipe files for an old recipe for ginger snaps. From memory she whipped up a batch of shortbread.

At her request, they sat in chairs in her sacred space, candles and the rock salt lamp bathed the room in soft flickering light. She'd built a fire and it too added to the ambiance along with some heat.

Three friends sharing a cup of tea, cookies and conversation. Relaxing, enjoying time with each other, thankful their bond endured.

"We need to do this more often." Lily reached for a ginger snap cookie and took a bite. "Delicious." A sip of tea came next. "I love how the hot tea melts the ginger and the flavors meld and dance on my tongue."

"My days have exploded with a toddler in the house. Matthew is installing baby gates everywhere because M2 has figured out how to get around any other barrier. I hope I've the strength and flexibility to step over them and then bend over and pick her up.

"I did put in a request for something that I can open instead of stepping over. He and M2 went shopping, came home happy and told me not to worry, they had it covered." A smile of remembering tilted her lips as she looked into her tea cup as if to see the scene again.

"Are we on for Sunday? I've not talked to Elizabeth or Gabriella."

"I did, Soph." Lily plucked another ginger snap from the plate. "E's flying to Italy tomorrow so she and Gabby can have some girl time."

"Where will Maeve be?" Diana nibbled her shortbread.

"Michael is keeping her. E's milk is drying up so they are already switching Maeve to a bottle. E's been using a breast pump and storing milk so they have some on hand. I think Matthew is part of the reason for Michael taking the plunge."

"What about Daniel?"

"Those kids are older. Michael'd have no problems there but a baby? Seeing Matthew with M2 in a front pack. Hearing him talk about taking her to work with him, well, taking her everywhere. The men are somewhat competitive."

Diana and Sophia laughed. "Somewhat?" they said in unison.

"Whatever it was, Michael will have Maeve and E will be with Gabriella."

"So do we want to be a fly on the wall when he changes her poopy diaper?" Sophia observed.

"E said he's a master at diaper changing and doesn't seem to mind the messy ones."

"Hunter will either be back or join us on that computer program."

"Then we're set." Lily bit into her third cookie. "Are you counting how many cookies I've had?"

"Of course we are." Sophia smiled and nudged the plate closer to her. "If there are any left, you can take them with you."

"Thanks. That may help me keep my hands off them unless Diana starts eating them. Then I'll have to chop off her hand." Lily patted the yet-to-offend hand. "Stick with the shortbread, it's delicious."

"I agree about the shortbread. And just so you know, I am not intimidated about the ginger snaps." Diana sipped her tea. "Have we decided where we're meeting on Sunday?"

"I'd like to offer my place," Lily said. "Eleanor is back with her daughters and Jackson could invite the men and children to movie time downstairs."

"Or they could all come to our place," Diana said. "And I'm sure Daniel could easily be persuaded to do "Grill Night" and we could join them when we're done. We wouldn't have to think about food."

A sharp pain stabbed Sophia's chest. Shooting pain ripped through her shoulder another buried in her abdomen. Sophia reeled with the impact. *Cam.* She tried to stand but fell back into the chair.

Wild with terror, she tried to get up.

Lily and Diana were beside her, their hands on her shoulders holding her down.

"I have to get up. Somethings happened to Cam."

They helped her to her feet and into the family room where her cell phone sat on the kitchen counter.

No messages.

She picked it up and dialed his number. It rang and rang but no answer.

Diana put her arm around Sophia's shoulder and Lily did the same saying, "Take a deep breath. You'll hyperventilate and be of no use when we find out what's happened."

"He's been hurt. Here and here." She touched the places on her body that still held the aftershocks of the assault. "I think he's been shot."

"Stay in the car," Cam ordered the young man on the ride-along. "No matter what happens do not get out. Is that clear?"

"Yes sir."

Cam exited his car thankful this kid was interested in law enforcement. He'd do what he'd been told.

A nerve twitched along his spine.

Something didn't feel right here.

"Need backup," he said into his shoulder mic.

"Where are you?"

"40th and Clemons"

"On its way," the dispatcher responded.

The guy had his arm around the woman's neck, holding her in front of him. Her head pulled back, the woman was on her tiptoes.

"Most problems can be solved by talking." Cam was alert but took a step closer. They were in that dim place between street lights.

"Fuck you!" The man dragged her back a step.

That bad feeling in his gut intensified. Nothing for it but to see if he could stall until backup arrived.

"You know sometimes things aren't as bad as they seem." Cam paid attention to his gut and quelled the urge to step closer.

A siren sounded in the distance. *Backup.*

Movement between cars across the street and behind the couple drew his attention.

The man pulled the woman back another step and earned Cam's focus.

A shadowy figure emerged from between vehicles parked along the road. Cam drew his gun just as a shot rang out. He staggered back with the impact when the bullet hit his left shoulder.

He managed to get his own shot off before the blast of the second shot slammed into his side. Collapsing against the side of the squad car, a third shot screamed past his ear as Cam slid to the ground, darkness claiming him.

"Officer down." The kid's words filtered through Cam's pain. Even though his breathing was shallow, the acrid smell of exhaust, the smoke from a wood fire registered despite the cold from the pavement that seeped into his bones. He couldn't seem to control his body. Was he dying?

Phia. If he could only see her one more time.

"Captain? Help is on the way." The kid's voice shook. "I have to stop the bleeding."

Agony seared through him as pressure was applied to his gut and shoulder.

A siren roused him, grew closer, then cut off.

Back-up.

The pain had eased. Had he passed out? He struggled to sit up. Nausea threatened. The pounding in his head, the ringing in his ear drowned out all other sounds. He couldn't die yet. He had to see Phia.

Big hands pushed him down. "Ambulance is on its way," a deep, unfamiliar voice said. "Hold on Captain."

More sirens wailed in the distance. He squinted up at two blurry faces. "*Phia*?"

Hands gently searched pockets, removing his cell phone.

"I heard four shots." The kid again. "I think one was the Captain."

"Good to know," the officer said.

"*Phia*?" He'd be okay with dying if he could just see her one more time.

"Do you know who this 'Phia' is?" the stranger said.

"I think he's asking for Ms. Stewart, she's my sixth period teacher."

Darkness hovered just outside Cam's consciousness. Would he ever see her smile, smell her vanilla scent, feel her warmth again?

"I don't see any Phia in his contacts," the officer said.

"I've got her number on my cell phone. Here it is. Sophia Stewart."

Thank God. He was so cold, and so tired…

Pain stabbed through the darkness. More voices, more hands. More flashing lights. The fire department and ambulance had arrived.

Cam heard voices but the pain blocked any words.

"Phia?"

"Captain, we've got her number. We'll let her know where you are. First we've got to get you to the hospital." Was that his back up or a paramedic? Who was here with him? The kid was but...

"Got an IV started, pressure bandages on wounds. Getting ready to transport. They're waiting for him at Fremont General. Let's get him on his way."

"One, two, three."

Cam knew they were going to move him, tried to be prepared for it. Brutal pain stabbed through him and red-rimmed blackness engulfed him.

Sophia was ready to call every hospital's emergency room. Something horrendous had happened to Cam but she didn't know what. His cell phone wasn't working. She called his office phone and left messages. She called the precinct but no one would say anything. She even tried the non-emergency dispatcher to no avail.

She wasn't his wife or even a family member so even if these people knew something they wouldn't tell her.

Either Lily or Diana stayed with her. Vaguely she knew when one stepped away. Now they bracketed her, arms around her to comfort.

Her phone rang. Before she could leap up, Lily did. "I'll get it and bring it back here."

Sophia heard Lily talking.

"Ashley checking in. She said she felt something was dreadfully wrong. I told her we'd let her know whatever we find out."

Another call came in. This one from Hunter who reported a sense of dark pain from Sophia.

"What's wrong?" Those two words texted from Ireland and Italy.

Hot tea in her favorite bluebird mug was pressed into her hands. A warm hand stroked her back or held her arm. Nothing touched the bone deep cold.

When her phone rang again, she looked at Lily who currently held it. "I don't recognize the number but it looks familiar."

Sophia took the phone. "Sophia Stewart."

"Ms. Stewart. Dr. Blackwell at Fremont General."

"Cam, are you calling about Cam? How is he?"

"I am calling about Captain Cameron Mitchell. Is that who you are referring to as Cam?"

"Yes, is he there at Fremont General?"

"He's on his way to surgery. He's asked for you which is why, if you can, it would be good if you can be here when he comes out of recovery."

"I can be there in fifteen to twenty minutes."

"Don't rush, Ms. Stewart. If you are here within the next couple of hours that will be plenty of time."

"I can do that."

"Now when you get here, you need to check in at the front desk. They'll know where he is. I expect he'll still be in surgery, or recovery or maybe in ICU."

"He was shot, wasn't he?"

"Yes, Ms. Stewart, he was shot."

"Will you tell him I'm coming?"

"I will be glad to tell him you're coming."

The call ended and Sophia surged to her feet. "I have to go. I have to be at the hospital when he comes out of surgery. I—."

"You do not have to nor will you deal with this alone." Diana still had her arm around Sophia's waist.

"At least not this time." Lily reached for the cell phone. "I'll put this in your purse along with your charger. You don't know how long you'll be there."

"What about a book?" Diana asked.

"We'll grab a couple of paperbacks. It probably would be prudent to take a change of clothes, toothbrush, etc.," Lily said as she followed Sophia into the kitchen.

42 ICU

Lily and Diana stayed with her, held her hand when the trauma surgeon sat to explain the injuries. Cam was listed in serious condition, his will to live a deciding factor. His family had also been notified and were on their way.

"His ex-wife and children?" Lily asked.

"At least some of the children. Don't know about the ex-wife. You need to know, Ms. Stewart that we're making an exception to the family and next of kin only rules because Captain Mitchell has been saying your name and once told you were here, appears to have calmed down."

"Where is he?"

"Recovery."

"Would it be helpful if Sophia were to see him in recovery so he knows she is really here?" Lily asked.

"It might. I'll check. If that is the decision, someone will come and get you. You need to be prepared for how he looks.

He's been shot and operated on. He has tubes running everywhere and he's hooked up to major machines."

"I'll be okay. If being with him helps, I can do that." Sophia mentally girded her loins for the worst.

Thirty minutes later three young adults charged into the waiting room. A nurse came out and they identified themselves as Ben, Beverly and Becca Mitchell, Cam's children.

As the three were settling themselves on the couch and chairs, another nurse came out. "Ms. Stewart?"

Sophia nodded. Shouldn't she say something to Cam's children? At least acknowledge them?

The nurse was waiting by the open door. "Follow me."

Cam comes first. I'm sure there'll be other opportunities for me to talk to them.

Probably because she'd prepared herself for the worst, when she came face to face with it, she managed not to cry out much less gasp.

"Cam, it's Sophia." She touched his cheek and leaned over to place a kiss on the nearer one. "I'm here. Know that if I'm not by your side I'm not far away. Know that I'm holding you in white light giving you time and space to decide if this is the time for you to leave or stay."

With the support of The Circle's energy, Sophia encircled Cam, his bed and herself in white light. The soothing energy helped her gain her emotional feet, to clarify for herself what her role was at this time and in this place.

"It's time." A quiet voice spoke near her ear.

Sophia turned to see the nurse who'd brought her to his room motioning her away. Leaning over the rail, she kissed his cheek again. "I'm still with you. Although I'm leaving your side,

I'm not far away." It occurred to her to mention his children were here but she didn't. *Something for the staff to tell him.*

"He was responsive to you so we're moving him to a room on ICU. When we have him settled in, you can spend a little more time with him."

Sophia found Lily and Diana waiting for her when she got to the waiting room. The other three occupants eyed her with suspicion.

"He's being moved."

Lily had her phone out.

Diana handed Sophia her phone with the text message screen lit.

They are asking about him.

They've guessed you are here about him also.

Heated words exchanged with nurse.

Doctor to come and talk to them.

Sophia handed the phone back to Diana inordinately thankful she hadn't said anything to Cam about them being here.

Taking Lily and Diana's hands she closed her eyes and concentrated on surrounding him in white light.

When the doctor came, he took the Mitchell children to a small conference room. Sophia heard the angry voices but also heard the fear beneath. *Do doctors and nurses hear that also?*

"Do they?"

"Do they what?" Diana asked.

"Do doctors and nurses hear the fear under the anger?"

"The good ones do," Lily replied.

"Those children are estranged from their father. To know he could die," her voice caught and she paused to steady herself, "must be intolerable.

"You know I love him," she admitted. "I tried so hard not to but it happened anyway."

"And he loves you, too, even though he tried very hard not to." Lily held her hand as the children followed the doctor into the room.

"Ms. Stewart, a word please." He opened the door into the ICU ward and motioned for her to go ahead. Looking back into the room he said, "If you create problems, I'll call security and have you escorted off hospital property."

Sophia looked back at the glowering angry faces. Her breath caught for three heart beats before it released. *Cam. Focus on Cam.*

The doctor said something to the nurse, wrote a note in the chart and then joined her. She'd settled in a chair and held his hand.

"He can hear you so talking to him is a good thing. Touching is also good so he knows you are here viscerally as well as aurally. He's heavily sedated so can't open his eyes right now but you'll see his lids flutter from time to time. That's normal.

"Any questions?"

"How long can I stay with him?"

"He can have visitors for ten minutes out of every hour."

"And if there is more than one person to see him, that ten minutes is divided?"

"Generally speaking, yes. Exceptions are made in extraordinary circumstances."

"Cam, I am stepping outside with the doctor for a few minutes and then I'll be right back. I won't be long."

"I know those are his children but we've never been introduced and I don't know if he knows they are even here."

"He knows. Come, I'll introduce you."

As soon as they were back in the waiting room, the doctor said "This lady is Ms. Sophia Stewart, a friend of your father's. You need to know that we are monitoring his reaction to visitors and if he shows any signs of stress or upset, your visiting privileges will be withdrawn. It is at the discretion of the ICU staff if the normal visiting procedures are altered in any way.

"This way, Ms. Stewart." The doctor led her back into the unit. "At some point they will speak to you and it may not be pleasant. I hope that will not deter you from visiting.

"The staff will be aware of what's happening and will call security if things begin to get out of hand."

How she ended up outside Cam's room, she didn't know. She heard words, followed directions and hand signs and trusted all would be well.

"I'm next to you again." She'd decided not to say she was going away or out or something that implied a real distance. What she hadn't decided was whether to tell him how much she'd missed him and how much she loved him. Never would she tell him how devastated she'd be if he chose to leave her, to leave this plane.

I have this time with him and it's more than I had with Jonathan. I will not waste it on past regrets or future worries.

"The peas we planted are beginning to sprout. This warmer weather will bring them on more quickly. Putting the string up is next. I must admit I like seeing the vines growing up along the fence. I wouldn't have peas this year if not for you.

"I've not planted beans yet. Gave all my vegetable starts to Diana and Matthew except for the squash. They are dividing things up with Ashley and Daniel and the kids. Seeing a tiny seed become a plant, grow, blossom, put out a tomato or a cucumber is like magic. I believe when children see the circle of life, they are more respectful of all of life because they experience the magic."

"Ms. Stewart, time is up."

"I'll be a few steps away, Cam. Rest now. Know that you are held in white light. Know that you are watched over, guided and protected while you decide your future. Know that whatever your decision, all will be well."

Animosity simmered in the ICU waiting room but the darker levels had dissipated.

"How is he?" Diana asked in a clear voice.

"He's heavily sedated. The only response has been the movement of one finger and then the numbers on all the machines he's hooked up to. I'm not sure what they're looking for but they know."

"Blood pressure and respiration respond to emotions, to stress." Lily said and patted the seat beside her.

"I told him about the garden. How the peas are getting tall enough they need to be strung up." Sophia swiped an errant tear rolling down her cheek. "I-I-I'd thought we might do that together. You know-know it was his idea at first. He wanted to coax me out of the darkness after the fall. I couldn't have-have done it myself and he-he-he knew that."

Diana sat on her other side and took her hand. "As best you can, put that behind you, Soph. Now is the time to hold him in the light."

Sophia let out a shaky breath. "I know." Closing her eyes she breathed in through her nose and out through her mouth, quieted her racing thoughts and found her center. Holding Lily and Diana's hands she pictured Cam. He looked down on her, a grin on his face. She couldn't hear his words but he was talking to her. Was this something that would come in the future? That wasn't for her to decide.

An hour later his children were led into the unit. While they went in as a group, Sophia knew they'd be in his room one at a time.

"I want to tell him I love him but is that fair?"

The startled looks from Lily and Diana had her adding. "Doesn't Cam need to decide if he wants to live or if this is the right time for him to go?"

Lily scooted her chair so she was facing her circle sister. Diana moved to sit on that chair's arm.

"Why would you not tell him? If it is his time to die, knowing he is loved by you will only make that easier for him."

"And knowing you love him, may be just the thing he needs to know to fight to stay."

"I'll ask the nurse what long term damage he can expect."

"If any," Lily added. "Don't think he'll be crippled for life, Soph. That won't help him."

"But he needs to know."

"Are you sure?"

"Yes that I am sure about. Whether to tell him how I feel? That wasn't as clear which is why I asked."

Grim faces were on the faces of the Mitchell siblings when they returned. A nurse followed them out.

"Here's the deal. You will not mention your mother. You will not complain. You will not bring up the past. If you cannot be positive in your interactions with him, you cannot see him."

"Ms. Stewart, please come with me."

"Why does she get to see him again?" Becca whined.

"Because when she is with him, he relaxes, breathes better. His blood pressure stabilizes."

Sophia was whisked into his room. "Ms. Stewart's back, Captain."

"I'm next to you now, Cam." She bent over and kissed his cheek before sitting down and slipping her fingers inside his hand.

"Your kids are so worried about you. You have a big heart, Cam. You know how to love and to forgive. Whether you decide to leave us now or stay with us, remembering how much you've loved them and still love them will make whichever path you take easier.

"A vision came to me a little while ago. You and I were in the garden. We were stringing up the peas. I couldn't hear what you were saying but you were laughing and I was happy."

It occurred to her to tell him she loved him but it didn't feel like the right time. She wanted to look him in the eyes when she said the words so he could see she meant them.

"Captain, Ms. Stewart is going to be nearby but we've a few things we need to check now."

Sophia stood, her hand still in his, leaned over and kissed his cheek. "I'm still with you."

"You're good for him," the nurse said as she escorted Sophia back to the waiting room.

"Thank you for saying that. His children need to see him too."

"And they will but in short increments. When he can tolerate more, they can stay longer."

"Do you know what long term problems he can have from these wounds?"

"I'll have the doctor talk to you."

"Thank you."

Grant and Hunter came in the morning. "Second shift?"

"Second shift bearing gifts," Grant said sitting a carrier with cups and a pastry bag on the small table.

"We asked about bringing a carafe of hot water so you can make your own tea. They said they have it available but I told them you needed filtered water. So, we got permission to do that. You can't take it into his room, but you can have it out here." Hunter opened a large bag and drew out a bag with her favorite teas as well as one of those pump carafes.

Two police officers came in. One of them went in to the unit the other stayed in the waiting room. "Ms. Stewart?"

"Yes?"

"Do you have any information about what happened last night?"

"No, I got a phone call from the doctor asking me to come."

"Do you know how they got your phone number?"

"Actually, everything happened so fast and I was so concerned, I never even thought about it."

The other officer came out, a serious look on his face a slight shake of his head as he stared at his partner.

"This is Ms. Stewart."

"Ah, the angel who used to send us cookies."

"I don't think baking a batch of cookies constitutes angel status." Sophia laughed. Out of the corner of her eye, she saw Ben straighten, a look of interest on his face.

"Those peanut butter chocolate chip cookies are sinful. You don't know how hard everyone worked to find out when the Captain would be bringing more in."

"When I'm home again, I'll bake several dozen and bring them to you."

"If you bake them, one of us will come and pick them up."

"But will the entire batch she baked make it to the precinct?" Grant questioned. "Or will they be held for ransom?"

"Good point." The officer's smile was brief.

"We came by to see how the Captain was doing. When he's able, we need to talk to him and get his statement."

Her gripped tightened on Sophia's hand, Lily asked "How was he found?"

"Kid doing a ride-along called it in. Captain had notified dispatch he was getting out, where he was and asked for backup, but the kid making the call got medical help there faster."

"Cam had offered students in my sixth period class the opportunity for a ride-a-long. I hope it wasn't one of them. That must sound awful."

"I'm sure it was one of your students, Ms. Stewart. No one knew what he was saying, but this kid did. He's the reason they could find you."

Around noon an older woman came in. Sophia guessed this was Cam's ex-wife, Betsy. She asked to speak to a nurse about Captain Mitchell. She handled things fairly well when she was told she could not see him. No tantrums or demands. After spending a little time with her children, she left.

His daughter, Becca's visit lasted less than a minute. She returned to the waiting room with a belligerent scowl followed by a nurse whose frustration was notable.

"What did you do?" Ben demanded.

"Dad has the right to know Mom wants to see him."

"Ms. Stewart, please."

"And then *she* goes waltzing in as if she's special. Well, she isn't. She has no right to—"

The door closed on the ranting.

"Hey Cam. I'm here beside you." Sophia kissed his forehead and smoothed her hand over his hair. Another soft kiss, this one on his cheek and she sat. "You are much in demand but I'm here to tell you that I have first dibs. Probably

Ben is next. Not sure about your two youngest. The nurses here are not just skilled in nursing, they are formidable when protecting patients. And that includes you right now."

How much to say?

Trust.

"Some of the machines you're hooked up to tell the nurses when you are upset or stressed. They are using that to decide about visiting. I've asked about any long term problems and a doctor is going to talk to me.

"Right now, I'm holding you in The Light. So are all of my circle sisters. Even Elizabeth and Gabriella in Ireland and Italy. Right now Hunter and Grant are in the waiting room. Diana and Lily stayed with me all night. Someone will be with me so I can be with you during these early days. I'm not alone, Cam and neither are you."

Sophia tucked her hand in Cam's. There were so many machines and lines, there weren't many places to touch him. When her time was up, she again kissed his cheek now bristly with whiskers and said the words that had now become a prayer. "Know you are held in healing light."

When next she counted the days, it was Monday. Diana had called school both Friday in the early hours of the morning and again earlier today.

Too worried about Cam, Sophia didn't even care about not being in her classroom.

Grateful she had a change of clothes, Sophia took advantage of the offer of a shower. She fixed her tea, read her book and waited for the next opportunity to hold Cam's hand and kiss his cheek.

Ben and Bev had approached her Saturday and thanked her for the cookies. Becca had flounced out. Sophia reminded herself she was the youngest and knew Cam the least.

Because he'd expressed doubts she was his daughter, Sophia found herself surreptitiously glancing in her direction.

She did look like her mother. Ben and Bev had his grin and Ben some of his mannerisms but she saw nothing in Becca that reminded her of Cam. *And it makes no difference.*

Bev and Becca left Sunday afternoon. Ben stayed. Lily had stepped out for a minute and she was alone with Cam's son.

"Have you known my dad for long?"

"I met him in November, so no, not too long."

"When I see him, I always tell him you're still here and I can see it eases him."

"I'm glad. And I'm sure knowing you are still here, eases him too."

"Are you nice to everyone?"

"Probably not, but I do try to be."

"Do you think Dad will make it?"

"I don't know. He doesn't seem to be worse."

"But he isn't better. The doctor said his will to live is critical to his recovery."

"I remember that." Sophia smiled. "He has a lot to live for."

"Maybe…he has you to live for."

"He has you and your sisters."

Sophia saw Ben's jaw clench and he looked away.

"Cam's very proud of all of you. He's talked about when you and Bev were born and watching you talk and take first steps. Actually that's backwards." She smiled. "Memories of those early days as a family are important to him."

"If he makes it, we'll make more."

"I know he'd like that."

Lily returned. "You may not believe it but the sun is out."

The nurse came to the door. "Ms. Stewart?"

Sophia sat next to the bed watching the monitors. "I'm here beside you." She stood and kissed his cheek, his forehead. "I've known for weeks that I love you. Of course I've been too nervous to say anything. Not really nervous, afraid is more like it. Loving someone is a wondrous feeling. The highest of highs but tinged with the possibility of the lowest of lows.

"You know that yourself. You love your kids. I've seen the pain being estranged from them creates. I've been talking to Ben. He wants to make more memories with you when you get out of here.

"I do too, Cam. I love you and want that vision of us and stringing peas to manifest.

"But more important, I want you to be happy, to rejoice in life whether I'm a part of that or not. I want you to live in the light and leave the darkness behind. The sun is shining outside today. Know that I hold you in the light of love. Know that I hold you in the white light of protection. Know that I love you."

43 When Dark Becomes Light

Pain jarred.

Soft voices soothed.

Darkness still claimed him.

Although he couldn't see it, Cam felt the light.

Sophia held his hand. She'd said she loved him.

Weak.

Did she feel him hold her hand back?

Someone else in the room.

"Captain Mitchell, if you hear me, open your eyes."

Open he commanded.

All there was was darkness.

"He can hear us." Sophia was talking. "I know he hears us even if he can't open his eyes. I thought I felt pressure, like he was holding my hand."

He was holding her hand.

"There, I felt it again. He does hear us. He is with us."

A kiss on his cheek held dampness. *Tears?*

So much he wanted to say, to hear. Did she still love him?

As if she heard his voice, he heard her say, "I love you, Cam. I'm right next to you. I'm never far away."

"I'll let the doctor know," the voice said.

"Since I've no idea how much you remember of all my chatting, I'll summarize. Today is Wednesday. It's been almost a week since you were shot.

"My student, Kyle, who was with you at the time you were shot, is okay. He came by Monday after school to see how you are.

"Ben has been here the entire time. He's a wonderful young man and you've every right to be proud of him. Bev and Becca were here initially and Bev's been back. Becca is angry that I'm here. I'm sure she'll spend time with you when you're better.

"They caught the man who shot you. You probably won't be surprised it was Randy Brown. One of those coincidences. Of course he recognized you and took his revenge. However, it was short lived. Mostly because you wounded him, they could follow the trail of blood. He'd didn't make it. Lost too much blood. Someone said he'd bled out.

"Oh, and you've had a steady stream of fellow officers stop by. They hung out with me or talked with Ben. You may remember that a couple of them came in and talked to you. So many lives you've touched, Cam.

"I am grateful to The Goddess that you've survived. I am blessed for each and every hour you've been a part of my life. I've learned so much from you. I love you. Not in a possessive way but in a sharing way.

"I see my time is up." Her soft lips pressed against his cheek and again on his forehead. He wanted her kiss on his lips.

Don't leave.

"I'm never far from you, Cam. Know that I hold you in the light of love. Know that I surround you in the white light. Know that you are in my heart."

A soothing blanket smothered the pain. Cam struggled to stay awake, to know when Sophia returned.

She is never far away.

44 Recovery and Rehabilitation

Recovering from multiple gunshot wounds was not a picnic. When he finally opened his eyes, Sophia was there. The next time he managed that feat, Ben's face filled his vision.

Cam clenched his jaw, gritted his teeth and grunted through the pain of moving muscles that had been on hiatus for too long. His head still pounded when he moved but he was grateful there was no permanent damage from the bullet that had cleaved a slot through his hair just above his right ear.

One of the first things he did when he regained his voice was send Sophia and Ben home. He rang for a nurse who assured them they'd be immediately notified if there was a downturn in his condition.

His emotions were strung taut and tears rolled down his cheeks when his Phia said she loved him while looking him in the eyes. Whatever had he done to be so blessed?

"Blessed, now I'm sounding like her." He smiled knowing she'd rubbed off on him. His worse fear was she become more like him, tainted by darkness and death.

"How are the peas doing?" He'd asked on a visit.

"With Kyle's help, I got them strung."

"He saved my life, Phia."

"I think you've saved his."

She'd seen his confusion. "Did you know that his mother has emotional problems?"

He shook his head.

"She does and he's been the parent to her and his two younger siblings. He didn't want the family split up so he didn't ask for help. The hospital ED social worker called child welfare on a hunch to see if his family had a history with them. A Ms. Haverstone was on duty. She knew the family well and actually had a fairly good relationship with Kyle's mom. With support, his mom has managed to keep her job and take care of her younger children. That means Kyle is not frantic about his siblings, where they will be living, what they'll have to eat."

Cam was not looking forward to the move to the rehab center but Lily had stopped by and told him the place he was being discharged to was a good one. She also said she'd stop by to see how things were going.

"Sophia doesn't need to—."

Lily had interrupted. "Oh, but she does Cam. She loves you and hovering is one of the primary ways those of us in The Circle show it."

He picked at the covers looking down hoping Lily didn't see the tears. He had no control of the damn things. Lily's hand on his shoulder got his attention. "Sophia loves you and because she loves you, you are stuck with the rest of us. When you can manage, the husbands, that's Jackson, Daniel, Matthew and Grant, will be stopping in to see how they can support you."

"They don't even know me."

"They know Sophia and since she loves you, you get a free ride on the basis of that."

"Not a free ride. If I hurt her, I'm toast."

Lily laughed. "Except they know if they hurt you and that hurts her they are toast." She flexed her arm and made a muscle.

"Girl muscle."

"Nope, loving woman muscle. It brings protective man to heel every time."

April 06, 2006

Cam was going crazy. He'd been in the rehabilitation center for less than a week. No contest it was the worst week of his life. Seeing people who'd suffered strokes, sustained significant head injures struggling to regain some part of their lives was so depressing he didn't want to leave his room.

"I'm good with people who broke a bone but the ones whose brains are affected? Phia, I just can't." He was sitting in his room, the door slightly ajar, staring out the window.

"Let's see if Lily has some other ideas. She worked miracles when Eleanor fell and even with her own accident, she didn't have to be in a rehab center. Don't give up hope. I'll call her tonight and see what she says.

"And you, you need to be cooperative. You can talk to the social worker here about figuring out another type of program."

"I'm not talking to anyone here but I will be cooperative."

Sophia leaned down and kissed him. He would have hauled her down on his lap and plundered her sweet mouth but that would take a strength he didn't have.

Another kiss on his forehead. "Something to look forward to when you aren't in such a public place," she whispered in his ear. "You've always like me nibbling on your ears. Do you think you'll still like that when you're better?"

He growled and she laughed.

The door opened wide and Ben was there with Bev and Becca. "I was just leaving. Your dad is on the grumpy side because he can't already run a marathon."

"You will pay Sophia Stewart."

"Promises, promises. You have to get stronger before you can catch me.

"He has cookies in the bottom drawer of the night stand."

"You owe me more cookies if these guys eat them all."

"Cam, you have company. Be a gentleman and offer them refreshments." Sophia crossed to where he still sat in his wheelchair, bent down and kissed his cheek. "I'll bring you another supply tomorrow."

He tried to be nonchalant but failed.

"It's alright to miss her, Dad." Ben said going for the cookies. "We'll leave you a couple for tonight." He grinned and passed the bakery box to his siblings.

Becca still sulked and tried to interject Betsy into every conversation.

"Your mom has remarried, Becca. I'm not going to be involved in her life nor is she going to be involved in mine. She has a life without me."

"Well that's because—."

"Knock it off, Becca. Just leave it. Dad has his life and Mom has hers. Whatever happened was years ago, decades ago actually. Let it go. Get over it." Ben stopped and looked at him. "Sorry Dad. Just get tired of the same old stuff.

"So how long do you have to be here?" Ben perched on the window sill, crossed his ankles and focused his attention away from his sister.

"Too long."

"Where will you go from here?" Bev asked.

"I know I can't go home. I'm not strong enough."

"Bet that—" Becca paused when the cautionary looks from her siblings zeroed in on her. "Bet Ms. Stewart would take you in. She seems like the type."

"I'll probably be here until I'm discharged home. Leaving here is an incentive to work harder on the exercises."

I'm a hellofa bastard of a dad. Could hardly wait for them to leave. He stopped the beginnings of a rant. *It's Becca.* He sighed. *And I don't even try to find a way to make friends with her.*

Grateful when a knock on the door brought in a couple of guys from the precinct, Cam offered them the last of the cookies. Listening to everything that was going on was interesting and boring. He really didn't care about any of that any more. An idea that came to him about another direction for his life was more and more appealing as the officers talked.

Looking out the window from his bed, he saw the moon through the tops of distant trees. He relaxed and let his mind wander free. Sophia was kneeling on the ground and looking up at him. He held string in one hand and looped it around a hook on the fence with the other. She was so beautiful. So happy. A laughed bubbled up from within.

45 Freedom for Leg Shackles

April 07, 2006

True to her word, Sophia came with two dozen cookies and Lily. They had a plan but before talking to the doctor, they wanted his take on it.

"You can have in-home physical therapy," Lily explained. "Through Home Health, virtually everything that is done here can be done at home."

Cam listened, thinking about spending his days in his apartment. Would that be better than being here?

"What do you think?"

Sophia was almost palpitating with anticipation. Something wasn't right. "Would you summarize this plan for me?"

Lily handed him a piece of paper. "It's all here. You'd be discharged to Sophia's and my care. I've a background in care or case management but you'd stay at Sophia's. Matthew or Daniel will build a temporary ramp so you can go out on the patio until you are strong enough to get around without a wheelchair."

"I already walk around here without one."

"But you have someone with you. Part of the deal is that you not be hiking around when you're alone. Sophia has asked to work half days. With her seniority that isn't a problem but you'd be on your own for four or so hours a day."

"I don't want you—." Cam started but stopped when he saw the warning flash in her chocolate brown eyes.

"I'm only doing what I want to do, what makes sense to me and what I can afford. By working half time, I still have my insurance benefits."

"She can't apply for family medical leave because you two aren't married," Lily put in. "If you can live with being at Sophia's, having a couple of the husbands stopping by at least in the beginning until you are stronger, being on your own for a few hours and being responsible for following through on exercises, etc., I'll start the conversation.

"If there's any part of this you object to or want to modify, just say so. For example: if you'd rather be in your apartment? Maybe one of your kids could spend some time each day or maybe off duty officers could."

"Can we talk?" He reached for Sophia with his right hand.

"I'll step outside." Lily pulled the door shut behind her.

"Are you sure this is what you want? I can get curmudgeonly you know."

"I do know but you'd be my very own curmudgeon."

"Don't say anything more right now." He got up from the wheelchair and sat in the room's largest chair. "Come sit with me?"

Sophia went into his arms, settled tentatively on his lap, her weight shifted to the right, she laid her head on his shoulder.

"I've missed this. I've missed you. I know I behaved badly, just leaving without telling you why. I worried I was bringing you into the dark with me. You'd always been so cheerful, so happy and positive. And then you weren't. I knew you had a concussion but I worried my negativity was rubbing off on you.

"The last night I stayed at your place after you fell asleep, I had the courage to whisper 'I love you'. You do know that, know that I love you, don't you?"

"I do know you love me. In some ways we are two of a kind. You told me you loved me when I was asleep. I told you I loved you when you were in a drug induced coma. What matters is that we've figured out how to say the words."

"If I move in with you, you know my kids will be around."

"I would expect them to be. My house and yard are big enough that I can find a place out of your way if that makes it easier for you. I like Ben and Bev. I think I'd like Becca if she let her guard down a bit."

"I have one condition before I say I'll take you up on the offer of your hospitality."

Sophia leaned back so she could see his face. "What?"

Cam knew tears were filling his eyes. "Just don't have emotions back under control yet."

Sophia kissed his cheeks. "You don't have to unless that is what's best for you."

"What's best for me is you. Will you marry me, Phia? I know I don't deserve you but if you say 'yes', I'll do my best to show you every day how important you are to me."

"You've heard the saying that actions speak louder than words? So my answer is in this action." Sophia held his face in her hands and poured her answer into her kiss.

"How soon?" Cam thought he could run a marathon his joy was so complete.

"Beltane. That's May 1st so not that very long to wait. A simple wedding, maybe on my patio?"

"Simple, are you sure?"

"Very sure. And Elizabeth and Gabriella will be in Fremont so The Circle will be complete."

A knock on the door sounded before it opened. Lily stuck her head in. "You've got company."

"Good, someone to share our news with."

He kept his right arm firmly around Sophia's waist pleased when she stopped struggling to get up. Cam was surprised to see Ben and Bev behind Lily. It would be easier to tell them without Becca here.

"I see the two of you have been talking," Lily said her smile dancing in her eyes.

"Phia has accepted my proposal of marriage." Layers of darkness faded, golden light bathed him. *This is what she was talking about.*

"When?" Lily asked.

"Beltane," Sophia answered.

"Plenty of time for The Circle to put a wedding together." Lily gave Sophia a hug.

"Let me go so you can talk to your kids."

The light did not abandon him when Sophia stood and moved away.

Ben smiled and shook his hand. "Good going, Dad."

Bev was not as happy about the news. "You haven't known her very long."

"In some ways I've known her a lifetime. There was a time when I was on the ground, before anyone got to me, I called her name and she was there. I could feel her with me. When I was first conscious, she was there. When I first opened my eyes, she was there. Even when she isn't by my side, she's never far away.

"I've lived in the dark, near death for too long. I don't want that life any more. I want to see the good in people. I want to celebrate life."

46 The Wedding

May, 01, 2006
Beltane

Sophia knocked on the bedroom door.

"Come in."

She cracked the door but stayed behind it. "Close your eyes."

"Why?"

"Because I need my morning kiss and you shouldn't see the bride before the wedding."

"It's important to you?"

"It is."

"Ready."

Sophia grinned at the sight that greeted her through the open the door. Cam was lying on the bed naked.

"Very tempting but I'm only here for my morning kiss."

He puckered his lips and made smooching sounds.

She laughed. Tears welled as the sound of joy came from deep within her. It had been a challenging three weeks while Cam continued to recover while living with her. Three steps and she was next to the bed. The mark above his ear was still visible and he suffered debilitating headaches. The neurologist had assured them it was not permanent. Red puckered skin on his shoulder and lower on his torso showed his body was healing and also how close she'd come to losing him.

"I love you." The quick kiss she'd planned morphed into a sweet kiss of joy.

"I love you more."

"It is your day to love me more." She kissed his forehead and smoothed her hand over his hair. "See you at the wedding." Sophia backed away, reluctant to leave. He'd only be alone for a short while but today of all days she wanted him surrounded by happy people.

The aura of darkness she'd seen when first they met still popped up from time to time but with a few hugs and kisses, it vanished.

A knock on the front door.

"Someone's here. I'll see who it is. Thanks for the preview." She pulled the door closed behind her and headed for the front door.

The plan had been that she'd drive to Diana's house but when she opened the front door, it was apparent that plan had changed.

"Come in." She stepped to the side to let Lily and Jackson in.

"Change of plans," Lily said as she hugged her.

"Where's the groom?" Jackson hung his jacket up on the hall tree.

"In his room."

"Has he eaten?"

"Coffee. He said he wasn't very hungry. And then he can't see the bride until the wedding."

"You go on, I'll see that he's fed, rested and ready for the ceremony."

"Thanks, Jackson." Sophia reached up and kissed his cheek. "I really appreciate what you and the other husbands are doing. He's still emotional and shaky at times. It bothers him."

"The Circle is waiting for you, Sophia. Go with Lily and know that Cam is in good hands. In fact a couple more hands have just pulled up."

Sophia picked up her purse and headed out the door with Lily as Giovanni and Grant came up the walk.

"We're late, you can kiss the bride later," Lily said and towed Sophia past the two men.

"I was worried about leaving Cam this morning. I'm glad you came a bit early."

"He will be surrounded by people who are very aware that he needs to rest during the day. By the way, there have been some slight modifications to the plans."

"Slight meaning you picked me up an hour early?"

"That and we aren't going to Diana's. To begin with we are all having an hour massage along with a manicure and pedicure. Then we're going to Elizabeth's where we've arranged for a catered meal. Something light.

"Then we are back on track with the original plan. Circle, dressing, wedding."

"We're spending at least three hours on pampering? We can't possibly have everything ready for the wedding at one."

"That's why the wedding is at four. That also gives the men time to transform your patio and backyard into the wedding venue of the century."

"But... ."

"Think back, Soph. Except for Hunter, we've all participated in creating the wedding venue in some way or another. And for her, we put together the reception she and Grant wanted."

"We did a magnificent job." Sophia smiled at the memory of Twinkle Toes festooned with yards of white and turquoise gauze, long tables with food, music and laughter. "It was all reflected in the mirrors which is what really set it off."

"We had the screen set up and Logan and Bill created that slide show of Hunter and Grant's lives. So many people just sat and watched it because it was so well done."

"Hunter glowed and Grant looked like the Cheshire cat. But Logan. Logan stole the show. Every time I saw her she was looking at her parents as if her every dream had come true."

"For her, I think it had. I know she'd like a baby brother or sister." Lily pulled in the parking lot of a mini-mall. "I don't know that Hunter and Grant have decided to even try or not. They are enjoying the time they have. Grant told Jackson it was Hunter's choice. He'd have a chance to see grandchildren. Plenty of opportunities for baby time. Maeve is here for now and they've offered unlimited babysitting to Diana and Matthew. Plus they've unofficially adopted Janeen, Jason and little Sophia."

"We're here?"

"We are. And it looks like we're the last to arrive."

Eleanor had returned from her visit with her daughters and Logan had been invited so there were nine of them.

They rotated through with three getting manicures, three pedicures, three massages and then moving on until three and a half hours later, they were all relaxed and sparkly.

Logan and Eleanor headed back to Sophia's and the other women headed to Murphy House. Within ten minutes of their arrival, the catering truck showed up. Croissants, fresh fruit, chocolate and a caramel dipping sauce for the fruit and scones, clotted cream and lemon curd.

A spirit plate was created, prayers of gratitude said and the plate was set on the back deck.

Sophia had a croissant and a pear and pecan scone with the clotted cream and lemon curd. The tang of the lemon curd woke up her taste buds and her mouth watered long after she'd swallowed.

"I've got smudge going," Hunter announced coming upstairs from the quarters she and Grant shared. The invitation to remain when Elizabeth and Michael resided in Fremont this spring was irresistible, especially with Maeve in residence.

Sophia waved the sage and pine smoke over and around her. She raised each foot and held it over the abalone shell where the smudge stick smoldered.

One by one they created their altar.

Sophia had brought her bluebirds, one for each direction and she'd also brought a bullet. This talisman of death was responsible for the life she would have with Cam because she doubted they ever would have found their way to this time and place without the tragedy of his near-death.

Over the last couple of days she'd pondered in which direction to put the bullet, deciding today on the East. The East was new beginning, new chances, spring, new growth and a new day. All of that and more was internalized in her wedding day.

Lily had her porcelain statue of the lioness and cub in the east. Elizabeth added her swan. Diana had a Siamese cat. Ashley, of course, a dragonfly. Hunter placed a stork and Gabriella a blue jay. The East was full!

But so were the other directions. Rose Quartz, Carnelian, Yellow Citrine, Jasper, a red crystal heart and acorns from The Sacred Grove graced the South.

Lapis lazuli, Black Tourmaline, Snowflake Obsidian, a Smoky Quartz 'Crystal city', malachite and blue lace agate filled the West.

A snowy owl, a polar bear, a selenite wand, a cathedral crystal, a phantom crystal and a crystal city anchored the North.

The center held the etched green crystal bowl from Ireland. Within it was a lit candle and a vial of water from The Sacred Grove's spring.

Elizabeth picked up the piece of multi-colored fluorite, their favorite talking stone. "I am so grateful to be here, to be in circle with all of us in the same place. I am grateful Gabriella is now so close we can see each other once a month and join with you all at that time. I am grateful I have Michael and Maeve and while my darling daughter is so very beloved, without Michael I would not be able to serve The Lady, spend time in The Sacred Grove and be Maeve's mother.

"So far our search for another soul to join our family has not born fruit. We are in trust that if another soul is meant to come to us, it will. There is no doubt that Maeve is a perfect match. She loves to make altars." Elizabeth laughed. "You should see her put her toy animals in a circle and then move them around ever so slightly until she is satisfied. Minutes go by and she just stares at it. Then she either destroys it or leaves it returning to it from time to time. Sometimes she leaves her creations up for a day or two. I'm so very blessed in all areas of my life. And if The Goddess is willing, by this time next year there will be another babe for me to hold."

The stone passed to her left and Diana. "Matthew and I have also been discussing whether to add to our family. Our answer is 'no'. We have Madison Michelle who loves her dad and mom and big brother—to be honest she loves the world. At my age the risk of complications in pregnancy is greater. While I've loved having this time with a little one, especially because Matthew is an exemplary dad, I don't relish the sleepless nights. I love teaching and my classes are in the evenings and Saturday so it's perfect for M2 to spend time with her dad.

"We are getting a dog. Matthew is building a run on the side of the house. There'll be shade from that maple tree and there is already a water spigot. He's going to put some kind of a tub thing nearby for the inevitable bath." She laughed. "He's very creative." A blush brightened her cheeks. "I'm done."

Hunter rolled the stone from hand-to-hand. "All this talk about babies. After spending time with Janeen and her baby, we were still conflicted but, at least at this point, we've decided there are things we want to do together." She smiled and winked at Elizabeth. "We've had an invitation to visit E and also Gabby. I don't relish traveling with morning sickness or heavy with child.

"Being here with E, Michael and Maeve in residence is giving Grant time to be with a baby without it being 24/7 for life." She smiled. "He's changed a few poopy diapers and has survived baby puke so I know he'd be a great dad to a little one. He seems more settled on it being the two of us for now, catching up on all those lost years after he spent a weekend in Eugene with Logan.

"One more thing. While the guys are all together today, Grant is talking to them about a place we saw at the coast. It will need renovations and an addition so it will accommodate everyone. Hopefully with Jackson, Giovanni, Matthew and Daniel they'll have ideas and we can move forward. Grant really misses the water."

Elizabeth reached for the stone. "He and Michael have talked. They took a flying trip to the beach to look over a five bedroom place. It has some land so it's possible to add on so there'd be seven en suite bedrooms."

"Hunter took the stone back. "I didn't know he'd talked to anyone yet or I would have mentioned it. Large great room with fireplace, wrap around deck. Jackson and Giovanni would design the addition. Daniel, Matthew and Grant would help with the actual build. If Michael is here and Cam is healthy, they can help also. But there will always be things like painting, hanging pictures."

Gabriella reached for the stone. "We could talk all day about this project but we don't have time and we don't know for sure what the guys will think. Well, actually we do. They'll all be on board.

"I can't believe how much our lives have changed in the past year. We'd just found Logan a year ago. And in twelve months, Hunt has found Grant, I've found Giovanni and Soph has found Cam. My prayer has always been," Gabriella's hazel gaze met Sophia's chocolate brown one, "for you to find someone to love you above all others, someone who could heal that last piece of your heart since Jonathan's death, someone who could give to you as much as you give to others.

"I look forward to you and Cam coming to spend time with us at the villa or at our Rome house." She laughed. "Just listen to me." Tears coursed down her cheeks, still holding the stone, she wiped her face. Elizabeth handed around tissue and Gabriella dried her eyes. "I'm a veritable water faucet these days." She caught the speculative looks. "No I'm not pregnant. I'm safe and I'm well-loved. I have so much my cup runneth over. I live in two beautiful homes. I have a staff who takes care of the houses and me. I lack for nothing because I'm married to the most loving and generous man in the entire world. Yes, even more loving and generous than any of your husbands.

"He loves me." She stabbed her fingers in her chest. "Supremely flawed and damaged me. For some reason he sees beyond all that crap. His love is so true there are times it terrifies me. And then I remember. I have him now and that is all that matters."

Ashley held the warm stone in her hand. "That is one of the great truths." She laid her hand on Gabriella's knee. "All we ever have is now. I could debate you on who has the most loving and generous husband." She gestured around the circle. "Actually I think we could all debate you on that score, but what is true is you have exactly the right husband for you and I have the right one for me and today we will bear witness to our Sophia claiming the right husband for herself.

"Rose has asked me to ask The Circle when she will be old enough to join us. I told her I would ask on her behalf but I also said no one could answer today because it is Sophia's day. She is good with that.

"Having my health is a gift. Having my husband and children healthy is a gift. Having everyone here, in person, is a gift. I am putting out a request that we purposefully plan to spend time together each week whether in ceremony or not…that isn't the issue. It's being in the same time and space with y'all. I'm grateful that our ability to connect energetically has strengthened. That certainly helps. But now, being in circle? My heart overflows with gratitude."

Lily pressed the heated stone to her breast. "It may be time to restructure The Golden Cauldron. When we first conceived it, there were just the seven of us. When we formalized it, I was about to marry Jackson. But now, with all of us married, more children involved and we've included the men in our ceremonies—unthinkable at one time.

"I'm not suggesting anything right now—but soon. While we are all together and after we learn more about the beach place." She turned to Sophia.

"You've become my dearest friend and without you we would not have each other. We've been through so much together, we've grown and changed, we've fought for ourselves and each other, we've struggled to overcome our fears and find a love that's steady and true, one we'd only dreamed of. And through it all, we've maintained The Circle. We are an awesome group of women. May your journey with Cam bring an abundance of joy and happiness."

Lily held the piece of fluorite up to the light. "I remember when you held a similar piece when we were newly formed. You said you chose this because it reminded you of the differences we brought to this circle. These differences and strengths have created The Circle, a group of women who know in their souls that together they can conquer anything." She chuckled and as she passed the stone to Sophia said, "Even hovering."

"I'm overwhelmed and even though I had thought about what to say, the words have deserted me. These past couple of weeks Cam and I have had time to talk about the present and the future. He isn't sure he wants to return to police work when he's released to do so—which won't be for some time. It will all depend on how much time before his retirement date. Leaving the force early would affect his retirement pay but we don't need much. The house is paid for. He can be on my insurance so that isn't an issue. Right now we don't know what his decision will be and that's okay. But if you would continue to hold him in prayer for him to see his future, I'd appreciate that. I find it impossible to do it in a neutral way because I want him with me for now and forever more.

"My life with Cam is a journey for me to be in the present. I think that is where my challenge with my garden has been this year. Gardens are about the future, about life continuing through the wheel of the year. Thank you for taking the plants and giving them life for this year. I did hold on to the various varieties of squash so I must have a bit of the desire to garden inside. No more decisions at this point. We'll see where I'm at next spring.

"I've always thought I'd teach until I died but after this spring I'm looking at my own retirement. I can retire with full benefits at fifty-two, that's only seven years from now. What would I do with my time? I don't know which is why I've not made a decision and I think that's one reason Cam hasn't made one either.

"The way the other men have included Cam gladdens my heart. I know their friendship is helping him fight off the darkness and embrace life. It isn't that they haven't had tough times, been in the darkness themselves but where they are now is in the light.

"I'm so blessed to have you all in my life. I've even forgiven you for hovering." She laughed. "I will admit that it is harder than it may seem to someone on the outside." She looked at Lily. "I truly was confused why you railed or glowered at us when all we were doing was helping." She patted Lily's hand and then looked around, her gaze resting on each dear face. "Now I know and should I ever need hovering again, I'll handle it better." Sophia placed the stone on the altar cloth. "What time is it?"

"It's time to get dressed and get you to your wedding." Lily stood. Arms raised in prayer they closed their circle with

"We are the light

"We are the source

"Through us love flows

"Throughout the world." And as was their tradition, the words were said times three.

Cars lined both side of the street near her house. "Who else is having a party?"

"I've no idea," Lily said as she pulled into the driveway and on into the garage. The garage door going up was a signal to those inside that the bridal party had arrived. Ashley's van pulled into the driveway. Between Lily's car and Ashley's van the seven of them easily made it to Sophia's.

The door to the house opened and Jackson stood blocking the view inside.

"They need one more minute, Soph." Lily waved to her husband and blew him a kiss.

He smiled and waggled his eyebrows.

With a courtly bow, he gestured for the women to enter the house. The drapes to the backyard were closed.

"Deja vu," Sophia said. "This looks like your wedding, Lily."

"Only in that the drapes are closed."

The women arranged themselves in order of marriage so Gabriella went first, followed by Hunter, Ashley, Diana, Elizabeth and Lily.

The drapes opened enough for the women to pass through. Sophia's view was blocked by her circle sisters. As each stepped onto the patio, someone offered an arm. She guessed it was her husband.

Her guess was right because as Lily came to the door, Jackson winged his arm and she took it. They waited for several seconds before stepping out.

Sophia gasped at what was before her. A raised circular platform with a canopy was in front of her living circle. The silver Victorian gazing ball had been exchanged for the green of spring. Large pots of vibrantly colored flowers flanked the platform and edged her patio.

Rows of chairs were set up on the patio and the lawn. Stunned Sophia stood and stared.

"Phia?"

Cam moved to stand in front of her. "Phia?"

"Cam, how did? How? But?"

"It's all for you, Phia. Come, take my hand." He held his left hand away from his side.

"Can you go so far?"

"To the ends of the earth if I'm with you."

"I love you." Sophia wrapped her hand around his arm gently positioning it against his body. She looked up at his clean shaven jaw. "I want to kiss you," she whispered.

"Wedding ceremonies take only a few minutes. I guarantee you a kiss you'll remember."

"So I have to wait?"

"You do."

They took it slow, that walk up the aisle. Sophia saw Kyle and other students from her sixth period class.

"The kids were all part of the ride-a-long program," Cam whispered.

Mrs. Deavers, the substitute who'd held her classes together was there. Sophia knew her being able to sub so regularly had meant they didn't lose their home. *Blessings come from tragedy.*

Eleanor, Logan, Charlie, James, Anthony and Rose were in the front row on the bride's side.

Ben and Bev were in the front row on Cam's side. Ben had visited yesterday and told Cam Becca wouldn't be coming. He'd told his father, he'd talked to Becca and told her Cam was her legal father but not her biological one. That Betsy was pregnant with her and Drake was her biological dad. He'd described her anger and hurt but relayed it was more directed to no one telling her. Now, it made sense she didn't feel the connection with Cam.

The rest of the seats on the groom's side were filled with fellow officers, some with wives or maybe girlfriends. She recognized two who'd spent time with her and visited Cam regularly at the hospital, rehab center and here.

Here was no longer her home. She'd thought about that for some time and talked to Grant about putting Cam's name on the deed.

"Would it bother you if something happened and this house went to his kids?" Grant had asked.

"Not really but I was thinking along the lines of what is planned for Lily's house."

Cam stopped. They'd reached the platform. Here was her present and her future. Judge Peterson stepped forward a smile on her face.

"Welcome, Sophia and Cameron."

Sophia wondered if Cam could make it up the one step after walking so far. He looked down, his Irish moss green eyes misted with tears. "I love you Sophia Camila Denton Stewart." He nodded and Jackson stepped forward. With his arm around Cam's waist, his other hand gripped Cam's right one and helped him up the step.

Cam was correct. The actual ceremony was short. Surprised when a layer of tension lifted when no one spoke up to object to this union, Sophia knew she had work to do regarding winning Cam's children over. Or maybe not. Maybe the only work she needed to do was love Cam.

"I now pronounce you husband and wife."

Cam's right arm swept her against him. He kissed her with fervor. Her arms slipped around his neck and she pressed close. This man was her present. She'd have however much time she had with him.

Hoots, hollers and whistles invaded her passion-filled mind. Cam broke the kiss but she hauled him back. Laughter surrounded them. White golden light enveloped them.

Trust. Always trust all is right and serves you. The Lady's voice echoed in her mind.

Sophia knew her face was flushed with a blush when she turned back to the group.

Jackson leaned over. "We're doing this a little different. Go with Lily."

Lily and Elizabeth linked arms with Sophia and started back to the house. Behind them, Jackson and Michael flanked Cam. Diana and Matthew and Gabriella and Giovanni followed. And last were Hunter and Grant. The only couple who'd never strolled down an aisle at a wedding together.

The drapes were pulled back, the sliding door opened wide. Cam sat on the loveseat. He patted the place next to him and Sophia sat, resting her head on his shoulder, holding hands.

Caterers swung into action. Chairs were quickly rearranged and small tables that must have been tucked away in the side yard brought out. Long tables held enough food for everyone here to stuff themselves and there'd still be some left over.

Someone had set two or three chairs in a semi-circle beside Cam so people could sit and visit, wish him well. As one seat was vacated it was immediately filled. The same set up was on her side. She had a chance to talk to each of her students and Mrs. Deavers whom she thanked for covering her classes for yet another week. She'd overruled Cam's insistence she return to her classroom Monday. That's another change in her life. She still loved teaching but it wasn't the only thing in her life she loved.

Kyle seemed so grown up today wearing a suit. She'd noticed he talked to some of the other officers and had heard him talking to Cam when he'd visited about being a police officer. *He'd make a good one.*

The biggest surprise was when Ben and Bev sat with their dad and included her in the conversation. When they stood, Ben had added, "We'd like you even if you didn't bake awesome cookies but I will admit it sure helps. Bottom line, you're good for him."

An hour later, the crowd had thinned out considerably. And two hours later only The Circle and their husbands remained.

Cam had moved to the recliner where he could more easily rest. It was still daylight but evening wasn't far away.

Jackson bent down and said something. Cam shook his head. If she had to guess, there was an offer to help him back to the bedroom.

"Time to leave the newlyweds alone." Diana announced. "The caterers have filled your refrigerator to the brim. You won't have to cook for a week."

Cam caught her attention. He crooked a brow.

She nodded.

"We'd appreciate your help in eating it. Way too much for just us. It's the least we can do for all you've done for us.

"Come around two tomorrow and we'll get the food out around four. That way there's time to talk. If you men had ideas bouncing around earlier today, so did the women."

She walked to the door, hugs and well wishes accepted from each of her circle sisters and their husbands as they left. Closing the door when the last one left, she set the perimeter alarm and returned to the family room.

Quiet reigned and she relished it. Cam was asleep in the recliner. Sophia curled up on the couch, her gaze trained on the man she loved. Another lesson she'd learned is that while love is never-ending, it is different. She'd loved Jonathan with all her heart but it was a different love than she felt for Cam.

Her love for Cam was more mature, not that her love for Jonathan was immature. She was a wiser woman now. She had an understanding of life and death she didn't have when she and Jonathan were married. And as important as anything was her spiritual growth. When Jonathan died, she didn't know anything had happened other than he was late and she was irritated and then worried.

When Cam was shot, she felt it in her own body. She loved both men but her connection to Cam was, well, very different than her connection to Jonathan. *Stronger?* She hesitated to use that word. *Perhaps not stronger but definitely very different.*

It was getting chilly. Taking the throw off the back of the couch she crossed the room to tuck it around him. A hand grasped her arm and pulled her close. Irish moss green eyes held passion in their depths.

"Hungry?" Sophia asked. "We've lots of food leftover."

"Hungry? Yes, I am but only for you. Help me up?"

Sophia helped Cam scoot to the front of the recliner and lever himself up. "Do you want to use your wheelchair? Make sure you don't fall."

"Until I'm stronger, I'll use it but tonight I want to pretend I'm a whole man."

Her arm around his waist, Sophia walked with Cam down the hall, past the spare bedroom and into what was now their room. "I'm not sure—."

Sophia kissed his cheek. "Remember how we do this. We go to bed, cuddle and talk and see what happens. I'm in no rush, Cam. If we are lovers tonight or tomorrow or not until next week, it makes no difference."

Cam held her, brushed her hair back from her face with his fingers. "I don't want to wait. I don't have to wait but I don't think I can be on top."

Sophia took his hand and led him to the bed. He toed off his shoes while she unbuttoned his shirt. Taking his shirt off, Cam eyed her hands as they danced over his pants, teased him while unbuckling his belt, and then unbuttoning and unzipping his pants.

"Can you take them off or do you need my help?"

"Gives me more energy to love you if you do it."

She pulled his pants down, his erection sprung free. She kissed the tip and stood.

At the foot of the bed she began to undress. She had to arch her back in order to unclasp her bra. Cam hissed as her breasts broke free. She'd worn an old-fashioned garter belt and put her foot on the bench at the end of the bed to unfasten and roll each stocking down. Cam's fascinated stare heated her core.

Sophia smiled. Aroused because her husband watched her undress? Yes, she was definitely aroused and so was he.

"We're supposed to talk first."

"I'm listening. What do you want to say?"

"I love you. I think I began to fall in love with you when you stood at the top of the path. You were my savior."

"I love you too, Phia. You are my savior, the best thing that's happened to me in a very long time. I was fascinated by you and your love of life. I was lost when you opened your house and your life to me, gave me a haven, a safe place away from the dark. I know I wouldn't have lived if you hadn't been with me."

"Shh," Sophia kissed his neck, his jaw, his cheeks. She nibbled on his earlobe.

"Are we done with talking?" Cam's voice was gravely.

"We are."

Get the Latest News about New Releases, Special Events, Special pricing/sales

You have just finished *Sophia,* the seventh and final book in the Original Sacred Women's Circle series. Be the first to learn about future releases such as prequels to the series in 2017, any pre-release pricing or sales and special events by signing up for my Newsletter <u>here</u>.

For More Information on The Sacred Women's Circle series check out:

My website: <u>www.JudithAshleyRomance.com</u>
My blog: <u>www.JudithAshley.blogspot.com</u>

Other Books in The Sacred Women's Circle Series:
<u>Lily</u>: The Dragon and The Great Horned Owl
<u>Elizabeth</u>: The Lady and The Sacred Grove
<u>Diana</u>: The Queen of Swords and The Knight of Pentacles
<u>Ashley</u>: Dragonflies and Dreams
<u>Hunter</u>: The Drum and The Dance
<u>Gabriella</u>: Chaos to Symmetry
<u>Sophia:</u> Every Ending Is A Beginning

A request:

If you enjoyed *Sophia*, please consider telling your friends and family and writing a review on Amazon, Apple, Barnes and Noble, Kobo and Goodreads. Reviews are a wonderful way to support me.

ABOUT Judith

Judith, in her real life, has been a part of sacred women's circles for over twenty years and knows first-hand how important spirituality is when dealing with life's challenges.

Her imagination has always been active and through books she's been a princess res-cued from the tower by the handsome knight, a missionary in India, explorer in the Amazon jungle, a priestess of the Goddess, and a nun to name a few. She's lived with people from all walks of life including different tribes of indigenous people on five continents in tents, wood cabins, igloos, castles, mansions, high-rise apartments, penthouses, dungeons, basements, and cottages.

Then one day in Judith's real life, the stories that make up The Sacred Women's Circle series flooded through her in daydreams, lucid dreams, and conversations so real at times she wondered about her sanity. It was a compelling experience! An experience that was a catalyst to starting her journey to tell these stories and see them published.

Judith's prayer for you:

Each and every day of your life may you find joy, may you see beauty, may you experience wonder, and may you know you are unconditionally loved.

For more books from the heart in fiction and non-fiction please visit Windtree Press

http://windtreepress.com

presenting life with imagination